The ceremony was over

"I don't know what it is we've stumbled into, but I'm thinking it looks mighty big, J.B.," Ryan said.

"Agreed," J.B. said, quickly glancing behind them.

The Armorer pointed to the open door ahead and Ryan took the lead, jumping onto the raised step and ducking through the door and into the car. J.B. followed, trotting up the step and out of the sunlight.

The interior smelled of incense, heavy and cloying, and thick drapes hung over the windows, blocking out the dawn light.

A lone figure sat at the table—a woman wearing a hood. She looked up as they entered, lit by the candle before her, and Ryan saw the deep lines of age crisscrossing her face.

"Come in, gentlemen."

Ryan glanced behind him, checking to see if the sec men had followed them into the car, but no one was there.

As they stepped closer to the elderly woman, Ryan saw what it was that sparkled on her cheeks— twin tears of blood. And then he felt the world drop from beneath his feet.

JAMES AXLER

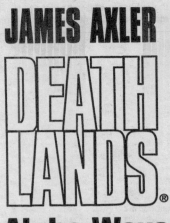

DEATH LANDS.

Alpha Wave

A GOLD EAGLE BOOK FROM
WORLDWIDE.

TORONTO • NEW YORK • LONDON
AMSTERDAM • PARIS • SYDNEY • HAMBURG
STOCKHOLM • ATHENS • TOKYO • MILAN
MADRID • WARSAW • BUDAPEST • AUCKLAND

Recycling programs
for this product may
not exist in your area.

First edition September 2009

ISBN-13: 978-0-373-62598-7

ALPHA WAVE

Printed in U.S.A.

Hitherto every form of society has been based...
on the antagonism of oppressing and oppressed
classes. But in order to oppress a class, certain
conditions must be assured to it under which
it can, at least, continue its slavish existence.
—Karl Marx and Friedrich Engels
The Communist Manifesto,
1848

THE DEATHLANDS SAGA

This world is their legacy, a world born in the violent nuclear spasm of 2001 that was the bitter outcome of a struggle for global dominance.

There is no real escape from this shockscape where life always hangs in the balance, vulnerable to newly demonic nature, barbarism, lawlessness.

But they are the warrior survivalists, and they endure—in the way of the lion, the hawk and the tiger, true to nature's heart despite its ruination.

Ryan Cawdor: The privileged son of an East Coast baron. Acquainted with betrayal from a tender age, he is a master of the hard realities.

Krysty Wroth: Harmony ville's own Titian-haired beauty, a woman with the strength of tempered steel. Her premonitions and Gaia powers have been fostered by her Mother Sonja.

J. B. Dix, the Armorer: Weapons master and Ryan's close ally, he, too, honed his skills traversing the Deathlands with the legendary Trader.

Doctor Theophilus Tanner: Torn from his family and a gentler life in 1896, Doc has been thrown into a future he couldn't have imagined.

Dr. Mildred Wyeth: Her father was killed by the Ku Klux Klan, but her fate is not much lighter. Restored from predark cryogenic suspension, she brings twentieth-century healing skills to a nightmare.

Jak Lauren: A true child of the wastelands, reared on adversity, loss and danger, the albino teenager is a fierce fighter and loyal friend.

Dean Cawdor: Ryan's young son by Sharona accepts the only world he knows, and yet he is the seedling bearing the promise of tomorrow.

In a world where all was lost, they are humanity's last hope....

Chapter One

Krysty's head throbbed. The pain had been getting steadily worse for the past three hours, ever since they had left the redoubt.

She gazed up as the sun poked through the angry clouds scudding across the violet sky, trying to keep her mind off the pain. As she did so, Krysty could hear the concern in Doc's voice as he spoke with Ryan and J.B. a few paces ahead.

"Look at her, Ryan," Doc said, gesturing over his shoulder at Krysty. "That's not a normal reaction. Something is clearly having a negative effect on our usually effervescent Krysty."

J. B. Dix, the armorer for the group, glanced briefly at his lapel pin rad counter, his walking pace, much like his expression, unchanging.

"Anything?" Ryan asked, though he already knew the answer. J.B. was a man of shrewd logic, and wouldn't even waste the intake of breath to confirm it unless the situation had changed. Ryan's single eye stared out across the empty landscape, before he turned back to address Doc. "Radiation's at normal, and there's nothing here we haven't faced a hundred times before. Dust and muties, mebbe, but nothing new."

"Sand," Doc corrected. "Not dust, Ryan—sand."

Doc was right. All around them, as far as he could

see, horizon to horizon, was nothing but sand. Sand and sand-colored rocks and sand-colored pebbles, gradually getting smaller and smaller until the pebbles were just grains of sand and the cycle started over again. It had been like that ever since the companions had stepped out of the redoubt eight miles behind them.

Ryan Cawdor marched ahead of the others with long powerful strides, his dark hair catching in the wind, the SSG-70 Steyr blaster swinging against his shoulders as he set the relentless pace across the wasteland.

Next to Ryan, dressed in a battered, brown fedora and a leather jacket far too heavy for the temperature, trekked J. B. Dix. Where Ryan marched, J.B. simply walked, light-footed and watchful of his surroundings, his movements economical and appreciably silent.

Then there was Krysty Wroth, the red-haired beauty who was Ryan's lover. She was a reliable whirlwind of energy and joy around which they all revolved. Strong, emotional, Krysty was a strange contradiction of facets. She had some mutie abilities—bursts of supernatural strength drawn from the well of the Earth Mother, Gaia; occasional prescience; and her mane of red hair, strangely alive and responsive to her emotional state. When Krysty was happy her hair shone like a beacon, when she was angry it crackled, curling like a vine around her head. Right now, her hair sat disheveled, drooping over her shoulders listlessly.

Dr. Mildred Wyeth walked with Krysty. Healer and caregiver, Mildred had never adopted the bleak outlook of the others. But she could still kill when the situation required it, and kill quickly.

Not as quickly as the albino Jak Lauren, the teenage survivor of unspeakable tragedy in New Orleans. Jak marched to his own beat. Even now he was off some-where, scouting ahead or checking behind them, out of sight, using the area's natural hiding places to camou-flage himself from possible predators. Ryan was a deadly killer, but at least he was stable. Trying to tame Jak was like trying to bottle a forest fire.

And then there was Doc himself, with his ornate walking stick and his centuries' old frock coat, his archaic turn of phrase. Theophilus Algernon "Doc" Tanner was an anachronism from a simpler age when wars were still fought face-to-face, man-to-man, not by the push of a button and the snuffing of ten thousand lives at a time.

"Doc, we go on," Ryan told him, snatching the man from his reverie. "You know what I'd give for her," he added quietly, glancing toward Krysty with his good right eye before looking back at Doc. "Whatever's affected her hasn't done spit to the rest of us, far as we can tell. Could just be a bad reaction to the jump. Catches all of us sometimes, you know that."

Doc nodded his agreement. Ryan was right. Nine times in a row you could step through that gateway, blast your atoms halfway across the old United States, and come out the other side as right as rain, just like waking up. Yet the tenth time could bring dizziness and nausea and a person might think he or she would never be able to stand again. Krysty just got trip number ten this time around. It would pass.

He looked back at Krysty and smiled reassuringly. It would pass.

JAK SPRINTED across the plain, clouds of sand kicking up in his wake.

He chanced a look back over his shoulder in an unconscious survival instinct, making sure that nothing was following. The razor blades and jagged glass sewn into the fabric of his camou jacket glinted in the sun until another angry, toxin-heavy cloud passed overhead, cutting off the light.

Somewhere off to his right—the north—he could see a storm in full fury, attacking the Earth like a cat playing with a wounded bird. Streaks of bloodred lightning flashed down, repeatedly punching at the ground. The storm was traveling away from him, farther into the north. Caught up in its fury, a full-grown man could lose a limb to those potent bolts of electricity, or have the flesh washed from his bones by the acidic content of the rain. But Jak knew something about weather patterns, however unpredictable others might think them; he could tell this one wouldn't be bothering them anytime soon.

He took a half step, skipping over the train tracks that ran across his path in the sand. Some tracks saw use here and there. When was the last time these saw use? he wondered. Like so much in the Deathlands, most train tracks were just another obsolete transportation system from a more complicated time. A time when the everyday had consisted of more than simply surviving another twenty-four hours.

What he had found out here, away from his friends, was worth further investigation. He couldn't quite tell what the thing was, but he knew that Ryan, J.B. and the others would be intrigued. So he ran, fists pumping, across the sandy plain to rejoin his companions.

"I THINK SHE'S GETTING WORSE," Mildred announced.

Doc slowed his pace and looked back. Mildred and

Krysty were fifteen feet behind the group now. Mildred was walking beside Krysty, an encouraging hand on her companion's elbow. Krysty had paled significantly, the blood drained from her face, and though she stood under her own strength, she did so with a hunch to her shoulders, as though suffering stomach cramps.

Doc raised his cane, went to tap Ryan on the shoulder before thinking better of it. You never quite knew with Ryan—his instincts were so sharp that he might just chill a man before acknowledging who the assailant was. Doc settled on a less invasive attention grabber. "Gentlemen," he called, "we have trouble."

Trouble. That was the watchword. That was the heart stopper. Tell Ryan that they had company, tell him that they had no food, tell him that they had radiation poisoning from the nukecaust, and Ryan would shrug and continue marching forward. But trouble was different.

Ryan stepped back to talk to Doc before the pair walked over to join Mildred and Krysty. J.B. remained at the front of the expedition, scouring the horizon in silence.

"What is it, Mildred?" Ryan asked.

"I think Krysty's getting worse," she told him.

Ryan looked at Krysty. Her muscles were bunched up, and she leaned her weight against the doctor. "You think, or she is?" he asked. It wasn't Ryan being rude; that wasn't his nature. Mildred knew that. There was just something in him, the way his brain was wired, that demanded absolutes. There could be no room for error, no room for questions or shades of gray.

"She's worse," Mildred stated firmly. "Without a full examination, I can't tell how much worse, Ryan, but she's definitely in worse condition now than when we left the redoubt."

Ryan turned to Doc, as though for a second opinion. Doc wasn't a medical doctor, his nickname stemmed from the Ph.D. degree he'd received from Oxford University, but he had wisdom and experience, and Ryan had always appreciated that.

Doc looked at Krysty for a moment, then turned to Ryan. "Her health is deteriorating," he decided.

"Open your eyes, Krysty, can you do that for me?" Doc asked the flame-haired woman.

Slowly, as though it caused her pain, Krysty widened her eyes from the slits that they had unconsciously become. Doc leaned in closer to look, and Mildred followed once he had stepped aside. The whites of Krysty's eyes had turned dark pink, bloodshot, as though irritated by smoke. Krysty blinked, her eyelids fluttering like a weathervane in high winds. Mildred told her that it was okay, she could stop now.

"Am I dying?" Krysty mumbled through dry lips.

"No," Ryan replied firmly, automatically, his single eye holding her gaze.

There was a long moment of silence until Mildred finally spoke. "It could be an infection. Food poisoning. Rad sickness—" she ticked them off on her fingers "—muscle aches, cramps, weariness. It could just be influenza. Right now I can't tell you. She needs a proper examination, which means you need to stop while I do that. It wouldn't take long, Ryan."

Ryan looked around, across the flat expanse of sand that surrounded them. "We can't stop here, Mildred," he told her. "This is a hopeless position if we need to defend it. There are probably burrowers here, and there's also—"

"Stop it, Ryan," Doc muttered. "Krysty's one of us, she needs…"

But Mildred butted in. "He's right, Doc. None of us will be any use to her if we're chilled," she stated. "Let's get to a campsite, a cave, a ville. I'll examine her when there's time.

"She'll be fine," Mildred added, turning to their companion. "Won't you, girl?"

Krysty nodded heavily, the hair falling over her face.

J.B. called back to them, keeping his voice low. "Jak's here," he said.

They all looked in the direction J.B. pointed and saw the little trail of sand kicking up in the wind as Jak approached.

The albino stopped in front of J.B., his breath ragged for a moment until he got it under control. Ryan and the others joined them, as Jak began to enthusiastically tell of his findings, gesturing repeatedly toward the northeast.

"Tall. Big tall," Jak began, the words stringing together into his own version of speech. "Towers into sky, like old Libberlady."

"What is it?" Ryan asked. "What did you see?"

"A tower, like skeleton, the air. Near it a ville."

Mildred sucked in her breath suddenly, so loud that the other companions turned to look at her. "A ville, Ryan," she said. "It is just what we need. I can examine Krysty there, it's ideal." No one spoke, and Mildred saw the doubt on Ryan's features. "We can all bed down there, maybe get more supplies," she added, a gambler trying to sweeten the pot.

"Could be trouble, Ryan," J.B. stated flatly.

Ryan looked in the direction that Jak had been pointing, weighing the options in his mind. Doc wondered if he should say something, like some old-time counsel for the defense, pleading with Ryan for the lenience of the court. Krysty needed to stop; in fact, all of them would benefit from it. But the Armorer was right, too—sometimes a new ville was nothing but chilling waiting to happen, and most villes didn't take kindly to outlanders, especially a bunch of well-armed nomads with nothing much to offer.

Ryan started to march to the northeast, the direction that Jak had come from. "Let's go look at this tower," he stated.

The others followed, with Doc and Mildred taking a position on either side of the sick Krysty.

IT TOOK FORTY MINUTES to reach Jak's tower with Ryan setting a brisk pace. As they got closer, they could see it resting on the horizon, its thin struts seeming to waver in the heat haze.

When they were fifty paces away, Doc stated his opinion. "It is just a pylon," he asserted.

J.B. didn't bother to turn back as he addressed the older man. "Then where are the lines?"

Shifting his grip around Krysty's back, Doc leaned his cane against his leg and held his free hand up to shield his eyes, staring at the towering structure. J.B. was right—there were no power lines, not even the trace of where they might have once attached.

Mildred's voice, urgent and quiet, broke into his thoughts. "Doc."

The old man turned to look at her across their suffering colleague. "What is—?" He stopped as the shiny red droplet twinkled in the sunlight, catching his eye. Krysty's nose was bleeding, a trickle of blood running from her left nostril, working its way to her deathly pale lips.

Doc started to call for Ryan and the others, but Mildred suddenly stumbled and Krysty lurched out of their grip, falling to the ground, making a muffled thump as her body compacted the sand.

Doc knelt, gently turning Krysty's head, pulling up her face. She spluttered, choking on a mouthful of sand. Mildred regained her balance and crouched beside them. "How is she?" she asked.

"She's breathing. Are *you* okay?" he asked Mildred.

Mildred brushed sand from her fatigue pants, little heaps of it sailing from the covers on the bulbous pockets. "I'm fine, I'm good. She just suddenly… I don't know, did you feel it?"

"She became deadweight," Doc responded, and immediately wished he had used a less resonant term.

Pulling an otoscope from her bag of meager possessions, Mildred held it to Krysty's eyes. Doc unfolded his kerchief, with its blue-swallow-eye pattern, and offered it to Krysty.

"I think I'm okay," Krysty told them both after a moment. "Just went weak for a second. Can you hear that? The noise?"

Mildred looked around her, then back to her patient. "There's no noise, sweetie. Just the wind."

Krysty looked confused, as though she would burst into tears at any second. "But it's so loud." She whimpered.

Doc looked at Krysty, a woman he had known for

more adventures than any man should have in a single lifetime, and his heart broke. Krysty Wroth: capable and beautiful. No, not beautiful—stunning. The stunning, utterly capable woman he had trusted his life to on more occasions than he could count on the fingers of both hands, was sitting in front of him, confused and helpless. He never thought he would see her like this.

Slowly, being as gentle as they could, Doc and Mildred helped Krysty off the ground. They didn't bother to brush her down, as there didn't seem to be any point. They just needed to get her moving, before she stopped moving for good. Together, they half carried, half dragged her toward the tower where the others waited.

"BIG, ISN'T IT?" Ryan said to no one in particular as the six companions stood at the base of the tower.

"Yeah, sure is," J.B. agreed, using the hem of his shirt to clean the lenses of his spectacles before perching them back on his nose. He took a step forward and stretched a hand toward the metal structure. He held it there, beside the tower, for a few seconds before announcing that there was no power emanating from it that he could feel. It was a quick test, hardly scientific, but it sufficed in the situation.

The tower rose forty feet into the sky. Built from struts of metal, like scaffolding, it looked somewhat like a power pylon, just as Doc had guessed. It was not a pylon, though. Up close, that was evident. There were no attachments, nothing feeding to it or from it. It was a free-standing, skeletal tower, roughly pyramidal in shape, albeit very thin. The base was only twelve feet square, and it closed to its tip very gradually.

A large metal canister, something like a prenukecaust oil drum, rested in the center of its base, half-buried in the sand.

The structure was utterly silent and displayed no moving parts, a surrealist statue on the plain.

Finally, Mildred spoke up, asking the question on everyone's lips. "Well, what is it?"

"Nuked if I know," Ryan replied.

Chapter Two

The companions watched as Jak clambered up the side of the structure, his hands clutching at the metal struts.

"Our Jak's quite the climber," Doc said in admiration when the youth reached the peak in a handful of seconds.

Both J.B. and Ryan had already run their lapel rad counters over the structure, making sure that it wasn't hot. Then they had tested the metal legs as best as they could, for electric current and magnetic attraction, as well as eyeballing for fractures or rust. It looked stable and had hardly been touched by the elements. The obvious conclusion was that it was newly built, but by whom and why, they couldn't tell.

"You see anything?" Ryan called to Jak at the top of the tower.

"Same," Jak yelled back. "All over same."

Mildred sighed, looking at the tower as Jak spidered down. "Ryan, we really need to get to that ville." She waited, looking at Ryan as he gazed at the structure. "Ryan?"

He nodded before looking at her. "Just seems wrong, leaving this tower here. Has to be here for a purpose, Mildred," he told her.

Mildred shrugged. "Maybe they tie their horses to it," she suggested, looking over at the tiny ville they could all see about two hundred and fifty yards away.

"Mebbe tie prisoners," Jak chipped in.

Doc's cheery voice cut through them, intentionally loud, like a wake-up call. "Perhaps we could just ask them," he suggested. The group turned to look at him. He was busy hefting Krysty to her feet once more, getting his arm beneath hers so that she could lean against him as she walked.

Krysty looked in no condition to walk. Dried blood married her face around her nose. The skin around her eyes was puffy and had darkened almost to black, and the whites of her eyes remained bloodshot red. Her flame-colored hair was a mass of tangles, twirling this way and that like the stems of a climbing plant. From the way that Doc carried her, it appeared that she had added weight somehow, her muscles no longer strong enough to support her.

Aware that he had everyone's attention, Doc pronounced, "Miss Wroth and I are going to make our way to yonder ville and ask some questions in the hopes of enlightenment." He struggled two steps with Krysty, and it was clear that he was taking all of her weight now.

J.B. had scrambled across to Krysty's other side. "Let me give you a hand, Doc," he told the older man, but he left it open, as though it were a request.

In the end, Ryan and J.B. shared Krysty's weight, relieving the older man as the group trekked down the incline to the ville. She had mercifully fallen into a slumber, and they carried her by shoulders and feet to make the journey easier. Mildred sidled up to Doc and gave him a wink. "You sly old coot." She laughed.

Doc shrugged. If it had been left up to J.B., they would still be studying the mysterious tower a month from now with Ryan deluding himself about Krysty's health. Krysty's problems, Doc had reasoned, were somewhat more pressing just now.

Head held low to his shoulders, Jak ran ahead once more, kicking up little puffs of sand as he edged sideways down the incline toward the buildings.

THE VILLE WAS SUNKEN slightly, located in a natural dip in the surrounding plains. It was made up of almost two dozen ramshackle buildings, constructed from scrounged wood and metal. The majority of the buildings were single-story, with only four in the center going to two stories along with a circular barn at the far edge of town. A high wall surrounded the whole settlement, and the companions could hear dogs barking furiously as they got closer.

The sun was setting when they reached the ville's high gates, turning the skies a burning red as it sauntered under the horizon in the west behind them. The sturdy gates were constructed of strips of rough wood tied together with old rope and held in place with rusty hinges. Twice as tall as a man, the gates were set within a similarly high wall constructed from a patchwork of materials. Opened together, the gates could let a wide wagon pass through into the ville, but they would be kept closed for most of the time to discourage possible looters.

Two sentries patrolled the top of the wall, and they came over to the edge of the gates when Ryan and his companions approached. "You want somethin', outlanders?" the sentry to the left called out, casually brandishing a large-bore shotgun over the rim of the wall. He was a heavy man, wearing a tattered, checked shirt and two days' worth of beard. Across from him, on the other side of the gates, a sallow young man dressed in similar clothing trained a wooden crossbow on the companions. Ryan judged that its range was insufficient to reach them as far from the gates as they were, and certainly not with any appreciable accuracy.

Ryan let Krysty's feet drop gently to the ground and waved his companions back, instructing them to wait as he went to speak with the sentry.

"We're not here looking for trouble," he began, holding his hands at shoulder height to show he held no weapon. The longblaster was clearly visible on his back, of course, and he had a blaster at his hip, but this was the Deathlands. The sentries would have been more suspicious of an apparently unarmed man than one who came at them blasters blazing.

The sentry on the left raised the muzzle of his weapon a little, encouraging Ryan to continue.

"My friend back there is ill," Ryan said, his gaze never leaving the man's eyes. "We come seeking somewhere to bed down, mebbe look her over."

The sentry with the crossbow shook his head, looking over at his comrade. "We don't got no healin' to give to outlanders," Shotgun stated bluntly, and his companion made a show of raising his crossbow higher, pointing it at Ryan's forehead.

"You best be on your way, One-Eye." The crossbow-wielding man chuckled.

Ryan didn't flinch, he just continued to look at the man with the shotgun. He bore these two no malice. They were just doing their job. Just protecting their own.

"We've got our own healer," Ryan assured them. The trace of a smile crossed his lips as he saw both the sentries look across to his companions, squinting against the setting sun as they tried to guess which of the ragtag group might have valuable medical skills. "Be willing to let the healer take a look at your people, too," Ryan suggested, "if you need that. Free of charge, if you can give us somewhere to examine our own."

The sentries looked at each another, muttered a few words that Ryan didn't catch. But he detected the change in atmosphere immediately, and leaped to one side as the buckshot exploded toward him with a loud crack.

The sentry with the shotgun bragged loudly as he targeted the barrel at the fleeing Ryan, preparing a second shot from the homemade weapon. "Think we'll just chill you and take your healer for our own, if it's okay with you, One-Eye!" He laughed.

Ryan had already loosed his 9 mm SIG-Sauer P-226 blaster from its holster. Straight-armed, he reeled off a single shot. The sentry staggered back, dropping the shotgun as it exploded in his hand, taking the full force of the Sauer's bullet.

Ryan targeted the second sentry, the one with the crossbow, but there was no need. J.B. had the man dead center in the sights of his mini-Uzi, Doc had his LeMat revolver aimed at the man, and Mildred and Jak had crouched around Krysty, poised with their own weapons—a ZKR 551 target revolver in Mildred's right hand, a .357 Magnum Colt Python in Jak's—to offer her necessary protection. Slowly, carefully, the younger sentry placed his crossbow on the ridge of the wall at his feet before raising his hands.

The sentry to the right, the one who had been holding the shotgun, cursed as he clutched at his bleeding right hand. But there was admiration in that curse as much as anger. "Black dust, but that is some good shooting, friend," he pronounced incredulously.

"For a one-eye," Ryan called back, keeping his blaster trained on the sentries, whipping it between the two.

The sentry laughed, the blood dripping from his hand where the homemade shotgun had been a few moments before. "Well, besides some dead-on shooting and a healer, you got anything worth my opening these gates for? Or should I go call me some reinforcements and see if we can't negotiate with you some more?"

Ryan looked at him, never lowering his blaster as he spoke. "Reinforcements won't be necessary," he told the sentry. "Like I said, we're not here looking for trouble. Just a hole to sleep in for me and my people. We're willing to pay for it, with ammo if you'll take it. Or we can walk away right now, and you've learned a little lesson in trying to take what isn't yours." Ryan's expression remained fixed as he watched the sentry.

The sentry smirked, nodding to himself. "You got ammo? Why didn't you say so earlier, One-Eye?" he asked. "We got the best nuking dog fights here, if you're a betting man, might even double or triple your wager if you bet as well as you shoot."

Ryan nodded, warily lowering his blaster. After a moment J.B. and Doc followed his lead, carefully relaxing, but keeping their weapons in hand in case things turned nasty again. "Triple at least, I reckon," he told the older sentry.

"Hell, yeah." The sentry laughed. "Now, my boy here is gonna open the gates, and everybody is going to just play nice. Sound okay with you and your people, out-lander?"

Ryan glanced across at J.B. and Doc to see if either would object. Then he answered by holstering his SIG-Sauer P-226. "You want my healer to look at that hand?" he asked as the younger man disappeared from sight.

The old sentry nodded. "I would be much obliged," he agreed.

J.B. AND DOC CARRIED Krysty through the open gates and into the tiny ville. She seemed heavy, a felled doe from a hunting expedition, as her feet dragged on the sandy ground. Mildred had suggested it would be easier to carry her by shoulders and feet, as Ryan and J.B. had when they'd brought her here from the tower, but Doc wouldn't hear of it. "Mayhap she cannot go in walking," he had told them, "but she will at least go in looking like she can walk."

J.B. agreed. Psychologically, it made sense to keep Krysty upright. That way she would appear hurt to the citizens of the ville and not dead.

The older sentry met them as they walked through the gates, his younger companion working the mechanism to open them—the gates worked on some kind of weighted cantilever system. J.B. made a mental note to examine it in more detail when the sun was higher in the sky. The old sentry had wrapped a makeshift bandage around his right hand, torn from the bottom of his checkered shirt. He smiled as he greeted Ryan and the companions.

"You sure gave my hand a walloping there," he told Ryan. "That was some nuke-hot shooting you did."

Ryan shrugged, not wanting to dwell on it, aware that the old sentry may yet be itching for payback.

"My name's Tom," the sentry went on, before indicating his younger partner beside the gate. "And this is my boy, Davey."

The younger sentry, Davey, brushed a hand through his hair and slowly eyed Mildred from the chest up. "Pleased to meet you," he finally said, oblivious to the others.

"Flattered," she responded with a fixed grin.

Tom carried on, pointing down the single street of the walled-in ville. "This here is Fairburn. Don't look like much, I guess, but we still call it home."

"It looks very homely," Ryan said. "I'm Ryan, and these are my traveling companions," he said by way of introduction, not bothering with anyone else's name. He would sooner they keep a low profile for now, at least as much as strangers in a walled ville could. "You said something about maybe having somewhere we could stay?"

Tom pointed to the center of the small ville, where the four twin-storied buildings stood. "There's an eatery over there. Can't miss it. Just follow your noses to the stink. Jemmy there will sort you out a room. Just ask at the counter."

As the companions made their way down the dusty thoroughfare, two dogs rushed over, yapping and snarling playfully, their thick, saliva-smeared tongues hanging from their mouths. They were mongrels, stupid and friendly, their tails wagging as they looked at the well-armed strangers. Jak issued a low growl from deep within his throat, and he narrowed his pure red eyes as he looked at the mutts. As one, the dogs turned tail and ran, seeking more willing playmates.

Doc looked at the sentry's bloodied hand as he

passed, hefting Krysty. "I do not imagine you have much call for renting out rooms here."

"Probably depends a little on who's on the gate," Tom agreed.

"Come over when you're ready," Ryan called back, "and our healer will take a look at that hand."

The companions headed into the center of the ville, with Krysty still lolling between Doc and J.B.

Chapter Three

A huge chandelier hung from the ceiling of Jemmy's by a thick, golden chain, its crystal droplets casting a flotilla of sunlight specks across the walls of the room where they rippled and bounced as if living things. The impressive chandelier was utterly incongruous, at odds with the simple, rustic design of the barnlike barroom.

Crude tables and chairs were scattered around the room, some simply upended wooden crates, seats ripped from old automobiles. A few men sat around, playing with stacks of dominoes or just jawing and drinking, mostly armed with remade revolvers, a couple of shotguns resting on the tables. Two women were propped at the bar, heavily made-up over expressions of utter disinterest. The wide room smelled of rotgut.

Doc and J.B. helped Krysty to the bar, which Ryan was leaning over, looking into the back room, trying to locate whoever was serving.

The two women propping up the bar looked at Ryan, then the older one—all of nineteen, perhaps—turned her head and shouted toward the back, her husky voice crackling like fire. "Jem, you got some new customers."

A moment later a woman came out of the back room, taking in the companions in a quick sweep of her hazel eyes before turning a bright, flawless smile on Ryan. She was dressed in a man's shirt, too large for her, with sleeves rolled up past her elbows, her dark hair tied back. Ryan guessed that she was in her early thirties, skin tanned and hands calloused from a tough, outdoor life. She tossed aside the towel she had been wiping her hands with and asked what she could do for everyone.

"We're looking to stop over in your fine ville," Ryan told her. "Could do with rooms if you have them."

"Here for the dogs?" the woman asked conversationally.

Ryan nodded. Behind him, J.B. had stepped away from the bar and was looking around the room, scanning for possible exits. Through the kitchen area behind the bar—where the woman had appeared from—he could see an open door leading to the backyard, the ground nothing more than sand. There was a well out there, really just a hole in the ground with a roped bucket beside it, framed by the open door. Off to the right of the bar, wooden stairs at the back of the room led up, and a second-floor balcony surrounded the room on three sides, with several doors leading off—most likely the lodging rooms for the establishment, transaction rooms for the two gaudy sluts working the bar. A door beneath the staircase proclaimed that it led to toilet facilities, though J.B. guessed it was probably nothing more than a fenced-in part of the backyard.

"You know how long you're here for?" Jemmy asked Ryan as he placed a few rounds of spare ammo on the bar. The ammo was useless to the companions, none of it fitting their blasters, but spare ammo served as the gold standard for the Deathlands.

Ryan looked around the room as though surveying the whole ville. "Nice place," he said. "Who knows? Mebbe a few nights. That be a problem for you?"

Jemmy was examining one of the bullets, turning it slowly in her hand to check for cracks or signs of tampering. "These new or reloads?" she asked him.

Ryan smiled, nodding. "Military issue," he assured her. "Predark."

"Two rooms, three nights," Jemmy told him, looking at the others. "After that, you come find me and we renegotiate. You'll have to share beds, 'cause that's all the rooms I got just now."

Ryan dipped his head. "We are much obliged."

Jemmy instructed one of the gaudies to watch the bar as she stepped from behind it and led Ryan and his companions to their rooms. Ryan took Krysty in his arms—armpits and knees—lifting her weight with ease as he followed the landlady up the creaking, wood staircase.

Jemmy's glance drifted to Krysty's Western boots with their elaborate Falcon wing designs up the sides, the silver toe caps smothered with dusty sand from the trek across the wastelands. "I like your friend's boots," she told Ryan as she led the way up the stairs. "If she's got no more use for them, I might be able to find you rooms for a whole month by way of trade."

Mildred held the woman's gaze for a second. "She's just tired," she told her firmly, then immediately regretted snapping, fearing it might make the woman suspicious.

J.B. nodded to Doc, gesturing to the open front door, before following Ryan and Mildred.

Taking his cue, Doc held out a hand to Jak at the bottom of the stairs. "What say you and I get us some refreshment, lad?" he announced in a loud voice.

The trace of a smile crossed the albino youth's pale

lips. "Been long walk," he said, nodding, then placed his back to the bar and watched the door while the teenage gaudy slut poured them two mugs of some locally brewed beer.

Doc was aware that the younger woman at the bar was watching him as he found a .22 round in his pocket for payment. "I trust this should be more than enough for our beverage, good lady, and I expect some local jack in compensation, as well." She checked the ammo suspiciously, then handed him several coins. Beneath the heavy makeup, he would guess she was no more than seventeen.

"You like what you see?" she asked, puffing out her chest and tilting her head to offer a well-practiced, co-quettish smile, her long brown hair falling across her face and bare shoulders.

Doc nodded, sipping at the brew. "I like the chande-lier. It's a nice touch."

The gaudy's expression dropped for a moment, as though unsure whether this old fool had understood her question.

Inwardly, Doc chuckled. It was desperately sad to see a girl this young forced into prostitution, and a part of him wished that things were different. But there was nothing he could do here; this was her life and the chances were slim to none that she would ever know any better.

"My friends call me Doc," he told her after a moment. "What's your name?"

"They call me Lois L'amore," she said, smiling. "That means 'love,' if you didn't know," she added.

Doc scratched his chin, as though deep in thought. "I did not know that," he told her. "How very unusual."

"Can I show you how I came by such an unusual name?" she asked him.

Doc looked her up and down, pity in his eyes. "Why don't we just leave that to my imagination?" he suggested before turning away. He heard the girl huff a sigh through clenched teeth.

Sniggering at the performance, Jak led Doc to an empty table set against one of the wooden walls from which they could watch the main door, the bar and the entrance beneath the stairwell.

JEMMY CLOSED THE DOOR to the upstairs room and left the companions alone. The bedsprings groaned as Ryan carefully placed Krysty on the rusting double bed, and Mildred sat beside her, placing a hand on the sleeping woman's forehead.

There were two doors in the room, one of which led to the second room that they had rented while the other led into a corridor that, in turn, led back to the balcony above the barroom.

J.B. poked his head through the door to the adjoining room, briefly giving it a once-over. It was much the same as the room where Mildred tended Krysty—a double bed, door to the corridor, a small basin sink that could be filled from the well as required, and a large window of sand-streaked glass. In the same spot over Krysty's bed there was an old road map showing the streets of Fargo, North Dakota, heavy white lines running on verticals and horizontals where the map had once been folded for ease of reference.

J.B. walked to the far door, turned the key in the lock then tested it, pulling and turning the handle three times before returning to Ryan and Mildred.

The frame shook and spewed sawdust with each pull on the handle. "These locks won't hold," he warned them. "If a gnat gets caught short, it could piss both doors open."

Mildred querulously looked up from the bed. "Are we expecting visitors?"

"Whether we expect them or not, won't make much difference if they come," J.B. insisted.

Mildred shook her head. "You're being paranoid. No one's looking for us out here."

"Paranoid's last to die," he reminded her, looking through the window across the main street of Fairburn. Out there, over the ridge of the wall, he could make out the tower in the dwindling sunlight.

Ryan spoke up, addressing Mildred. "Sentry Tom might yet decide he owes me a gutful of buckshot, Mildred."

Mildred started to reply, then checked herself. They were all tense, worried about their colleague. The best thing she could do would be to give Krysty a thorough checkup, see if she could pinpoint what had laid the normally healthy woman low. Mildred picked up her backpack, then searched through the contents of her med kit for a pocket thermometer and her otoscope.

J.B. looked across, an apology tightly held behind his eyes. "You need help?" he asked.

Mildred shook her head. "Maybe get her boots off, try to make her comfortable." J.B. and Ryan knelt at the end of the bed and stripped off Krysty's boots.

IT WAS THE SCREAMING that finally woke Krysty.

Her eyes opened as tiny slits, and she warily scanned her surroundings. It was a well-honed survival instinct—

she couldn't remember what had happened or where she had fallen asleep.

She was in a simple room, the planks that formed its walls visible in the flickering candlelight, never having been painted or even varnished. She could see two figures across the room. One was a huge bear of a man, his back to her, rippling muscles well-defined where his vest top left his arms bare. He was looking out the window of the room at the night sky, stargazing.

The other man was sitting at the end of the bed, stripping and oiling a revolver. Krysty shifted her head slightly, trying not to attract her captors' attention. Her head felt muzzy as she did so, like moving through water. The blaster was a .38-caliber Smith & Wesson 640. Her blaster. These psychos planned to chill her with her own blaster!

She struggled to move, but it felt like she had been drugged. Her limbs felt so heavy she could barely shift them. And the screaming—the screaming was getting louder. She could hear it, penetrating the very core of her being, like something in her womb, waiting to be born. What was going on? Were there other women like her, trapped, drugged, helpless, waiting for these stupes to hurt them, to chill them? Why else would they be screaming? She needed to get out of there, right now.

She tried clenching the fingers of her right hand, willing the muscles to move, and felt nothing more than a twitch. A twitch and a wealth of pain, as though the muscles of her arm had been dipped in acid, burning through the nerve endings, a ripple of agony. She bit her lip, holding back the scream.

Then a door to her right opened, a brighter light from outside bleeding through for a moment, and another figure was framed in the doorway. She couldn't make out the backlit features, but the silhouette was plainly that of a woman, short and muscular. She held a large bowl of something, and from the way she carried it, it was likely full of liquid. More of the acid, perhaps, to drench her muscles in, to keep up the agony.

The woman put the bowl down; Krysty heard it being placed on the cabinet beside her ear, heard the liquid sloshing within. And then the woman reappeared in her line of sight, reaching for her face, a rag of cloth in her hand, dripping from a dunking in the bowl. Gaia, no! The woman planned to burn her face with the acid. What kind of monsters…?

In her mind, Krysty begged Gaia to help her, calling on all her strength to try to push herself off the bed, attack the woman with the acid cloth, stop the madness. Stop the bastard madness.

MILDRED REACHED DOWN, placing the damp cloth on Krysty's forehead. She'd obtained a bowlful of cold water from Jemmy, wishing she could add the simple, twentieth-century luxury of ice.

Nothing had changed in the three minutes that she'd been gone. J.B. continued stripping and cleaning Krysty's weapons, greasing each segment from the container of oil he habitually carried in one of his voluminous pockets. That was his way of showing he cared, she knew. No point getting her through this only to have her blaster jam up, he had told her.

Ryan, meanwhile, stood looking out the window, watching as the street filled with people. It was about 8:00 p.m., and they'd been advised that the dogfights would kick off at 8:30 p.m. sharp. It was obviously a big slice of local action. A barker poised at the entrance to the open-topped circular barn at the end of the street was enticing passing trade to place early bets. The bar downstairs had got busier, too.

Stupe really. If they had arrived a couple of hours later than they did, the whole face-off with the sentries could have been avoided. Seemed the ville of Fairburn opened the gates at night.

Mildred stopped woolgathering as she felt something cross her hand where it mopped the cool water across Krysty's brow. She looked at her hand and saw the streaks of red crisscrossing it—Krysty's mutie hair was wrapping around Mildred's hand like a creeping vine, surrounding and trapping it, its silken threads exerting considerable force. "Ryan, look," Mildred whispered.

Ryan turned, and J.B. was already out of his seat, standing beside Mildred, a protective arm reaching for her.

"What is it?" Ryan asked. "How is she...?"

"I think she's waking up," Mildred told them softly, carefully excising her hand from the tangle of hair that had smothered it. "Come on, Krysty," she said in a louder voice, "wake up now. It's okay. Time to wake up now. Time to wake up."

Krysty's green eyes blazed open, full of fire and pain, and she sat up in the bed in a great spasm of her muscles, choking and coughing all at once. Mildred sat beside her, watching as the statuesque woman coughed and spluttered some more before taking gasping lungfuls of air as though she had nearly drowned. Krysty stayed like that for almost three minutes, doubled over herself, taking great, heaving breaths, unable to speak or to even acknowledge their presence. Finally she looked at Mildred, her face flushed, her shoulders hunched as she tried to breathe.

"Take it slowly, Krysty," Mildred told her calmly, "there's no need to rush. We're safe here. It's just us."

Krysty looked around the room, seeing J.B., Ryan, returning to look at Mildred. "Wh-what," she began, her voice a pained whisper, "what happened to me?"

"I'm not sure yet," Mildred admitted. "Bad trip through the gateway maybe. You were pretty out of it for a while there."

Krysty nodded, hugging her knees to her chest. "I thought I was going to be chilled," she told them, genuine fear crossing her features at the memory of the hallucination.

"No," Ryan assured her. "No chilling today."

Krysty nodded slowly, her movements birdlike, twitchy.

"Here," Mildred said, handing her a glass of water, "you should drink something. It'll make you feel better."

Krysty took the glass in both hands and it almost slipped from her grip, but she managed to clench it and raise it to her lips. Mildred, Ryan and J.B. watched as she sipped at the water, tentatively at first, before finally taking a long swallow. She greedily finished the glass, letting out a satisfied exhalation afterward, before handing the empty glass back to Mildred. "So much better," she told them, a smile forming on her lips.

Grinning, Ryan leaned across and put an arm around Krysty. She returned the gesture, and they sat there, silently hugging for almost a minute while Mildred and J.B. looked uncomfortably away.

Finally, Krysty spoke up, still holding Ryan close to her. "We're safe here, aren't we?"

Ryan assured her that they were. "Jak and Doc are just downstairs, keeping an eye on comings and the goings, just to be triple sure."

Ryan felt Krysty's head nodding against his shoulder, relieved by his words. Then she spoke again, quietly, her voice so confused she sounded like a little girl. "Then why is everyone screaming?" she asked him.

Chapter Four

Jak and Doc had spent much of the past three hours watching the passing trade at Jemmy's bar and, despite the small size of Fairburn ville, they had both been surprised at the surge in customers as the day stretched into evening. Doc had made some efforts to talk with the locals, joining in with a couple of hands of dominoes with some of the older men, and losing with good grace.

Jak had silently watched the room while the older man went about his business. The youth could scout for a man across two hundred miles with no more clues than a snapped twig and some churned-up mud once in a while, but he would never be one to put people at their ease. Part of that, Doc reasoned, came down to the lad's appearance—whip thin, with alabaster skin, a mane of chalk-pale hair and those burning, ruby-red eyes. Doc was no domino expert, but he knew a lot about people. Gleefully losing a little jack to Sunday gamers was a sure way for an old man to ingratiate himself.

Doc had asked his questions in a roundabout way, just another chatty wrinkle passing through the ville. But he'd deftly turned the conversation to the subject of the strange tower outside the ville, and he'd met with what he could only describe as a polite silence. He hadn't pressed the issue. Instead he'd set about buying drinks for his new friends and losing a couple more rounds of dominoes.

Jak had watched the whole performance with amusement. When Doc finally returned to his table, loudly bemoaning that the domino game was getting too rich for his blood, he and the teen had ordered a plate of food and discussed Doc's conclusions while they waited for news on Krysty's condition.

"The truth of it is," Doc began, "I do not think anyone hereabouts actually knows what the dickens that towering doohickey is for."

IN THE UPSTAIRS ROOMS, Mildred and J.B. were looking at each other while Ryan gently eased Krysty away from him so that he could see her face.

"What did you say?" Ryan asked as though he disbelieved his own ears.

"I just want to know why everyone is screaming," Krysty said quietly.

Mildred spoke up, her question holding no challenge, no judgment. "Who's screaming, Krysty? Are *we* screaming?"

"No." Krysty breathed the word, shaking her head. "Not you. Out there. Outside. Can't you… Can't you hear them? The screams?"

J.B. addressed the room. "Krysty's always had real sensitive hearing," he stated. But Krysty was shaking her head, her vibrant hair falling over her eyes.

"What, Krysty?" Mildred asked. "What is it?"

"It's not far away," Krysty told them, unconsciously biting at her bottom lip, tugging a piece of skin away. "It's right here, all around us. You must be able…you must be able to hear it. Tell me you can hear it. Tell me."

No one answered, and the room remained in silence for a long moment, the only sounds coming from revelers downstairs. Krysty's breathing was hard, ragged, and it was clear that she was trying to hold back her frustrated anger.

Finally, Mildred reached across for her, and Ryan moved out of the way, stepping from the bed. "You're okay," Mildred assured Krysty. "It's nothing, I'm sure. It's nothing, Krysty, I promise you."

Quietly, J.B. led Ryan into the adjoining room and pushed the door between them closed. "This ain't nothing," the Armorer told Ryan flatly in the darkness.

Ryan half nodded, half shook his head, the leather patch over his left eye catching the moonlight from the window. "What do we do now, old friend?" he asked quietly.

"She's not one of us and no more crazy right now than that old coot downstairs," J.B. said, the trace of a smile on his lips. "We've carried Doc when he's been ranting and raving and vision questing all over time and space. You know we have. We'll take care of Krysty."

J.B. turned to the window of the darkened room, looking out at the street. There was a party atmosphere out there now, maybe fifty or sixty people milling around. Street vendors had appeared, selling roasted nuts from open barrels of fire, hunks of meat on sticks.

Ryan joined J.B. at the window, taking in the scene. "Quite the party ville we've found ourselves in," he said, not especially addressing the comment to the Armorer.

J.B. nodded. "I wonder how much of it is connected

with *that*," he said, and his index finger tapped at the glass, pointing to the towering scaffold in the distance.

Ryan turned to look at him, concern furrowing his brow. "You think that tower thing could be connected to Krysty?"

"It's all connected, Ryan," J.B. assured him, as he continued to point at the unmoving tower outside the ville walls. "You just gotta connect enough of the dots."

DOC, RYAN AND J.B. jostled through the crowds as they made their way along Fairburn's main street. Night had long since fallen, and with it the temperature, turning their sweaty afternoon trek into a distant memory. Though the sky was dark, the street was well-lit by oil lamps and naked flames atop haphazard lampposts.

More than seventy people milled around, and tense excitement was in the air as they waited for the dog-fights to begin. People were still arriving, out-of-towners on horses that they weaved through the crowd toward a corral set up at the end of the dusty street.

"You know," Doc pronounced as the companions joined the forming line outside the large, circular shack at the end of the street, "I am starting to conclude that this is not such a bad place." Ryan and J.B. looked at him quizzically, until he continued. "The people seem friendly and well-nourished, they have food and they're making a go of entertaining folk, too. Mayhap a nice place to settle, build a shack." He shrugged.

Ryan's expression remained stern. "And the price is Krysty?"

Doc sighed. "She's getting better, Ryan. She's going to be fine, I'm sure."

Ryan nodded.

J.B. spoke up as the line finally started to shuffle through the entrance to the circular barn. "Just keep alert, see what you can find out about the thing out there," he reminded them, referring to the towering scaffold.

The group had had a hasty meeting after Krysty had woken. They had been in Fairburn for three hours, and the purpose of the tower had nagged at J.B. the whole time, rattling in the back of his brain like an itch he couldn't scratch. Doc's findings, or lack thereof, had only served to worsen that feeling in the Armorer. Mildred had determined that Krysty would be fine; other than the auditory hallucinations—acousma, Mildred had called it—Krysty seemed normal now, just exhausted. The latter was probably down to dehydration, and, Mildred argued, that may even be causing her acousma.

"A dose of bed rest and you'll feel much better," Mildred had assured Krysty, though she had insisted on staying at the woman's side, just in case. Jak had agreed to stay with the women while the other three went off to speak with the locals.

"Roll up, roll up," the barker at the entrance called as Ryan's group reached the front of the line. He held out a rubber stamp glistening with dark ink and asked them for the minimal entry fee. Doc paid with some of the jack he had received at the bar.

The atmosphere inside the circular building was stuffy, despite an open skylight at the center of the roof. In the middle of the room was a round pit, twelve feet in diameter with a floor covered in straw and sawdust. Two mastiff dogs were held in cages at opposite sides of this arena, and they growled at each other meanly through the metal grilles of their holding pens. A low wooden fence surrounded the pit, thin struts acting as bars to prevent the animals from getting out once uncaged. The rest of the room was built with a regular incline, raising the floor from the pit to the outer walls, providing the standing crowd a good view of the action without obscuring the people behind them. Two men worked through the crowd, money and stubs exchanging hands.

"Which one do you like?" J.B. asked Doc and Ryan.

Doc craned his neck, trying to get a better look at the vicious-looking mastiffs. One of the dogs had an ugly scar across its flank, and a streak of white fur covered its left eye, while the other had a dark, dappled coat of fur, browns and grays and blacks, like it had been rolled in ash. "I am no expert in such matters," he admitted, "but it seems that the one on the left is the spitting image of our esteemed leader."

Noticing the white patch of fur across its eye and the scarring on its body, Ryan laughed in agreement. "That's the one we should bet on," he agreed, clapping Doc on the back.

J.B. went to speak with one of the bookies while Doc and Ryan split off into the crowd.

"Ladies and gen'lemen!" a man's voice called from the center of the pit, and the crowd hushed, with just a few conversations continuing as whispers. Doc looked at the man. He was dark skinned with a stubble of hair upon his head, dyed scarlet with food coloring. He had dressed in a patchwork of bright clothes, a long jacket with metallic buttons that twinkled as they caught the flaming lights of the room, striped trousers and bright shined shoes. He held a cane similar to Doc's own, and used it to gesture around the room as he went into his pitch, addressing specific members of the audience as his cane singled them out. This man acted as the ringmaster, working up the excited crowd to fever pitch before the dogs were released.

"We got us two magnificent brutes to start things off tonight," the ringmaster announced. "Killers, the both of them, let me assure you." He flicked the cane toward the caged mastiff with the white stripe across his eye, running the cane along the bars of the cage, antagonizing the beast. "The Streak here, he's eighty-eight pounds o' pure muscle. Those jaws chomp down on your arm, your leg, let me assure you, you would need some serious medical attention, my friends." The man moved across, glaring at the other dog, banging his cane on the top of its cage before launching into similar patter about that hound.

Doc stopped listening, checking the room to try to work out where the ringmaster had appeared from and, thus, would likely disappear to. He spotted a curtained-off area across the circle from the entrance, and pushed and excuse-me'd his way toward it while the ringmaster continued his lecture.

Finally the ringmaster finished his spiel and bared his teeth at the caged animals one last time before reaching for the fence surrounding the arena. Two dog handlers, thick gloves on their hands, leaned into the arena and prepared to unlock the respective cage doors. "Unleash the hounds!" the ringmaster hollered, ending with a wolflike howl before leaping over the fence. The crowd held its collective breath as the cage doors were raised and two short-haired bundles of rage and fury leaped into the arena, scrabbling for purchase on the sawdust as they snarled at each other.

The ringmaster ducked his head low and made his way to the curtained area at the edge of the room, never once bothering to look back. Doc stood there, leaning both hands on his cane, its silver lion's-head handle glinting in the light.

"Hot diggety, but that is one nice cane you've got there, sir," Doc announced as the ringmaster walked past him, pulling the curtain aside.

The ringmaster stopped, turning a querulous face in Doc's direction. Doc weaved his cane back and forth where it stood on its point, making the lion's-head catch the light. "Well, thank you," the ringmaster said as he looked at Doc, then down at the head of Doc's ebony cane. "You not here for the fight?"

Doc shrugged. "I decided to save my money for a later duel. I figure that the odds may become more agreeable as the evening wears thinner."

The ringmaster nodded. "It's a sound plan. Lot of people just come for the spectacle. They're out of jack by the time the real action kicks off."

A cheer surged from the crowd as one of the dogs attached its jaws to the neck of the other, tossing the wounded animal around the circle. The ringmaster pulled back the curtain and gestured inside. "You wanna talk a little out of people's way?" he suggested.

"Much obliged." Doc followed the ringmaster through and found himself in a small dressing area in a corridor, a mirror propped up against a crate. Farther along the corridor were four cages, holding two pit bulls, a ridgeback and what looked like some kind of cross-breed Alsatian-cum-wolf.

Doc had handed the ringmaster his swordstick and he waited patiently while the man examined the lion's head atop it. "This is some fine workmanship," the ringmaster admired. "Are you in the market to sell this?"

Doc tried to look noncommittal. "A man has to eat, my friend."

The ringmaster smiled. "That he does. What do you want for it?"

Doc pointed a thumb back to the curtain. "Mayhap nothing if my strategy pans out. Who knows when Lady Luck will smile?"

The ringmaster reluctantly handed the cane back to Doc. "Lady Luck, she can be an unfaithful mistress. If you do find you want to sell it, I would be very interested."

"That's mighty kind," Doc said, nodding to himself as he strode back toward the arena. As he reached a hand up to part to curtain he stopped and, as though in afterthought, turned back to the ringmaster. "I guess I'll know when you're here by the beacon."

The ringmaster looked at him. "The beacon?" he asked, puffing at the cheroot.

"You know," Doc said, "the tower. I did not see it myself, got here early, but you light that when it is fight day, am I right?"

The ringmaster laughed. "That ain't nothin' to do with me, man. Nothin' to do with anyone, far as I can tell."

Doc scratched his head, further messing his already unruly white hair. "Then what's it there for?"

"You know, I don't think anyone in this whole ville knows the answer to that. When it first appeared some of the good men of Fairburn tried pulling the thing down. Succeeded, actually. Then the outlanders come and shot six men—" he snapped his fingers "—like that. Chilled 'em, stone cold. Told us we were not to touch the towers again."

"Towers?" Doc asked, emphasizing the plural.

"I hear they're dotted all over," the ringmaster told him. "Near the tracks. That's how they travel, you see? By the tracks."

Doc was mystified, trying to recall if he had seen any tracks while the companions made their way to Fairburn. "I am surprised they can find them," he said after a couple of seconds' thought, not really sure what he was referring to but hoping it would entice the other man to tell him more.

"Oh, they worked damn hard gettin' those tracks in serviceable condition," the ringmaster assured him. "'Round here wasn't so bad. The tracks were just a little buried by the dust storms, I think. But some places they must've had to rebuild them pretty much from scratch."

Realization dawned on Doc then. "You mean, the railroad tracks."

"Too right I do." The ringmaster spit. "Couldn't travel around in that monstrosity otherwise, could they?"

Doc shook his head in agreement before turning back to the curtain. "I shall get back to you about the sale," he told the ringmaster, "if my bets do not pan out the way I would surely like them to."

"Good luck," the ringmaster told him, and Doc was touched—it sounded like he meant it.

Out in the main room, the crowd was whooping and cheering. Doc scanned them, looking for Ryan or

J.B. among the sea of heads. He spotted Ryan almost immediately, the tall man towering over the crowd around him. He seemed to be talking with a pretty blond woman, but when Doc got closer he realized that his friend was trying to extract himself from the conversation.

"Excuse me, madam," Doc said loudly as he interposed between the lady and his friend.

Ryan scanned Doc's face. "What news, Doc? Any success?"

"A little. Let's find J.B. and I'll explain it to you both at the same time."

KRYSTY SUDDENLY SAT UP in bed, tilting her head as though to catch a faraway sound.

Mildred put down the book she had been reading. "What is it?"

"Something," Krysty began slowly. "Something's out there." She looked at the window, and Mildred's gaze followed.

Half dozing in a seat in the corner of the room, Jak shook himself and was suddenly wide awake. "What?" he asked the women simply.

"I can hear it," Krysty told them both. "Coming closer now. Screams all around it, like a blanket. A blanket of agony."

Mildred looked at Krysty, wondering what it was that she thought she could hear. Her companion looked disheveled, black rings still heavy around her eyes, her rosepetal lips so much paler than normal. "There aren't any screams," Mildred assured her. "It's just your mind playing tricks. Try to forget about it now. Try to keep calm."

Krysty slowly sank back onto the bed, calming her breathing with an effort. "But they sound so close," she mumbled.

"I know, Krysty," Mildred told her, taking one of her hands in her own. "Just try to rest, recover your strength. And in the morning it will all be over. No more screams, I promise."

Jak was standing by the window, his nose pressed to the glass and a white hand pushed against it over his brow, trying to block out his own pale reflection. He craned farther, turning his head sideways to see a greater distance. Then he said a single word. "Screams."

Mildred turned, shocked. "What? What did you say?" she asked him.

The albino teenager didn't move from the window. "Screams. Coming."

Mildred stood beside him, peering over his shoulder. She knew that Jak had incredible eyesight, almost superhuman, which was decidedly odd for an albino. That very ability had saved her life more than once, an early-warning system for all of the companions. She tried to follow where he was looking, squinting to discern whatever he had seen. "What is it?" she asked.

"There," he said, jabbing his finger toward the skeletal tower that loomed over the ville wall. Mildred followed as Jak traced his finger along the glass. "See it?"

"What am I looking for?" she asked, unable to identify anything unusual in the darkened landscape beyond the wall.

Jak turned from the window, glancing at Mildred before marching to the door. "Lights," he told her.

"Wait, you can't just…" Mildred began.

"Have to," Jak told her. "Find out. Tell Ryan." He left the room, quietly pulling the door closed behind him.

Mildred turned back to the window, pushing the side of her face against the cold glass as she tried to locate whatever it was that Jak was investigating. Almost a minute passed, her breath clouding against the glass before she spotted it—a tiny flicker of crimson light, there and then gone, out in the far distance. She watched for it in the darkness, her heart fluttering anxiously in her chest, until it suddenly reappeared, larger and presumably closer. It wasn't just one light. Now she could make out there were three separate light sources, infernal red and traveling side by side. "What the hell is that?" she muttered to herself.

JAK'S HANDS WERE STRAIGHT, held like blades to cut through the air as he ran across the street and into the shadows between the buildings beyond, taking the most direct route to the wall and the lights beyond it.

When the high wall came into view, Jak assessed it, mentally calculating where the ridges, the natural hand- and footholds in the wood were. Wiry and thin, it was easy to mistake Jak Lauren for a younger boy, but in reality his body was a powerful tool, not an inch of fat on the whole frame; he was built sleek, like a jungle cat.

With three quick steps Jak was up and over the wall, the soles of his boots barely glancing off the wooden surface as he sprang up it, just quiet tapping sounds to mark his passing. He dropped to the other side, landing in a crouch, his weight distributed evenly. Then, without a second's hesitation, he was running again, his flowing mane of hair a snow-white streak cutting through the darkness.

He focused on the lights approaching across the

dusty plain, flaming red and satanic. When he turned his head he could just barely make out the sounds, as well, carrying uncertainly across the flatland with nothing to amplify their echo to his ears. Most of all, however, he felt its approach, heavy on his booted soles, a tremor through the dirt, rumbling across the land.

"A TRAIN?" J.B. repeated.

Doc looked around the crowded room, wondering how much of this they wanted to announce to the strangers around them. He stood with J.B. and Ryan near the back of the crowd, close to the lone entry and exit door. "That is what the man told me," he explained, gesturing with his hand that they keep the volume of their conversation low.

"It's not the first time we've come across one," Ryan reminded him.

"Yeah, I know, but you've got to build tracks and grease points, there's a shed-load of maintenance with just the physical upkeep of those tracks, let alone finding or building an engine to run on them." He whistled softly. "It takes some doing." The companions had seen trains operating before, but they were rare in the fractured landscape of the Deathlands.

The three men stood in silence, each turning over the prospect in his mind. Finally, Doc spoke. "What if they are using the old tracks, prenukecaust. Could that be done?"

J.B. adjusted the spectacles on his nose, wiping away the sweat that had pooled under the nose clips. "It's possible, Doc. Usually it was the transport links that were the first to go, targeted by the Reds."

"When we got here," Ryan stated, "you said that this place had avoided much of the bloodshed and bombing."

J.B. nodded. "Never been here myself, but I heard that North Dakota got mostly passed over. Too far north, I guess, and nowhere near the big conurbs. Weather got scragged, of course, but that's all over Deathlands. That's global."

Suddenly the crowd surged, clapping and cheering, and the three men turned to watch the action in the sunken arena. The darker-coated dog had just sunk its huge teeth into the neck of the dog with the white blaze. White blaze made a whimpering noise, a nasty choking sound coming from his throat as specks of blood amassed around his opponent's fangs. He tried to pull away, but the other's jaws were locked tight, unwilling to release him. The dark furred dog pushed the sharp claws of its left forelimb into the other's chest, tipping him over, still clinging to his neck with powerful jaws.

J.B. turned away from the action, leading the way to the door. "Looks like you lost your bet, Ryan," he said.

THROUGH THE WINDOW, Mildred watched the red lights getting larger as they closed in on the ville. There were more of them now, and she could see that they made up some kind of pattern across the front of a large, dark shadow, low to the ground, with numerous wispy lights trailing behind. The shadow was moving steadily toward the ville, not especially fast, just steady, relentless.

A moving speck caught her eye, lightly colored against the night-dark sand. Jak. He was running an intercept path across the plain, torso held low to make him less visible, a smaller target. He ran with considerable speed toward the red lights.

The flames of hell danced in those lights, Mildred was sure of it.

THE GROUND ALL around Jak was vibrating now, shuddering as the monstrosity lumbered toward the ville. He narrowed his eyes as he ran toward it, trying to see past the bright glowing spots that covered its leading face. A vast shadow plowed relentlessly onward behind those crimson spots, the grim reaper stalking the Deathlands.

Fifty feet away, Jak suddenly threw himself to the ground, hunkering down, working his elbows into the sand to create a ridge in front of him. He reached to his belt, pulled the Colt Python, reassured by the weight in his hands.

The shadow trudged closer, belching smoke and fog into the night sky. Jak watched the glowing slits approach, like multiple eyes in the front of the creature. And behind, the metal carapace, some terrible insect grown vast.

It was a train like Jak had never seen. Painted black, sulphurous eyes glowing like embers across its engine, dragging its bulbous cars like pregnant women being pulled by their hair, stretching back along the tracks farther than Jak could see. And on the front, perversely, was a mutie woman carved of wood, her bare breasts pushed forward to lead the way, her torso morphing into reptilian scale as she disappeared into the engine housing, lit only by the reddish-orange glow from those hellfire slits. The woman's face was a picture of agony, mouth taut in silent, never-ending scream, bloodred tears painted from her straining eyes.

As Jak watched from his meager hiding place, he realized that the train was slowing and that people were being disgorged from its bloated cars.

Chapter Five

Jak lay perfectly still, the Colt Python resting in his right hand, watching the hideous train pull to a halt beside the skeletal tower. A dozen men had leaped from the first two cars as the train slowed, all of them armed and several brandishing their blasters in readiness, as though they expected an attack. The men spread out across the area, checking, Jak realized, for people who might be hiding, checking for people like him. He hunkered down lower, wishing for better cover in the open plains. For the moment, the armed men remained close to the tower, which was two whole car lengths away from Jak's current position. Despite leaving it open to the elements and to attack through the day, they had arrived to protect it now—and Jak's curiosity was piqued.

The train lurched to a halt and a huge cloud of steam burst from the funnel atop its insectlike engine. For a moment Jak watched it through the cloud, like trying to make out faces in the fog, until the steam disbursed, filling the atmosphere all around with a malodorous mist that irritated his nose and throat. Burning—the train smelled of burning.

Instructions were being shouted now, and more people were stepping from the train. The first group had been fighters, sec-men types, well-armed and well-muscled, men of action. But the second group was made up of more general body types.

Two shirtless men were struggling with a cylinder less than three feet in length. Jak guessed that it wouldn't reach to his waist if it was stood on its end. But seemed to be heavy—the men struggled with it, walking in irregular spurts as they carried it to the tower, quick discussions preceding each movement. A sec man followed them, casually holding a short-handled club, shouting instructions.

Three others followed, two men and a woman, looking nervously around as they left the security of the train. One of the men looked quite a bit older than the others, wispy gray hair blowing around on his balding head, glasses perched on his nose. The other two were younger, midthirties perhaps—about Ryan's age. All three looked uncomfortable as they walked warily to the tower, taking care not to slip on the dry, sandy ground.

While they made their way to the structure, Jak turned to examine the train. It stretched off down the tracks for a seemingly impossible length. Its details lost to darkness, Jak could see faint lights burning in the cars as it waited down the length of railroad. He held a thumb up to his eye, trying to estimate the length of this beast of chrome and steel, but there were no landmarks to adequately judge it by. A quarter mile, perhaps a little less—that would be his guess. Helluva train.

None of it matched. Though too dark to make out the detail, even with Jak's unearthly vision, he could clearly see that the cars were constructed ad hoc, random pieces of junk transformed into containers to travel the metal tracks. Some were straight conversions, old train cars pulled out of the enforced retirement of the Long

Winter. Others looked like they had been constructed by a blind man dancing a jig in a junkyard, choosing pieces wherever he tripped, bulbous or holed or both, only their wheels fitting the gauge of the tracks.

Noise came from some of the lighted cars, laughing and shrieking, people having fun, their voices and the sound of clinking glasses carrying to Jak over the empty plain now that the shuddering train had ceased generating its arthritic cacophony of movement.

The three people had reached the tower beside the nose end of the train, and they called out and pointed at the ground around the base of the tower. The younger man was setting up a small tripod, unfolding a large sheet of paper that he held out to the width of his arm span and consulted diligently—a map, Jak realized. The woman joined him, jabbing at the map, then pointing at the sky above them, and the man nodded his agreement. Then he crouched slightly, and put his eye to a small metallic box that rested atop the tripod. His right hand fiddled with a knob sticking from the side of the box, and Jak realized that this was some kind of seeing device that he was lining up to check on his whereabouts or the whereabouts of something important to the man and his team.

Meanwhile, two burly thugs worked at the oil drum canister that rested at the base of the scaffold tower. At first Jak thought they were trying to move the half-buried can, but then he saw them remove the large metal plate that formed its lid.

One of the men at the tower put his fingers to his lips and loudly whistled. The cry went out. "More light!"

There was movement to Jak's left, farther down the train, and two men wheeled a cart from the fourth car down an unfolding ramp and across the dirt. As they passed Jak, barely eight feet in front of his hiding position, he could clearly see the cart. Set on a rig on top of it were three, heavy, round spotlights of the type found in theaters, and a petroleum generator rested on the cart's base. When they reached the site of the tower, the genny was switched on and it began to chug loudly, spluttering as it started converting fuel to power, filling the air with the rotting fruit stench of petroleum. The spotlights came on in a blaze, dimming a moment, then reaching full intensity. The cart was positioned so that the spots pointed at the open canister at the tower's base. People milled around, blocking Jak's line of sight.

The albino teen looked around, conscious of the guards patrolling the surrounding area. They seemed fairly lax, as if they weren't really expecting trouble, and Jak reasoned that they had had trouble in the past and had dealt with it in a definite manner, the way that scared interested spectators away from future excursions. Whatever, he needed to get closer to the tower, to see for himself exactly what these train people were doing here. If he could see what they were up to, he might have the answer to what the tower actually was, its purpose.

With a swift check over his shoulder, Jak pushed himself off the ground and scrambled across the plain toward the tower, keeping clear of the glowing red lights cast by the holes in the train's carapace.

He was just forty paces from the tower, then thirty, twenty, and suddenly he had almost run slap-bang into one of the huge sec man dressed in muted colors and holding an a longblaster. Jak dropped silently to the ground, and was reassured that the sec man showed no reaction. Swiftly, Jak clambered away on elbows and knees, the noise of his movement masked by the vibrating gasoline generator.

Jak watched as the three nervous types instructed the others. The woman dipped a thin line of metal into the buried canister, and when she pulled it out it glistened with liquid. She looked at the dipstick for a moment, and the older man with the wispy gray hair spoke to her, writing the reading into a book he had produced from his jacket pocket. He showed her the page and the pair consulted for a half minute. Then the older man pointed to the two shirtless men who had hefted the heavy, three-foot-high cylinder over and instructed them to bring it to him.

Their companion continued to check through his tripod's eyepiece, occasionally pulling away and using his fingers to count off some calculation, his lips moving.

The two shirtless men had brought the cylinder to the area beneath the tower, and wedged it into the dirt as they stood waiting for further instructions. The older man leaned down, clutching at a muscle in his back and wincing before he adjusted the glasses on his nose to read off something from the side of the cylindrical tank. Satisfied, he nodded and consulted with the woman and the tripod man. There was a hasty discussion, with a lot of arm waving, but Jak couldn't hear what they were saying over the noise of the genny running the spotlights.

After a while, one of the burly sec men stepped over, his face angry, and jabbed at the older man with a meaty paw. The older man checked his wrist chron and nodded in supplication.

Jak watched as the shirtless men tipped the cylinder toward the open barrel in the ground. The younger man who had set up the tripod shouted a single word, loud enough that it carried to Jak's ears. *"Careful!"* Jak shook his head, brushing his white hair from his face unconsciously as he tried to discern what it was that the group was doing. They had unscrewed a cap at the top of the smaller cylinder and were carefully tipping it until a thick drool of liquid poured from it into the barrel beneath the tower. The liquid didn't pour easily— it had lumps in it and it trickled from the cylinder spout in fits and starts. The gunk was a grayish color, glistening in the harsh spotlights.

Suddenly the operation was called to a halt, the older man, the younger man and the woman all calling for a stop at the same time, shouting over one another. The shirtless men stopped pouring the liquid from the cylinder, tipping it backward until it rested upright again on its base, denting into the sand. One of the shirtless men leaned down, screwing the black cap back on, while the woman tried her dipstick in the liquid of the barrel once again. Satisfied with her findings, she nodded and gave a thumbs-up.

The older man and the woman turned, walking slowly back to the train, deep in conversation. The other man was busy folding the legs of his tripod back together and inserting it into a plastic carry case. An instruction was given by the thug who had pressured the group—a foreman of some kind, Jak reasoned—and the genny was shut down. The lights dimmed and went out, and the generator shuddered a few times before finally sitting still on the cart.

The whole mysterious group was making its way

back to the train and it was time for Jak to make his way
back, too, to tell Ryan and the others all that he had witnessed. He couldn't begin to fathom what it all meant,
but he trusted that Ryan and the others would make
sense of it given enough information and time. The
barrel of liquid seemed vital to the operation—was that
somehow connected to the tower, beneath the sands,
where they couldn't see?

Jak eased himself backward, crab-walking, his belly
touching the ground as he pulled away from the train
and the tower, back toward the ville wall. The crew was
getting on the train, and he could hear the engine being
stoked with coal, building up a head of steam to get it
moving once more along the metal tracks. And then he
heard another sound: the familiar click as a blaster was
cocked behind his ear.

"Don't move, Whitey." It was a man's voice, impa-
tient, anger barely held in check.

Jak spun, flipping onto his back and unleashing a
blast from his Colt Python without even stopping to
think about it. One of the sec men was standing there,
right behind him, surprise on what remained of his face
as the large-bore bullet drilled through his head. The
boom of Jak's blaster echoed across the plain, and he
dropped all pretence of stealth, leaping up and running
toward the gates of Fairburn.

The sec men from the train reacted swiftly, a half
dozen of them chasing the fleeing teenager across the
sand, shouting to one another as they zeroed in on him.

Jak looked over his shoulder, dodging as a well-
muscled man in a torn T-shirt made a grab for him from
over his right shoulder. The man missed, his hand
clutching at Jak's leather jacket. He pulled his hand

back with a shriek, blood pouring from the lacerations where his fingers had gripped around the razor blades and sharp edges of glass and metal that Jak had meticulously sewn into the fabric.

The wounded man reached for the blaster in his hip holster, but the foreman was beside him now, barking instructions. "Keep him alive," he called loudly, so that all of his crew could hear. "One like that, be a lot of use to us."

Jak tossed his arms back, the Magnum blaster still in his right hand, keeping his balance as he skirted down the slope that led to the walled ville in front of him. Two more of the train sec men appeared from the shadows to his left, and one of them tossed something in Jak's direction. Roughly the length of a man's forearm, the thing looked like some kind of nightstick in the light cast over the wall. Jak ducked his head, swerving to avoid it as it hurtled at him. The nightstick clattered to the ground, missing him by inches, and Jak continued to run.

The gates were closed. There wouldn't be time to negotiate with the sentries now, so Jak would have to use his speed to clamber up them, the same way he'd negotiated the wall to get out here in the first place. He was scanning the gates, looking for potential handholds, when something hit him in the left shoulder. The other sec man had to have had a nightstick, too.

Jak staggered back, raising the blaster and targeting the two men who charged him. His first shot slapped the lead man off his feet, creating a vast hole in his chest as he fell to the sand. But by then the second was on him, and the handblaster was useless. Jak swung his left fist at the sec man, the man's stubbled face leering at him as he lunged at the teen with a dagger. The fist connected, caving in the man's nose. The sec man staggered backward, clutching at his bloody nose, but Jak could feel a nasty throbbing in his left arm. The hit with the nightstick had caught his shoulder, and the surge of adrenaline was already passing, leaving numbness in its wake.

More guards were arriving, appearing from the shadows all around, eight of them, then ten, with blasters and knives.

Jak stepped backward, Fairburn's gates looming over him, his hands at his sides. He dropped his Colt Python to the sand, then raised his right hand, open and empty. His left arm sagged, unmoving.

Chapter Six

"My sweet Lord," Mildred murmured as she watched from the window. She stood immobile as the train pulled away and watched it slowly ease along the tracks, away from Fairburn.

Finally she turned and looked at Krysty, who was hunched on the bed, her knees pulled up to her chest in fetal position, her hands over her ears. "Come on, Krysty, time to go," Mildred said firmly.

Krysty sleepily opened one eye, mumbled something incoherent.

Mildred crouched at the side of the bed, running her hand over Krysty's fevered brow. "I'm sorry, Krysty, but we have to go. I have to find Ryan and I think it's best if you stay with me. You understand that, don't you?"

Krysty slurred her answer, still struggling to shake off her sleep. "O' course," she said around her thick tongue. After a moment she opened both eyes and pulled herself up, swinging her legs and feet over the side of the bed. "What happened?" she asked as Mildred passed the woman her cowboy boots.

"They took Jak," Mildred stated bluntly.

"So," Doc asked the others as the three of them walked back toward Jemmy's bar and hostelry, "what did you two find out?"

J.B. shrugged. "Nothing we didn't already know."

As they crossed the street—now empty but for a lone, hopeful street vendor, still roasting nuts over an open barrel—they saw Mildred burst from Jemmy's, followed by a tired Krysty. J.B. ran the last few steps to meet them, and Ryan and Doc increased their pace behind him.

"What's going on?" J.B. asked Mildred.

"Jak's gone," she told her audience. "He jumped the wall, to get a closer look at that monstrous thing that—"

Doc interrupted her. "What 'monstrous thing'?" he asked.

"The train," Mildred said breathlessly. "Didn't you see it? Didn't you hear it, at least? It shook the ground, Doc."

"We were in the arena, the dog fight," Doc explained. "'Twas mighty noisy in there, the crowd all excited and the hounds going at each other hammer and tongs. Quite the experience."

"Which way did he go, Mildred?" he asked, all business again.

Mildred hefted the backpack on her shoulder, pointing in the direction of the tower. "The train stopped beside the tower, and I think they did something to it, I'm not sure what. It was all very quick, like they had done this before. The whole operation took no more than four minutes. Jak was out there the whole time, he'd sneaked up really close so he could observe and report back, figured it was something worth knowing about." She stopped, calming her breath. "But they took him, Ryan. They took him and then they left." She pointed in the direction that the rails led.

"Fireblast!" Ryan cursed, taking brisk strides toward the gate.

J.B. called after him. "What are you planning on doing? Chasing after him on foot?"

Ryan stopped, turning back to J.B. and the others. "Well, what would you suggest?"

J.B. smiled as he indicated the corral behind him with his outstretched thumb. "I would suggest that we travel in style."

Ryan was already sprinting down the street, heading for the corral at the far end, and J.B. kept pace with him. Mildred looked torn, her head flicking to watch Ryan.

"Go," Doc told her quietly. "I shall take care of Krysty." She looked at him, an unspoken question on her lips, and he shook his head. "Now that she is on her feet again, I think we can just about take on the world between us. She will probably be carrying my weary bones by the time we catch up to you."

"Thank you," Mildred called as she sprinted down the street after Ryan and J.B.

While their companions raced to the corral, Doc led Krysty in the opposite direction, telling her that they needed to reach the gates. She rushed along in his wake, struggling to keep up.

At the gates, Doc studied the cantilevered system for a few moments. One of the sentries atop the gates—a strong-looking farmhand, twenty-one and toughened up by a life of manual labor—noticed him and made his way down the wood stairs, calling to the old man. "Hey, hey, what do you think you're doing? Do I even know you?" he asked.

In a single movement, Doc snapped his cane open, revealing the sword blade hidden within, and had it pointed at the young man's throat. "I will be requiring these gates to be opened instantly," he explained.

His mouth agog, the young sentry glanced at the blade that was poised at his neck, then collapsed in a dead faint.

From the other end of the street Doc could hear the fast beating hooves of horses. As if to clarify what he already knew, Krysty alerted him. "Here comes Ryan."

Doc squinted at the lock, trying to fathom how the system of pulleys that opened the heavy gate worked, then he shook his head and pulled his shining Le Mat revolver from its holster. "Rope A, fulcrum, point B..." He shrugged and blasted a hole through the middle of the rope with a single load from the weapon's shotgun barrel.

There was a second sentry, an old man dozing atop the sill beside the top of the gates. He was startled awake by the thunderous sound of Doc's percussion weapon, and the first thing he saw was the gate swinging toward him, the taut rope that held it in place gone slack. The sentry backed up, forgetting where he was, and fell from the top of the wall, the full nine feet to the hard ground. He landed with a thump, rolling on the ground in pain. And then three horses galloped past him, their hooves bare inches from his skull, as the riders left the ville.

The gate open, Doc was rushing back down the street with Krysty at his heels. "We need to get transport of our own, Krysty," he called to her as he led the way to the corral that Ryan and the others had just raided.

The surge of action seemed to be doing Krysty good. Her cheeks were flushed, and she seemed more alive now than she had in the past nine hours.

"Do you feel up to riding a horse?" he asked her.

"I feel as if I am flying," she replied, "floating on a vast lake. It's all so unreal."

At the gates to the corral, Doc looked around at the tied horses. "I would be inclined to take that as a 'no,' my dear," he decided, "but please feel at ease to disabuse me of that notion if you so wish."

She screwed her eyes closed, trying to feel whatever it was that was inside her. "I can still hear the sounds, Doc," Krysty said. "The screaming."

Doc spied a pony and trap in one corner of the corral and began to walk toward it. "In which case we shall be a little more sedate in our pursuit," he told Krysty, untying the pony's reins. He looked around the corral, wondering if he had missed anything. Slumped on the ground by a sack of feed was the stable boy, a large jug resting on his stomach. The boy was perhaps thirteen years old, and he stank of pear cider.

"Hyah! Hyah!" Doc shouted as he whipped at the pony. He and Krysty were on their way, speeding down the street and through the gates.

Doc gave one last look over his shoulder as they rushed out of Fairburn. He had liked the ville, as it had something of his home-town values about it. Sadly, they probably looked down on horse thieves, he reasoned as he urged the pony and trap past the gates and up the incline in the direction of the tracks.

As they bumped up the incline, Krysty called loudly for him to stop and Doc turned to her. He was hesitant to call a halt to their chase so soon, but he also worried about the young woman's health. She looked okay, tired but otherwise well, but Krysty called again for him to stop, shouting to be heard over the racing hoofbeats.

Doc pulled back on the reins, until the pony staggered to a stop. "What is it, Krysty? Are you...?" Doc began, but the woman was already out of her seat, running back toward the ville. Doc admired Krysty as she ran; there was something of her lithe grace returning to her muscles, though she seemed a little unsteady as she wended toward the open gates of Fairburn. She was twelve feet behind him when Doc saw her bend and take something large and shiny from the ground. Then she turned, ran back, and Doc saw that she clutched Jak's .357 Magnum Colt Python blaster.

"Jak would never forgive us," Krysty told Doc as she climbed into the seat beside him. She didn't need to finish the sentence; Doc agreed one hundred percent.

He urged the pony toward the horizon. The train was nowhere in sight and neither were their companions. They had a long ride ahead.

RYAN, J.B. AND Mildred rode side by side, urging the stolen horses beneath them with kicks and slaps. To their left, the train tracks continued in a slight curve across the sandy landscape, barely visible in the moonlight.

J.B. was trying to get the facts in order in his head. "You say they *took* Jak with them?" he asked Mildred, raising his voice to be heard over the loud hoofbeats on the packed ground.

She turned to him, her beaded plaits whipping across her face. "Definitely. I saw a half dozen of the crew lead him back to one of the cars, then push him inside."

"And he was still alive? They hadn't chilled him?"

"They took him alive," she assured J.B., "but I don't know how long they'll keep him that way."

Ryan continued to look to the horizon as he chipped in on the conversation. "Why would they want him, Mildred?"

"I wasn't close enough to hear what they said," Mildred reminded him. "I could barely make out what was going on once they flicked the spotlights off. All I know is that Jak ran to the gates and a group of men followed him. I heard two shots and then the men reappeared, marching Jak to the train."

"J.B.?" Ryan called for the Armorer's opinion.

"Who knows why anyone would want Jak," J.B. answered.

"If he's still alive," Ryan stated, "we'll find him. And if he's dead, then we are going to chill every last sec man on that train."

THE SEC MEN HAD MARCHED Jak beyond the locomotive engine and the first ten, wheeled units that it pulled before one of them opened a door and shoved him into a car. Jak had kept his head low, hands weaved behind his neck, left arm burning with pain, and tried to keep track of everything he saw.

The engine had been painted a matte black so as not to pick up reflections. It shrugged off the moonlight, a shadow looming large against the indigo sky. Holes had been molded into its casing through which burning coals glowed reddish-orange. It was almost forty feet, tip to tail, and the majority of that space was dedicated to burning the fuel that powered it. An open plate at the end showed where the engineer worked the controls. Above the engine, near the strange figurehead that jutted from the front, a wide chimney belched puffs of steam while the vehicle stood at rest. Once it got moving again, that smokestack would blast a dense fog into the air around the train, just as Jak had seen on its approach, creating a misty cloud through which it seemed to battle to its destination.

Behind the engine stood a chrome container unit and Jak guessed that this held the fuel that powered the beast. It was a long unit, almost as long as the engine itself, and Jak could see putrid yellow symbols indicating radioactive material within as well as the coal.

Cars followed. The first was a flatbed, open to the elements with a large cannon affixed to its surface. If necessary, Jak guessed, this would be the first line of defense should any unwelcomes approach the steel behemoth.

After that, a series of boxes on wheels, glass windowpanes catching the moonlight. Jak guessed that these held equipment since one of these cars was where the spotlight trolley had appeared from.

The next two cars looked similar to each other, like large wooden crates with narrow horizontal slits where the planks met, and a set of steps at each end leading up to an open doorway. Inside the first doorway, Jak saw a sec man watching the group that passed with the prisoner. The man held a large-bore shotgun in his hands and trained it on Jak as he passed.

Jak stumbled up the steps as he was pushed roughly into the second car, though he felt grim satisfaction when he heard his assailant's wail as he cut himself on his deadly jacket.

Inside, the interior was intensely dark, and Jak blinked his eyes several times in an effort to adjust. Out in the open had been dark enough, but the inside was pitch black.

Then a man behind him lit an oil lamp and followed Jak up the steps. "Come on," he growled, "git in there."

Jak looked around the narrow car. Floor-to-ceiling grillwork stood immediately in front of him with a bolted gate in its center. The grille acted as a cage, closing off four-fifths of the car. Through the grille, Jak could see eyes staring at him—scared, timid eyes, wet with tears.

As his guard jostled him forward, the oil lamp picked up more of the room and Jak saw that the eyes belonged to about eight or nine children, dressed in dirty rags and cowering as far from the mesh gate as they could. The room stank of their own feces and urine, and Jak could see cockroaches and other small creatures moving around the stained floor of the cage. As he watched, one of the filthy children reached out, trapping a roach in his fingers before devouring its squirming body.

"Welcome to your new home, sonny." The guard with the oil lamp laughed behind him, his breath rancid as it spewed over Jak's shoulder.

Another sec man had joined them, and he unbolted the gate, brandishing a remade Beretta blaster at the children in the cage. "These here are your new friends," he told Jak, pulling back his hand to push the albino inside. He looked at Jak's coat with its decoration of sharp edges and obviously thought better of it, choosing to wave the blaster in Jak's face instead. "You get inside." he told Jak.

Jak looked at the blaster's muzzle, then up at the sec man's eyes, and a snarl crossed his lips. The sec man backhanded him across the face, and Jak stumbled backward into the caged room, twirling around before slumping down hard on his rear. The guard pointed the

Beretta at him, arm outstretched, aiming it at Jak's forehead.

The albino teen sat still, watching the man's eyes, waiting for that flash of determination that meant he was going to pull the trigger. Nothing. Just a bluff. A wicked smile crept across Jak's face and the man growled, lowering the blaster.

And then Jak saw the twitch in the eyes, the defining moment, and the man pulled the trigger after all, burying a slug deep in his chest.

Chapter Seven

The horse's hooves thundered against the ground beneath her as Mildred and her steed tried to keep pace with Ryan's horse. J.B. and his own horse had deliberately dropped back behind the group, and the Armorer had his mini-Uzi hidden in his lap, covering his companions in case things got bloody.

They could see the train ahead now, a little below them where the ground sunk. The companions charged downhill, following the tracks as they endeavored to catch up.

Mildred could hear the noise of the train over the frantic hoofbeats of her mount, rattling the metal tracks with a regular clacking sound. As she closed with it, the racket became louder. Close by, the train stretched onward as far as Mildred could see; it was only when they were on the higher ground that she had had any inkling as to the length of the metallic beast.

Ryan leaned in low to his steed's neck, letting the wind from the train's slipstream pass over him. There were three horse lengths between him and the rear of the moving train, and he urged his horse on with a kick of his heels in its flanks.

A man crouched atop the train, holding a longblaster pointing into the air. Rearguard, obviously, but a pretty stupe one in Ryan's opinion. The man was paying no attention to the track behind the train, and the noise of the train's passing masked the galloping approach of the horses across the sandy plain; enough at least that the man didn't bother to check. Ryan knew the type—he was lazy because he was bored by the routine.

The one-eyed man was in reach of the train now, though the horse kept shrugging away as Ryan guided it toward the moving vehicle. He patted the horse's neck, trying to calm the animal, as he pulled the reins to the left, guiding the horse closer to the back of the train. There were no doors here, no way in from the rearmost car, but he could see bars of metal stretch up the side—a ladder.

Ryan reached out for the nearest of the horizontal bars as the wind whipped all around him, slapping him in the face and pushing his reaching arm backward. The one-eyed man urged his mount on with another jab of his heels. He needed to get up that ladder and kill the sentry before the sec man knew what was happening, otherwise the whole crew might be alerted. Ryan reached again for one of the metal rungs and felt his little finger whisper against it. He stretched his arm a little farther, teeth gritted as he strained his muscles for the extra reach, and suddenly snatched the rung in a firm grip.

Taking all of his weight on his left arm, he kicked the horse away beneath him. Suddenly he was dangling by one arm, watching his mount run off into the wilderness, the ground hurtling three inches beneath the toes of his combat boots. The instant stretched for an eternity, and he swore that he heard Mildred gasp behind him, despite the relentless noise of the tracks and the howling wind shrieking in his ears. Then he had swung his other arm around and he was climbing the ladder, pulling himself up as his feet swung over empty space.

The muscles in Ryan's shoulders and across his chest burned as he pulled himself up the ladder, looking down to ensure that his feet found the lowest rungs. As soon as his feet were planted, Ryan relaxed a little, his pulse pounding in his ears.

He powered up the ladder, hurled himself over the rim of the car and onto the roof. The sec man with the longblaster rifle turned as he heard or felt Ryan's boots slap down on the roof. He made to cry out, but Ryan's fist pounded into the man's windpipe before he could even stand.

The man fell backward, dropping his blaster over the side of the hurtling train. He scrabbled, arms flailing, spluttering where his throat had been bruised, but he regained his balance and pulled himself to a crouch at the edge of the narrow rooftop. His eyes fell on Ryan, assessing the stranger, and he tried to speak. The words came out as a croak, their meaning lost, and the man began to gag, looking at the roof like a drunk who had lost his bearings.

When the man looked up again, he saw his one-eyed assailant was on top of him, casting a low punch into his belly. The breath whooshed out of the man, and he felt something burn where the blow had connected.

Ryan stepped back, yanking the blade of his panga from the sec man's gut. A dark flower blossomed on the man's shirt where the blade had pieced his flesh, and Ryan watched it expand in the dull moonlight. The sec man reached for his stomach, looking at Ryan with fear in his eyes, then he keeled over, collapsing to the roof.

The wind streaming in his dark hair, Ryan walked across the car roof, placed his boot against the man's thorax and shoved the heel into the man's body, tipping the guard over the side of the train. He watched as the man bounced along the tracks two, three times, before finally coming to rest as the train sped away. J.B. and Mildred were trailing along the left edge, urging their mounts to keep pace with the train. Ryan's boarding, start to finish, had taken three seconds.

Ryan crouched and looked down the length of the roof and along the consecutive rooftops that traveled up the line ahead of him. There were a few sec men on the nearby rooftops, but none close enough to cause the companions any problems. Ryan scrambled across the roof and, lying flat on his belly, dipped his head over the edge and checked each side in turn. They were the same, a simple ladder arrangement built into the metal sides about two-thirds of the way along the car. In the dark it was hard to be certain, but the car appeared to be made of molded steel, cold to the touch.

Halfway along the roof was a lumpy square, and Ryan crawled swiftly along to examine it: some kind of drop-down hatch. He put his ear to the entryway and listened for any echoes coming from within. Ryan failed to discern anything, but the train was loud on the tracks, the wind loud in his ears, and the whole thing was shaking worse than a gaudy slut with an armful of jolt on payday; he couldn't be certain.

He quickly worked his way back to the ladder on his left, the right-hand side of the car, and looked over the side. Mildred's horse was keeping pace, and she was looking up at Ryan, waiting for his signal. He held his open hand out to the side, fingers splayed where

Mildred could see them against the inconstant moon, then bunched it into a fist and pumped the fist down as though pulling an overhead cord: *come on.*

Clutching her horse's neck, Mildred shrugged the bag from her back and held it up against the side of the car. She traveled as light as she could, but there was important medical equipment in it that she'd gathered here and there during her travels.

Ryan leaned down and grabbed for one of the backpack's straps, yanking it onto the roof. He rested it there as quietly as he could, trusting its weight to keep it secure for the few seconds it would take to get Mildred aboard. Then he reached back over, his chest flush against the rooftop, and stretched his left arm as far down the ladder as he could, securing himself to the roof with his free hand.

It took two tries, but Mildred's reaching hand finally locked on to one of the low rungs of steel and she pulled her body, still atop the horse, closer to the train. Her mount shook its head back and forth, trying to keep away from the rapidly moving train as Mildred took her right foot out of the stirrup and shifted her balance in the saddle. Her right arm darted out and she clutched at Ryan's forearm. His hand gripped her own forearm, their wrists touching, and he held her steady as she leaped across the gap between horse and train, the ground hurtling beneath her.

Mildred swung awkwardly for a moment, scrabbling to find the rungs of the ladder with her feet, but Ryan's grip held firm and she realized that she had ample time to find proper purchase and make her way up to the roof. Ryan held her arm the whole time, as solid as an oak, his grip never faltering, and Mildred finally swung onto the ladder and held it firmly.

When she let Ryan's forearm go, he continued to clutch her until he was sure that she wouldn't drop, then his grip loosened and she pulled her right arm to the rungs of the ladder and yanked herself up. Ryan smiled at her from where he lay atop the roof and she breathed a word of thanks as she pulled herself over the edge to join him.

"Easy pie," he assured her as she pulled her backpack back over her shoulders and tightened the straps.

J.B. was next, passing up Ryan's SSG-70 Steyr blaster before he clambered up the ladder. Before long the three of them sat together on the roof establishing their next move in a series of rapid hand gestures.

Ryan indicated the roof hatch, and they moved toward it in walking crouches. The three of them surrounded the hatchway, each assuming his or her role for the next part of the operation. Mildred unholstered her ZKR 551 Czech-built .38 caliber target revolver, pointing it so that it would be aimed directly into the space below once the hatch was removed. J.B. set his Uzi on the surface of the roof, close to hand, and placed both hands ready to unfasten twin catches on the hatch.

Ryan had resheathed his panga and now held his SIG-Sauer. The blaster had a built-in baffle silencer that worked sporadically, and it would prove necessary if they were to execute their plan quietly. Mildred and J.B. were there for backup, but if Ryan could take out any guards with a passable degree of silence they would be better placed to continue their operations unnoticed.

Ryan held his left hand above the hatch, silently counting down from three on his outstretched fingers. On one, J.B. flipped the latches, and on zero he had the hatch pulled back toward him, opening the doorway in the roof.

Feet first, Ryan dropped through the opening, quietly landing in a crouch and steadying his blaster hand with his left, swiftly rotating on his heel to take in the confined space of the car. The room was dark, the only light coming from the night sky through the open hatch directly above him. He could sense objects all around him. A few glints of metal caught his eye, but he couldn't see anyone else in the car. He held his breath and listened, blaster still in the ready position. Nothing. He was alone.

He called to the others, his voice a low growl, confirming the all clear and instructing them to join him. Mildred dropped down first, her target revolver still in hand, and J.B. followed, Uzi at the ready.

"Dark as a blacksmith's rag in here," J.B. muttered as he pulled the roof hatch back in place. He fiddled in one of his jacket pockets for a moment and produced a glow stick with an audible snap. The glow stick emanated a dull, green iridescence, filling the car with long shadows.

Ryan scurried to the front end of the car and stood next to the metal door that had appeared with the increase in light. He put a hand on the doorknob, slowly increased the pressure on it and felt the door give, opening a bare inch. He pulled the door closed again and examined it for a locking device of some kind, but couldn't find any bolts or turnkeys. "Door's unlocked," he told the others bleakly.

"One of us needs to watch that at all times," J.B. decided. "Can't be entertaining uninvited company."

Mildred sat cross-legged on the metal plate floor four feet in front of the door and held her ZKR 551 loosely in her hand, her eyes focused on the door handle. "Got it," she said. "You boys look around, see if there are any toys to play with."

Ryan and J.B. checked the small room rapidly as the glow stick continued to fizz out its greenish hue. The walls held strong steel shelves at the tail end, and the shelves were piled with train parts in various states of deterioration. Some even looked shiny new. There were heavy wheels for the rolling stock, jars and other containers filled with rivets, nails and screws; large sheets of metal lay atop one another in a huge stack, and J.B. found another group standing in one corner, wedged in the gap where two shelving units met. They located three acetylene torches for welding, and J.B. shook one to see if it had any fuel in it. Hooks and chains were attached to ceiling racks, and they rattled with each movement of the car.

"Storeroom," Ryan announced.

"Repair shop," J.B. agreed. "These people are well prepped for life on the move. Smart place for it, too, all this heavy metal at the back of the train—it would do double-duty as armor if someone tried a rear assault. They've thought this through." He looked around the cramped room, calculating how much material was held here. "Probably not the only one though, train this size."

"Any medical supplies?" Mildred piped up, never looking away from the door she guarded.

"Nothing seen," Ryan confirmed.

"We've got everything we need to barricade both doors," J.B. said, "but I don't know if there's any real reason to do so."

"Safety?" Ryan suggested.

"How safe would it be if someone plasts the car and unhooks the couplings?" J.B. asked in reply. "Find ourselves in a hot coffin with both exits well fortified to stop us getting out in a hurry."

"Point taken." Ryan nodded.

"So," Mildred asked, "what do we do? Take it one car at a time?"

"No," Ryan said firmly. "We'll just look around for now. Make some decisions once we get the lay of the land."

J.B. was opening the containers, seeing if anything else was stored in them besides screws and rivets. "Do you remember which car they took Jak into?" he said, addressing Mildred while both of them continued on their designated tasks.

"It was relatively close to the front section, about the tenth or twelfth car from the engine," she told them. "I didn't really get a sense of how long this thing was until we were above it."

"Yeah," Ryan grunted. "We need a way to get to the right car. Any ideas?"

"Along the roof?" Mildred proposed.

"Lot of sec men up there," Ryan said, shaking his head. "Can't rely on all of them sleeping on the job like my pal back there."

"If we knew what was in the car…" J.B. trailed off, turning the idea over in his mind.

"Reckon we're going to have to find out," Ryan stated after a moment.

"Reckon we are at that," the Armorer agreed.

Chapter Eight

They were about ten miles out from Fairburn, traveling in a southeasterly direction. "Mostly southerly," J.B. decided, consulting his tiny compass by the eerie light of the glow stick, "but I saw some curvature to the tracks that suggests we'll loop to the east." The three of them were pondering their next move in the cramped storage car.

"Ultimately, we are going to have to get much closer to the front if we're to locate Jak. That means working through the car somehow. Any idea what we can expect to find there?" he asked Mildred. "You're the only one of us that saw the folk who work this thing."

"Quite a few sec men came off the train when it stopped…" Mildred began.

"How many is 'quite a few'?" J.B. interrupted.

"More than a dozen, but I didn't count them on or off," she admitted. "I was trying to keep one eye on Krysty."

The hard look left Ryan's face for a moment. "We understand, Mildred. Go on."

"I saw maybe fifteen men, some of them were giving out orders, I think," she said. "Our window really was quite a long way from the action, Ryan. The whole plan was that Jak would do the scouting and report back."

"Pretty thin plan," J.B. concluded in a growl. He was

leaning against one of the walls, flattening out a dent in the brim of his fedora.

"Well," Ryan decided, "I guess we are going to have to take us a look-see outside, see how far we can get."

"Pretty soon someone is going to notice that the rear-guard's gone," J.B. stated, pointing to the roof. "It's pretty dark out there but they will notice if they don't see a body sitting up top."

"What are you saying?" Ryan asked.

"One of us should get up there, keep their head down and hope they don't get challenged, least till Doc gets here," he stated evenly. "Anyone want to play ringer?"

Mildred piped up. "I'd like to keep an eye out for Doc, make sure Krysty is all right."

J.B. considered that for a moment. "Ryan?"

"Your build is closer to their lost comrade, J.B.," he told his friend.

J.B. stepped across to the roof hatch and reached up to unseal it. "Good point," he acknowledged before climbing out of the hole.

Ryan offered his hand to help Mildred off the floor. "Ready, Mildred?"

THE TRAP JOSTLED over the rough ground as Doc urged the pony on in pursuit of the train. "How does it feel now?" he asked Krysty as he struggled with the reins.

"It's a lot better," she told him, pulling her jacket around her to stave off the cold wind that had whipped up around them. "My head feels much clearer now, like the pressure's going away."

"Any thoughts about what was causing it?" he asked her.

"The closer we got to that ville, the worse it became."

"And now that we have departed the area..." Doc continued, seeing the logic.

"Mebbe there was something there affecting me," Krysty suggested, pushing her hair away as it blew into her face. "Never felt that before."

"It is certainly most peculiar," he acknowledged. "And yet Fairburn seemed—almost impossibly— normal. Friendly place, a real sense of community."

Krysty barked out a laugh. "Perhaps I've been on the trail so long that I cannot bear to be near normality."

"It was not just hallucinations, Krysty," Doc reminded her, steering the pony around a large ditch in the terrain. "At one point when we were nearing the ville in question you were beset with a sudden, inexplicable nosebleed. That is more than a simple adverse reaction."

Krysty shook her head, mystified. "I don't even remember. Did that really happen?"

Doc nodded. "Something in that ville was working its way deep inside you," he told her, "and removing you from there has proved itself a most fortunate decision."

"What about the train of screams?" Krysty asked thoughtfully after a moment. "Could that have done something to the wiring in my head?"

Doc looked across to her. "I have considered that possibility, but it does not ring true. You were affected long before the train came to Fairburn. In fact, you were at your worst long before the engine appeared. If anything, its appearance coincided with an overall improvement in your health."

"Apart from the imaginings of my ears," she reminded him.

Doc encouraged more haste from the pony, snapping

the reins and shouting encouragement to the creature before turning back to Krysty. "Do you still hear it now?"

"A little," she told him, "if I listen for it. But it's real quiet and far off now. What's gotten into me, Doc?"

Doc shook his head. He had no answer.

THE WIND BLEW in Mildred's face as she stood in the open doorway to the lattermost car on the train. When she looked down she could see the ground rushing beneath the cars, the metal tracks two parallel streaks caught in the periphery of the green light cast by J.B.'s ebbing glow stick.

Two feet ahead of her, close enough to reach, stood another open door, mirroring the one she stood in, the entryway to the next car in the monstrous train. Ryan had just stepped through it and disappeared into the dark shadows within.

Mildred crossed the gap and stepped through the open door, her target revolver held upright in a two-handed grip. She took an immediate side step to the left the second she was through the door, flattening her back against the metal wall of the new car.

The car seemed to be about the same width as the one she had just exited, and she could just about make out trace lines of bluish light trailing along the sides. Other than that, the room seemed to be in utter darkness.

Ryan's voice came from the shadows ahead of her: "Clear." Mildred would place him at maybe fifteen feet ahead. "Keep going, watch the crates."

Crates? Mildred held her eyes closed for several seconds. When she opened them she could see more clearly in the dark, narrow room. Shadowy shapes stood in the darkness, large square blocks lining the walls, some spilling across the central area of the room.

Enshrouded in darkness at the far end of the car, Ryan was almost invisible, the only hint of his existence coming from the indigo sky reflected on his belt buckle when he turned to call her. "Come on, Mildred. Let's go."

Mildred pushed the door behind her silently closed, then walked the length of the car to join Ryan at the next door.

THEY CHECKED FIVE CARS, each subsequent car increasing the tension in Mildred's mind. The whole while, Ryan remained calm, treating the opening of those doors as routine.

The cars had been stuffed with various supplies, all of them ephemera one might associate with the construction of steam engines and train tracks. There was a lot of unpainted metal, sheet steel and solid pig iron, cut into various shapes and sizes for ease of storage or for specific uses. Ryan proposed that the majority of it was probably intended for what would basically amount to patching the engine and cars as required, and Mildred had voiced her wonder that the train was built so shoddy as to need a constant repair kit to hand.

"What's the weather like in the state of North Dakota, Doctor?" Ryan had asked her.

"I don't know," she replied without really thinking.

"Me neither," Ryan said. "But I've seen toxic clouds full of pollution and radiation right across Deathlands, and I don't imagine that Dakota is somehow different. Wind blows the wrong way, you could probably see whole hunks of this train burned through by an acid storm."

Mildred nodded, looking around the car they were in, seeing the supplies in a different light. "Pays to be prepared," she agreed, with new understanding.

Three of the cars had had at least one window, one of them had one whole side devoted to reinforced glass. When Mildred had taken a closer look she had recognized a sticker still adhering to one of the panes—this was windshield glass designed for automobiles before nuclear eschaton had changed the world. Never used for their original purpose, the windshields had been placed upright and secured by welded spots to form the joins.

Mildred and Ryan had stopped and looked through the safety glass for a half minute. He was watching the curve of the train, looking for nearby roof guards ahead of them against the moonlit sky. She watched the countryside whiz past in the darkness, noticing the outline of trees against the horizon. The terrain was changing; they were moving out of the bland desert that had covered the earth from the Minot gateway to Fairburn.

When they reached the sixth door, Ryan paused. He was standing on a minuscule sill below the far car's door, no more than a lip of metal where the door and floor failed to meet correctly, the ground between the tracks hurtling by four feet below him. He turned back, stretching one leg across the gap between the two cars and wedged his foot there, propping himself over the open gap.

"I don't like it," he told Mildred quietly.

"Should we go back?"

Ryan hung between the doors a moment, considering options. Finally he stepped back into the car with Mildred, closing the door behind him. "We've been lucky so far," he told her quietly. "No sec men, nobody.

I saw a light under that door, so it's likely there's someone in there. Mebbe a whole mess of someones."

Mildred nodded glumly. "We'll have to face them sooner or later. We could wait for Doc and Krysty, have J.B. with us, too, and go in guns blazing."

"Or we could do it quiet," Ryan said, clearly thinking out loud. "Stealth, just the two of us."

"And maybe not need to do it at all."

"What?" Ryan demanded.

"I was just thinking about the problem being two doors," Mildred told him, and then realized what she had said. "Back in medical school one of my lecturers told me an anecdote about trying to find an obstruction in a patient's large intestine. He was using a tiny camera that fed through a thin wire inserted in the patient's mouth, but he and his team just couldn't find whatever it was that was causing the patient so much trouble. 'And then,' the lecturer had told us, 'I remembered something quite fundamental about the human body.' and he pointed to his anus."

Ryan smiled. "So the doctor put the camera…"

Mildred nodded. "The lesson that he taught the class that day was to always remember that the body is three dimensional. If you can't get in one side, alter the tangent of entry." Mildred pointed to the door at the far end of the car, the one through which they had entered. "Every car we've been in after the first has had two doors besides the sliding side panels, Ryan."

"Some of them have had three, one in the roof or one in the side," Ryan reminded her.

"You enter that car through the back door here, where it's all unmanned storage lockers on wheels," Mildred said, "whoever is in there is likely going to wonder where your gateway is, am I right? But if you enter via the front door…" She held her hands open, as though the whole strategy was obvious.

Ryan's single eye burned into her. "Up, over, down, through the door. Then we introduce ourselves to the local players."

"Without arousing so much suspicion," Mildred finished.

"The real question is," Ryan decided, "whether we can *go* up and over." He went back to the door between the cars and gestured for Mildred to keep well back. She stepped backward to the center of the car, still clutching her target revolver, and tried to remain alert as Ryan disappeared out the door.

Ryan had lifted himself so that his head was above the rooftops of the cars both fore and aft. He checked the one behind first, saw no one there, then his head whipped around and looked at the rooftop of the car he intended to cross. Empty.

He dropped back to the rear car and encouraged Mildred to follow him. Then he was back out the door, lifting himself up the fore car by the strength of his arms alone, letting his legs swing below him until he could kick them over onto its roof. Mildred watched the feat of strength, realizing that Ryan had done it to avoid kicking at the car and alerting its passenger or passengers.

She looked behind her and reached up for the top of the open door frame of the car they were leaving. She pulled herself up on the swinging door, using the handle as a footrest, and got her knee up on its thin top ledge. From there she could reach the opposite roof with ease, and she pulled herself onto it, crossing the gap quietly.

Ryan waited there, crouched and looking back and forth, up and down the moving train as the wind caught at his dark hair. "Sec man two cars behind us," Ryan whispered, "another at twelve o'clock, three lengths ahead."

Mildred squinted, trying to make out the dark figures against the night sky, noticing the light cast from the windows of the car below them on the ground beneath. "Got them," she told him quietly.

"Don't think either of them will give us trouble, as long as we move quick," he suggested. "It's dark and it's noisy out here, and they're probably posted to look over the edge for attacking locals or muties."

"Not checking tickets—got it."

Together, the pair prowled across the curved rooftop in quick, quiet steps. Halfway across they dropped to the roof and lay flat. Ryan held Mildred's hips as she dropped her head over the side of the train and looked in a lighted window—just a fraction of a second to assess the scene before she reappeared on the roof. "Compartments," she whispered to him, then they got up and made their way stealthily to the far end of the car.

At the other side, Ryan dropped like a stone, there one second, gone the next. Mildred dropped flat on the roof surface again, bracing her legs and swinging down. She hung upside down between the jostling cars in front of the door, blaster ready. Ryan pulled the door open and entered, with Mildred hanging there, covering his back.

Ryan clutched his blaster as he stepped into the car. The walkway stretched along the left wall, which had three large windows evenly spaced along it. To the right were compartments, just as Mildred had advised: glass partitions in wooden frames, their contents hidden by heavy, moth-eaten curtains. There were four compartments in total, and each had a glass-and-wood door in its center. This was, Ryan realized, a genuine train car, salvage scrap put back on the tracks, probably two hundred years after it had originally seen use.

Noises came from the compartment closest to him, and he silently walked the length of the corridor, stopping and listening at each of the doors to confirm whether they appeared to be occupied.

After he had checked them all, listening at the doors and peeking through gaps in the curtains, Ryan silently indicated for Mildred to join him. Swinging on the door frame, hands clutching the top, she dropped to the floor of the car very quietly, closed the door behind her and unholstered her revolver once more. The corridor shook from side to side with the movement of the train as Mildred sneaked silently along, and she held her arms out to keep her balance without raising the alarm.

Ryan stood outside the third compartment, his back to the glass wall, blaster held shoulder high. Mildred stood opposite the door to the compartment, her own revolver ready, and nodded firmly at Ryan. It was clear that he intended to enter, and that Mildred was his backup; he didn't need to state it out loud for her. He put his left hand on the door handle and shoved the sliding door aside with a noisy clatter on its tracks, raising the SIG-Sauer and entering the room in a series of swift, fluid movements.

The small compartment was dimly lit by an ornate oil lamp hanging low on the ceiling. A bunk stood to the right, a curtain pulled across it, and to the left a chair sat in front of a small shelving unit with a mirror and a large washbowl. A large, curtainless window—almost the whole width of the compartment—looked out across the passing countryside, dabs of green speckled between the sandy-yellow soil. There was movement in the bunk behind the curtain, and a hand appeared, hairy knuckles reaching to pull back the curtain.

A gruff voice came from behind the curtain as it swept back. "Who the...?" But the man didn't get to finish his sentence. Ryan had shouldered the bunk's curtain aside and leaned one knee on the man's chest, thrusting the blaster into the occupant's face. An ugly face glared back at Ryan from the wrong end of the barrel, piggy eyes narrowed in reams of pallid flesh, unshaven jowls hanging heavily beneath.

The man's eyes were full of questions, all of them murderous, but he remained silent as he looked at the one-eyed man bare inches above him. Behind his attacker he watched a curvaceous, dark-skinned woman pad into the room, sliding the door back into place and adjusting the curtain to ensure no one could peek in.

J.B. KEPT LOOKOUT AT THE BACK of the train, unconsciously checking the hilt of the Tekna knife he had hidden in one sleeve. The wind whirled all around him, making sound an unreliable indicator. Behind his round spectacles, his eyes flicked back and forth, and he spent equal times watching ahead and behind him as the train thundered across the ragged landscape. He was doing a commendably more vigilant job than the sec man that Ryan had dispatched, and the irony of that didn't escape him.

On the horizon, where the deep blue of the sky met

the solid black shadow of the earth, J.B. spotted a movement. The train was going downhill, a subtle incline, and it meant that he was looking upward. The moving shape looked like a box, and J.B. narrowed his eyes to try to bring it into focus. The box was being pulled with some speed across the bumpy plain, and J.B. concluded that a single horse was at the front of it. He watched for almost two minutes before he decided that the pony and trap was following them. Because of the curvature of the railroad tracks, their pursuers could cut out vast chunks of the journey, straight-lining where they circled, and this was being used to help the vehicle catch up to them, slowly but surely. The jackass way of doing things like that had all the hallmarks of Doc, J.B. realized. Still, if it worked…

J.B. looked behind him, thinking about the car below and whether there was anything he could use in there to help Doc and Krysty get on board—rope, mebbe, or some kind of wire he could turn into a lasso. As he looked behind he saw a man approaching—one roof ahead and closing the distance carefully, keeping his balance low with a crouching shuffle of movement. As he watched the man approach, J.B. eased his index finger beneath the trigger guard of his Uzi, felt for the reassuring weight of the Tekna knife in his sleeve.

"Nate?" the man's voice carried to him on the rushing wind. "That you, Nate?"

Whoever was approaching him, it wasn't Ryan Cawdor.

Chapter Nine

J.B. sized the man up in his mind watching him jump across the gap between the car and land at the end of the one J.B. waited atop—about six feet tall, maybe 240 pounds, all of it solid muscle. He moved like a big cat, instinctively balancing on the moving rooftop. He wore a revolver under his arm, holstered in a shoulder rig, and the barrel to a larger blaster could be seen over his shoulder where it hung on his back by a thick leather strap. As the man closed the gap between them, J.B. could see pitted scarring on his cheeks, awkwardly catching moonlight.

"Nate?" the man asked again, deliberately keeping his voice low. He was just a few paces from J.B. now, trying to make him out in the darkness. "Hey, you ain't Nate," the man finally said.

With the butt of the Uzi resting on the car roof, J.B. had the man perfectly in his sights. But he waited, not pulling the trigger. The man had realized that he wasn't "Nate," but he hadn't made any move for his own weapon.

"What happened to Nate?" the man asked, his dirty blond hair blowing around his face.

In his mind's eye J.B. saw the sec man falling from the train after Ryan had knifed him in the gut, a bloody splash oozing over his shirt. "Stomach problem," he stated.

"Little wonder." The man laughed, clearly at ease with the stranger. "All I see him eat is crap." He crouched and held an empty hand out to J.B. "Givin. Sean Givin."

J.B. rested the Uzi on the rooftop and shook the man's hand. "John Dix," he told him. "You my relief?"

"Yeah, man, and— Did you say your name was Dix? You're not Tish's old man, are you?"

"Cousin," J.B. said. He had no idea who Tish was, but it seemed that Sean Givin was happy to fill in the details and provide far more trust and alibi than J.B. could have asked for.

Sean shook his head, relieved. "Phew, thought I'd just walked into an ambush for a minute there." He looked around. "I didn't walk into an ambush, did I?"

J.B. reached across, giving the sec man a friendly punch on the shoulder. "Hey, what my cousin does is up to her. None of my business," he confirmed.

A line of bright teeth appeared in the moonlight as Givin smiled. "I'm real sorry I'm so late, man," he told J.B. "You go get yourself some sleep. I got this covered now." He pointed out across the land behind the train, not really looking.

J.B. got to his feet. He was rapidly considering what to do next. Doc and Krysty were on their way, and the last thing they needed was a firefight with this stupe. At the same time, if the Armorer chilled him now he'd only up the possibilities of raising suspicion. The ante had been raised high enough with their boarding the train, and the trusting sec man's naivete had granted him a lucky break.

He made his way to the far end of the car roof, looking back at Sean Givin sitting there, the wind catching his long blond hair. Doc or Krysty could handle this dope, and neither of them would be stupe enough to approach the train without checking for guards. For now, J.B. was going to have to retreat and see if he could locate Mildred and Ryan.

"WHERE ARE WE GOING?" Ryan barked at the man in the bunk, pushing the barrel of the blaster further into his forehead so that the man sunk down in the pillow. "What is this train's destination?"

The man in the bed stuttered, fear overcoming his ability to speak. "I—I—I…"

"Where?" Ryan barked again, but the man failed to provide a coherent reply. "Listen, you little worm. That thing you feel pressing against your forehead is the end of my blaster. I'll shoot what little brains you have right out the back of your head and no one will hear a damn thing over the racket of the engine, no one will come running. So you answer my questions now or you're going to have yourself one bastard headache. You understand?"

The man gave a slight nod, the pressure of the blaster causing more pain as he moved his head. His whole face had turned very red with the pressure placed on him, the blood rushing to his head.

"So," Ryan asked again, "where?"

Ryan watched the man blink rapidly, his tongue struggling around his mouth. "Forks, man," he said, his voice trembling. "The Forks."

"And where the rad blazes is that?" Ryan asked, and he looked across to Mildred who stood at the mirror, ignoring the man in the bunk.

"North? South?" Mildred shrugged, filling a disposable hypodermic syringe she had taken from her med kit. "I really don't know. I can't think of any Forks. Maybe it's a nickname."

Ryan breathed a sigh through gritted teeth before turning his attention back to his captive. "I'm looking for a friend of mine. He was taken on this train against his will."

The man in the bunk just looked at Ryan with those wide, scared eyes.

Ryan continued, gouging the barrel of his blaster into the man's forehead once more. "What are you? Sec man? Is that it?"

"Yeah," the man breathed, clearly terrified.

"You take prisoners? You do that?"

"Sometimes," the man croaked. "Just kids though."

"Just kids?" Ryan repeated, scowling.

The man struggled to breathe. "Mebbe sluts sometimes, I'm not...not sure."

"Be sure," Ryan warned him.

"Yeah. Gaudy sluts. Good-lookin' girls who should be gaudies. You know, guy?" the terrified man pleaded.

"No," Ryan shook his head. "My friend is young-looking, very distinctive. He's an albino. You know what that is?"

The man tried to shake his head but Ryan's blaster point held him firm. "No."

"Means he's white," Ryan told him. "Pure white, like snow. You get snow here? You've seen snow?"

"I see snow," the man agreed. "Wintertime."

"My friend's skin and hair are colored like snow. You wouldn't miss him."

"I don't..." The man in the bunk tried, but couldn't seem to finish the sentence. His eyes fluttered.

"You don't remember, you haven't seen him? What?"

"I ain't seen no one, man," the man croaked. "Please don't chill me," he added, his voice high and squeaky.

Ryan took the blaster away from the man's head but continued to point it at his face. "You are going to have to remain very quiet for me if I'm to let you live." The man nodded, his lips clamped shut, and so Ryan continued. "And you are going to have to prove irreplaceable in your helpfulness to me and my people. Think you can do that?"

The man's eyes flicked across to his right, looking above his head for a fraction of a second, then he looked back at Ryan. "Anything," he said. "Anything at all."

Ryan stepped back slowly, his SIG-Sauer still trained on the man's face.

"I can sedate him, if you want," Mildred told Ryan. She had found some ancient sedatives during their rummaging in the remains of military hospitals and the like, although she wouldn't want to vouch for the reliability of these medicines these days. Sedatives, like everything else in the Deathlands, inevitably expired.

"I don't think that will be necessary," Ryan told her. "Our friend here just wants to play along. Isn't that right, friend?"

The man spun in the bunk, launching his right hand at a cubbyhole above his shoulder, obscured from view by the pillows of the bunk. "Screw you!" he croaked, pulling a snub-nosed .38 weapon from the cubbyhole and swinging it around to target the intruders.

Ryan's bullet drilled through the man's forehead in an instant, and the man's blaster hand continued to swing around but his fingers never pulled the trigger. The back of the man's skull opened up as brains splattered across the bunk, the pillows and the beechwood wall behind. Though loud in the contained area of the cabin, the noise of the blaster was negligible outside thanks to the racket of the train rocking along the tracks.

Mildred held her breath, looking at the scene for a moment as the man's body twitched, its life departing. "I thought we could sedate him," she said quietly, "if he became rowdy."

Ryan sighed. "Didn't seem like the sedating type, Mildred," he told her, his blaster still trained on the body in the bunk as a final muscle spasm jerked through it.

After a moment Ryan opened the door slightly, poked his head out and checked the corridor. No one was coming.

He stepped back into the compartment and holstered his weapon in his belt. "J.B. is probably getting concerned," he told Mildred.

THE SWEAT WAS FOAMING on the pony's coat as Doc urged more speed from its tired legs. They had been racing across the North Dakota plain for far too long, and the animal was near exhaustion. It couldn't take much more of the grueling punishment. Its legs looked unstable as it ran, threatening to buckle as it dragged the trap behind it. However, they were definitely gaining on the train now. Doc could see its obscene length slithering along the tracks, a giant, black caterpillar crossing the land, smoky steam belching from its foremost segment.

"I think it may actually be slowing," Doc said to Krysty, his eyes fixed ahead, watching the train in the distance.

When Krysty didn't respond, he voiced his observation louder, above the loud tattoo that the pony's hooves were banging out on the hard-packed earth. They had hit a few pockets of grass here and there, and the land was definitely getting greener, the soil more fertile. Doc turned to Krysty, then, and saw she was slumped in the seat beside him. "Krysty?" he asked, letting go of the reins with one hand and reaching across to shake her gently by the shoulder. "Krysty, dear? We're almost there. Try to stay awake."

Krysty's head weaved atop her neck as she returned to consciousness. She looked at him, bleary-eyed. "D-Doc?" she groaned. "Is that you?"

Doc glanced ahead—just level fields here—then took the opportunity to look more closely at his companion. "Krysty, are you feeling unwell?" Mentally he added the word *again*.

She shook her head, not in answer to his question, he realized, but to try to bring reality back into focus. "The screaming is louder," she told him, so quietly he had to strain to hear her over the drumming sound of hooves.

"We're getting closer to the train," he explained. "Perhaps we were wrong in our earlier summation. It seems to be having some affect on your faculties, after all."

Krysty looked ahead of them, eyes focusing on the train in the distance. "It's that, but it's not just that," she said after a moment's consideration.

"What do you mean?"

"It's so hard to tell. My brain feels like it's on fire," she said hesitantly, struggling to find the right words of explanation. "But there's something… I can't tell if it's just inside me now, alive and eating away at me."

Doc reached his free hand across to Krysty, patting

her lightly on the shoulder. "You poor child," he said. He watched, horrified as she winced at his touch. "My profuse apologies," he told her, immediately withdrawing his hand.

Krysty closed her eyes a moment, and when she opened them Doc could make out the watery tears in the moonlight. "It hurts so much," she said.

Silently, Doc agreed with her. It hurt him, too, deep inside, seeing his companion in so much pain.

"HEAR THAT?" Mildred asked.

Ryan cocked his head, trying to filter out the sounds of the train to divine something new. "What?"

"High-pitched squealing. That's brakes," Mildred told him. "We're slowing down."

Ryan moved across the tiny compartment and looked out the fly-specked window. "You're right," he said, examining the landscape as it passed. "Any ideas why?"

Mildred shrugged. "Pit stop, station." She thought for a second, then added, "Food run?"

"Doc found out something earlier," Ryan said, "and never had the chance to tell you. There are other towers. That's what he was told."

Mildred felt a chill come over her, hugged her arms around her as she stood next to Ryan while he watched through the window. "It doesn't surprise me," she stated. "I didn't give it a thought until you said it, but it doesn't surprise me, not really."

Ryan continued to stand at the window, looking this way and that, trying to make out details in the moonlight. As she watched him, Mildred realized just what it was he was really looking for. Krysty and Doc, who were still somewhere between here and Fairburn.

Maybe they never even left the walled ville. After Doc had opened the gates it was very possible that they had both wound up at the end of the hangman's rope, vandal and accomplice. Mildred pushed the thought from her mind, and then her voice broke the silence. "You know, Ryan," she said, "I shouldn't have left Krysty."

She watched Ryan standing there, looking out the window, his face away from her, the moisture in his breath steaming the cold glass. He gave not so much as a nod of acknowledgment to her statement as the sound of the brakes grew louder, their scream becoming increasingly shrill as the train pulled to a stop.

Mildred took two steps forward, unable to stop herself moving as the train stopped. Ryan, she noticed, didn't move at all. His thick legs were planted, rock-solid, on the floor of the train, his uncanny sense of balance holding him firm.

Once the train had stopped, Ryan turned and went to the door. "Come on," he told the doctor, and stepped from the compartment, SIG-Sauer blaster back in his hand.

Mildred followed him, and they jogged down the corridor toward the door through which they had entered the car. As they reached it, the door at the opposite end opened, and Mildred spun, dropping to one knee and targeting the newcomer with her revolver. J.B. stood in the doorway, his own weapon—the compact Uzi—in ready position. When he saw Mildred and Ryan he lowered the blaster and gave a single, firm nod.

"We stopped," Ryan told J.B. as they returned to the door at the front.

The Armorer nodded, tight-lipped.

"We're a long way from the front," Ryan continued. "Going by what Mildred said, I'd guess that's where the action is. We were planning to go take a look-see, find out what's what." He opened the door, then reached up to the roof of the car. In a moment, Ryan was up and over. Once there, he lay down flat and looked up the length of the train. It was too dark to make out details. He unslung the SSG-70 Steyr and rested it in front of him, then looked down the powerful scope, adjusting it until he could see to the front of the train.

A handful of people were walking around, most of them armed sec men. A few others rushed back and forth, receiving orders from a dark-haired foreman who held something shiny and metallic in his hands— probably a blaster, Ryan guessed. The one-eyed man panned the scope slowly across the area, tracking a group of three, serious-looking people, a dark-haired woman and two men, one of them older and sporting wispy, white hair. Lit by the glowing light of the train engine, Ryan watched as this group made its way to an area off to the side of the tracks. As they left the faint light of the engine, he lost them. Then a bright light suddenly broke the darkness in the scope's image. The train people had a method to light the area. A little pool of light as bright as day had appeared where the group waited.

Ryan watched as the group had a quick discussion, gesturing to something to the right. He panned the scope slightly, and there it was. Spitted in the X of his crosshairs, gleaming in the brilliant light as it lunged into the sky, was another skeletal tower, just like the one outside Fairburn.

"Fireblast," Ryan muttered.

Chapter Ten

While Mildred kept watch, J.B. joined Ryan on the roof of the car to discuss the situation. Ryan continued to watch the activities through the scope on his SSG-70 Steyr blaster as they talked, trying to fathom what the operators of this mechanical monstrosity were doing.

"So, why did you come find us, J.B.?" Ryan whispered.

"My position got relieved. Sec man came over, spoke to me. Saw nothing out of the ordinary in my being there. I told him I was filling in."

There was frantic activity through the scope as Ryan watched. A group of the raggedly dressed sec men leaped from the train and ran toward a nearby copse. The remainder of the group continued to work at the tower. "Something's going down," Ryan said. "They have a big sec force, easily infiltrated."

"That's my conclusion, too," J.B. agreed. "None of them are uniformed. Walk tall, they won't bother us, I'm thinking."

"Sounds risky," Ryan stated, "but we need to find Jak, and I don't think we have a lot of options here."

Ryan continued to watch the activity through the scope, never shifting his position.

J.B.'s gaze swept the rooftops of the train in the moonlight, pinpointing where the roof guards waited.

"Any sign of Doc?" Ryan whispered.

"I think I saw him and Krysty," J.B. said, checking the rear cars, trying to see beyond but finding only darkness below the moonlit break of the horizon. "Looked like a pony and trap. Not much of a vehicle for the long haul, but should be enough to get them here. 'Specially if we're stopped here for a while."

"You think she'll be all right?"

"Ask a Mildred," J.B. told him. "I don't know."

DOC PULLED AT THE REINS, slowing the pony's charge. They were close to the train, barely two hundred yards away, and Doc knew that it was only the cover of darkness that granted them protection. Above them, the silver moon danced through the clouds, its light sporadically bright on the landscape.

Doc could see a man on top of the last car of the train, cast in silhouette against the indigo sky. The old man pulled the pony to a halt and spoke rapidly to Krysty.

"I need you to look for me, Krysty," he told the sick woman, "locate the sec men."

Krysty lay there, slumped in the seat beside him, her head lolling on her shoulders, her eyes scrunched tightly closed. Doc wondered what folly had made them think to move her from Fairburn, and to let Mildred leave her side. She had seemed better, he reminded himself. What had happened? What was going on with Krysty?

Doc snapped the reins and the weary pony trotted forward once more, approaching the train while thick clouds obscured the moonlight.

"MUTIES." RYAN BIT OUT the word, and J.B.'s head whipped to look in the direction that Ryan was watching through the powerful magnification of his scope.

"Where?" the Armorer asked, his vision unable to pierce the darkness around them.

"Trees, two o'clock," Ryan stated. He watched through the scope as a group of sec men fought with the naked, humanoid figures. The muties numbered more than fifty, and they moved with grim determination. The sec men's bullets slowed them, but the few they felled would collapse for a moment only to struggle back up and continue the attack. Scalies, probably, thick leather skin protecting them against small blaster fire.

Suddenly, Ryan rolled over and shifted to a sitting position, looking at J.B. with his single, piercing blue eye. "Time to find Doc and Krysty," he said.

They leaped from the roof, returning to Mildred where she waited in the car beneath them. "Back of the train, Mildred," Ryan told her.

"What is it, Ryan?" Mildred asked as they turned to jog through the car.

"Mass chilling going on outside," Ryan explained. "We need to get Krysty and Doc onboard before someone chills them, too."

"I didn't hear anything," Mildred said, following them into the car with the car windshield wall.

"It was up front," J.B. told her. "Mutie scuffle. We're best keeping out of it."

"But if they spot Doc…" Ryan stated, then left the inevitable conclusion unsaid.

When they reached the penultimate car, Ryan clambered up between the coaches and took to the rooftops again, with Mildred and J.B. following. The sec man,

Sean Givin, was still atop the roof of the last car. "Hey, man," Givin began as they approached, "what's—?"

He never finished the question. A 9 mm bullet from Ryan's SIG-Sauer blaster drilled through his left eye.

Ryan jumped across the gap between rooftops, scanning the horizon as the sec man dropped onto his back, crashing onto the metal roof with a loud thump, a mosaic of blood splattered across the left side of his face. "There," Ryan called, pointing to the left of the train. J.B. and Mildred followed where he indicated, spotting the pony and trap bumbling toward the train from the shadows.

J.B. was down the side ladder in an abbreviated second, waving his arms above his head to show Doc it was safe to approach. Ryan looked up the length of the train, aware that the roof guards had to have heard the single shot, wondering how long they had before another guard became suspicious.

THE SEC MAN HAD LEFT the children in the twelfth car alone. The group had sat there, huddled together as far from the pure white youth as they could get. All of them watched the thin figure lay there, saw him jostled with the heavy movements of the train as it had hurtled down the tracks. They watched him roll away from them, toward the front of the train, when the brakes were applied, until he finally rolled over, slapping softly into the grille mesh when the train stopped.

His eyes were closed and he hadn't reacted when his body had hit the ringing metal of the mesh wall, not even with a grunt of expelled air. Some of the younger children were crying quietly, but that wasn't so unusual. Everyone in the cage had shed some tears after they had been snatched from their home villes or their arduous lives on the Dakota farms. But it was hard to see in the vague light that peeked in through the open door of the car with the racing wind of movement, and no one had wanted to approach the strange youth with the face of alabaster.

Humblebee, nine years old and a passenger on the train for three long days, finally plucked up the courage to ask the question that had been troubling her. Her voice came out quiet, as though she was afraid of breaking something with it. "Is he...a ghost?"

One of the younger children—Francis-Frankie—started to wail when he heard her say that, and Marc, who was almost fourteen and was used to taking care of whining younger siblings, scooted over to Francis-Frankie and told him not to cry because it was a stupe thing to do. Francis-Frankie sniffled back his crying, but it made him cry more, so Marc punched him on the nerve below the shoulder, giving him a dead arm. That shut Francis-Frankie up.

Humblebee didn't want to say it again. She had this idea that if she said it, it might just come true anyway, even if it hadn't been true before. She looked at the ghost boy slumped there, unmoving, and closed her eyes tight, trying to picture the car before he came, how it would look if he wasn't lying there now. It was like the monsters under her bed back home in Brocketville; if she thought about it hard enough, if she really believed, then they stopped being there after all and she could go to sleep.

But when she opened her eyes again, he was still lying there. She screwed her eyes up tight and whispered, "Go away," but he was still there when she looked again. So she had to ask the question again.

"Maddie?" she asked, frightened to take her eyes off the stationary white figure on the other side of the car.

Maddie was Humblebee's best friend on the train. Maddie was as old as Marc, but she was clever and funny. She had made up stories to help Humblebee sleep on her first night on the train, after she'd been snatched by the train pirates. "What is it?" Maddie asked after a few seconds.

Humblebee could tell that Maddie was watching the white-skinned boy, too, that she didn't dare avert her gaze from the stranger. She was behind Humblebee somewhere, and Humblebee wished she could hold hands with her now, when she asked the scary question again. "Is that boy a ghost?"

"I don't think so," Maddie decided.

"Why is he so white?" Humblebee whispered. "He looks like a ghost."

Marc's funny, high voice broke the stillness after a moment. "I think he might be dead," he announced.

"He's not dead," Maddie stated firmly. "Don't say that, it's a horrible thing to say."

Humblebee looked at the ghost boy, trying to see if he was breathing, but she couldn't see any movement. "That man shotted him," she told them.

Marc sniggered nervously. "If he wasn't a ghost when he got on he prob'ly is now. Chilled."

Maddie shushed them. "Stop it."

Francis-Frankie was sniffling when he spoke up, his voice, as ever, an irritating whine. "Why would they give us a ghost?" he asked. It struck Humblebee as a

very intelligent question. Why would anyone give you
a ghost?

"For eatin'," Marc decided, and he padded toward
the white figure in the corner of the cage.

Francis-Frankie started wailing again when he
heard that.

J.B. HELPED RYAN WRAP a blanket around the corpse of
the pig-eyed sec man he had shot and shove it into the
overhead luggage rack. They used the soiled sheet from
the bed to wipe blasted brains from the wall. Then
Mildred helped Krysty into the bunk.

The companions had moved in silence through the
cars, alert to possible discovery.

Once they reached the perceived safety of the compartment, a hushed conversation brought everyone up
to speed.

Mildred sat with Krysty, speaking soothing words as
she took the woman's temperature. The compartment
was cramped now, with five living people and one
blanket-wrapped corpse vying for space. Ryan stood
with his back to the door, his weight against it and his
heel dug against the sliding edge so that no one could
force his or her way in. Doc and J.B. stood together by
the window, watching Mildred work on their other companion.

"Why has the train stopped again?" Doc asked.

"There's a tower up front," Ryan told him.

"Another one?" Doc asked, his incredulity raising
his voice. He had been the first to hear that there were
probably more towers, but it still seemed unexpected
somehow. He came from a different time, the 1800s, and
it was hard to discard his instinctive assumption that

trains stopped at stations. "I did not see it," he concluded.

"Long way to the front," Ryan explained.

"How far?" Doc wanted to know.

"Over a quarter mile," J.B. chipped in. "Hard to tell with a dark, moving object, no landmarks."

"By the Three Kennedys," Doc muttered under his breath.

They felt the train begin to thrum. The engines were warming up, and the powerful shuddering was followed by gradual movement as the mighty engine began to pull its burden, very slowly, forward.

J.B. gestured to the dead sec man in the overhead luggage rack. "Might be easiest to toss the body overboard once we pick up speed. Cloud cover may hide it, but if not, anyone who sees it will probably think he's slipped. Don't reckon they'd stop the train to check on one man."

"Have you located Jak?" Doc asked.

"Not yet," Ryan replied. "Mildred thinks he's close to the front, mebbe ten or twelve railcars from the engine."

"How far away is that?" Doc asked, looking from Ryan to J.B. to Mildred.

J.B. answered. "Reckon the train's about sixty cars in total, front to back. So far all we've seen is storage, but as we get nearer the front we can expect to see more people. The bunks here won't be the only ones," he said. "There's a sec here, but they're badly briefed. I passed myself off as one of them with the rearguard, didn't even raise an eyebrow. Figure if we keep our heads down, no one will question me or Ryan."

"We'll work through the cars," Ryan added, "try to find Jak. We'll plan it from there."

Doc was shaking his head, clearly deep in thought.

"What is it?" Ryan asked him.

"The lad is plenty resourceful," Doc told them. "He may well have found his escape route and be off the train already."

"In that case he'll find us," Ryan said firmly. "Or we'll go back to Fairburn, make our apologies, and wait for him to appear. Last rendezvous protocol, Jak'll follow that."

"Assuming he is on the train, however," Doc mused, "how long do we have to find him?"

"Sooner the better," Ryan said, as though it was the most obvious thing.

"You have missed my point, Ryan," Doc told him. "This train has to go somewhere, even if it is just to refuel. The next stop may very well put us in a situation we are ill-prepared to handle. There could be a thousand armed sec men waiting at the end of the tracks for all we know."

"And my point stands," Ryan stated. "The sooner the better."

J.B. took a long breath, thinking it through. "Doc's right, Ryan," he said, "We may not be able to just rush Jak off. Might be a shedload more to it than opening a door."

Mildred had been listening throughout as she tended to Krysty in the bunk. "The previous occupant of this bunk told us they were heading to the Forks," she said.

Ryan nodded. "Mean anything to you, Doc?"

In his previous life, Doc was a well-traveled man, as well as a well-educated one. He stood by the window now, the dark countryside speeding past as the train rocked from side to side, trying to place the name. Many things had changed with the nuclear devastation of the United States of America; place names had been corrupted or simply vanished to the mists of time, and new settlements had popped up, named for their barons or the local geography or a dozen other reasons. Doc tried to picture the map of the Dakotas, North and South. There had been a glorious map on the wall of one of the lecture halls of Harvard, and he had spent brief moments studying it when he had been waiting for class to start.

"Grand Forks," he told them with certainty in his voice. "Up here—" he gestured in the air, still seeing the map in his mind's eye "—in the northeast of the state."

"We're traveling south," J.B. pointed out, producing a folded booklet from his inside breast pocket, "but there's a curve to the tracks, could be taking us easterly, hard to say yet."

"The redoubt that we exited said Minot on the wall," Ryan added. "Whereabouts is that?"

J.B. placed the washbowl on the floor and laid a map on the small desk it had sat on, flattening the paper with a sweep of his hands. Doc looked over J.B.'s shoulder and Ryan took a single, small step away from the door to join them.

"Here's Minot," J.B. said, pointing. "Northwest. And Grand Forks…here, a hundred and fifty miles as the scud flies. But if we're looping around—" he drew a rough circle with his fingernail, following the state boundary "—who knows. Could take a week or more, especially if we're stopping."

Ryan addressed Doc, stepping aside as Mildred joined the group at the little desk to see the map for herself. "Know anything about this Grand Forks place, Doc?"

Doc shook his head. "I am afraid I've never been there, or if I have I do not remember doing so. It is still hard to remember much of what I've done," he continued, "some of it is so vivid, my times with Emily and the children, but other things…" His voice trailed off and Ryan nodded his understanding to the older man. Doc's memory had fractured somehow, due to the time jumps that had been thrust upon him. It seemed a cruel kind of senility to force upon the intelligent old man, and Ryan knew that it caused Doc much frustration, even if he didn't voice it often.

Ryan spoke then, addressing everyone, his firm voice steady. "We get Jak, we do it quiet and we get off. If we don't go looking for a ruckus, we can hopefully avoid getting ourselves into one. Low profile, all the way." He looked across to where Krysty lay in the bunk. She seemed to be sleeping, but her fists were clenched tight, nails digging hard into her palms. "Mildred, you're going to have to do what you can for Krysty until we get off this thing. J.B. and I'll scout the train. Doc, I don't think you'll pass for a sec man, sorry to say. So that puts you on watch for Krysty and Mildred."

"And two more delightful companions no man on Earth could ask for," Doc announced, bringing a smile to Mildred's face in spite of herself.

"Same rules as ever," Ryan reminded them. "Everyone's backup. We're three people down, with both Jak and Krysty out of action, and someone watching her at all times. So we don't draw any attention we don't need."

"Do you think this cabin is safe?" Mildred queried.

"Storage cars behind might be safer," Ryan admitted, "but we have to think of Krysty's comfort. Plus, at least we're out of sight unless someone actually comes through that door." He gestured to the single door of the tiny compartment. "We'll live with it unless something more secure presents itself.

"How's Krysty?" he asked Mildred.

"Her health's declining again, Ryan," Mildred admitted. "I can't see what the pattern is, but she's almost as low now as she was when we reached Fairburn."

"I have hypothesized," Doc explained, "that it may be something to do with the towers, but since we do not know where they are nor what they are doing, it is hard to come to a definite conclusion."

"It's a sound theory," Ryan stated, "but why would it affect her and not us?"

Mildred looked at Krysty, then back at Ryan and the others. "It's hard to say, Ryan. Anything I tell you now would have to be pure guesswork."

"No point," J.B. confirmed, and they all agreed to let the matter rest.

In the bunk, Krysty clawed at the remaining blanket, her hands scrabbling at the material, a soft groan coming from her mouth as her breathing became more rapid.

"Keep her comfortable," Ryan told Mildred, his own frustration boiling into his abrupt tone for just a second.

"I'll try," Mildred assured him, resuming her vigil at the side of the bunk. She could almost feel the cold breath of the Grim Reaper blowing softly over her shoulder, standing just beyond the edge of her vision, waiting to claim Krysty for his own.

Chapter Eleven

After a short discussion, the companions had decided to sleep in shifts, making room where they could on the floor of the cramped cabin. Ryan had been keen to continue the search for Jak, but eventually recognized his need for sleep after some persuasion. Inside, all he wanted was to get out there, find Jak and get off this awful train, but as soon as he sat on the floor beside Krysty's bunk he felt his muscles locking, his head getting heavier as tiredness caught up with him.

Sleep was welcomed by all of them. The trek across the wasteland outside Minot had been exhausting, and none of them had had time to stop for very long except for Jak back in the Fairburn lodging room. J.B. and Mildred took the first watch.

The train stopped three more times during the night, and each time whichever of the companions was on watch had sneaked outside to see what was happening. The train people were working on more towers, though Mildred noticed they passed several others without halting.

Doc was awake for one of the stops, and had taken Ryan's blaster scope to observe the action at the front of the train, much as Ryan had earlier. The land was becoming greener, and they had passed occasional tributaries of clear water, shining in the moon glow, sometimes even crossing them over rickety bridges. The tower stood near one of these tributaries, set back twenty feet from the rail tracks. When Doc looked at the magnified image, he realized that this tower was still under construction, its skeletal frame ending roughly, not reaching to the high zenith of the others. The foreman of the sec team spoke to a man whom Doc realized had already been on-site, and the three intellectual types had joined in with a flourish of maps and notations passing between them. A small construction crew sat waiting to go back to work—just three men, including the one who spoke with the train people.

Doc recognized the rumbling sounds of the engine as it warmed up once more to leave, its brief stopover concluded. He jumped back on the train from his crouched position beneath, bringing the longblaster with him, and returned to the compartment. He stood at the window, a step back so that he wouldn't be seen, and studied the tower as the train trundled past. The construction crew was already back at work, the bright blue jets of welding torches clear in the darkness. "Curiouser and curiouser."

THE COMPANIONS WERE awake when the rays of dawn peeked over the horizon and began to shed light in the cramped cabin. The air in the enclosed space had become warm and stuffy, smelling of sweat and leather from their boots. Krysty sat up in the bunk, her knees pulled tight to her chest, gently rocking with the movement of the train. Mildred had asked if she wanted a sedative, as she had several different types in her bag, but Ryan had rejected the idea. "If trouble comes calling we'll need her awake," he told them, even though it meant leaving Krysty in pain. If they had to make a swift exit he didn't want to have to carry Krysty if he didn't absolutely have to.

Doc told them about the construction work he had seen during the night.

J.B. tried to marry the readings from his minisextant with the topographical information presented on his creased maps, but he couldn't work out precisely where they were yet, let alone where the towers they had passed were located.

The train pulled to a halt just as Ryan and J.B. were checking their weapons in preparation for their search for Jak. Mildred stood at the window, looking up and down the tracks to try to see what was happening.

"Another tower?" J.B. asked.

Mildred shook her head. "Can't see any."

Ryan slung the SSG-70 Steyr, rolling his shoulders to accommodate the familiar weight, and indicated that Doc and J.B. join him as he entered the corridor beyond the cabin. The three of them paced swiftly down the corridor, and Ryan opened the door at the end and lowered himself down between the adjoining cars.

The one-eyed man pressed against the forward car, looking toward the front of the long vehicle. First J.B., then Doc peeked out to see what he was watching. All around the train, at a distance of roughly twenty yards from the tracks, stood a fence. Pieces of corrugated steel stood next to wire mesh and wood panels, and some of the fence was made up of tree trunks, branches removed but left rooted where they grew, the panels of the fence slotted around them. The fence never fell below seven feet in height—not an impossible climb, by any means, but certainly a deterrent. A few sec men strolled slowly around the perimeter, blasters in their hands. A set of chain-link gates had been closed at the far end, behind the train. The compound made an effective stopping point, easily defended from local interference, but Ryan realized it might also double as a prison for him and his companions if they weren't careful. The air held that fresh smell that Ryan associated with the ocean shore.

Doc's whispered words broke into Ryan's thoughts. "Some kind of stopover," he said, incredulous.

"Saluting the dawn," J.B. concluded, "like dirt-poor primitives."

Ryan beckoned J.B. forward, and together they sneaked silently alongside the train toward the ceremony, leaving Doc to wait at the juncture of the cars. Doc stepped back into the shadows, removing the LeMat from its holster and resting it easily against his leg. Should anyone question the older man's presence he wanted all of his options within easy reach.

Ryan and J.B. walked past eighteen cars, two of which had rounded sides, making them bloat outward like a well-fed boa constrictor, and both men silently committed the details of each one to memory. As they neared the dawn ceremony, Ryan turned back to his partner and whispered from the side of his mouth, "This is not a good idea."

J.B. continued walking straight ahead, his gaze set on the participants of the ceremony as they laughed and spoke among themselves. "Too late now," he said.

"Ho, brothers," called a bald sec man when he spotted them. Ryan and J.B. felt a wave of relief when the man offered them no challenge, but Ryan could see the tremoring in the man's stance that indicated jolt dependency. High on an ultimately lethal drug, the man was probably not the most observant of the train crew. "You're not late, they ain't 'peared yet."

They noticed that other sec men were still stepping from the train, joining the pack that waited in the rising sunlight, and several musicians stepped from the bloated cars carrying simple instruments—fiddles and guitars—with which they entertained the crowd as they walked through. Ryan counted around eighty sec types in all, as well as the gaudies and a handful of weaker-looking men who were mistreated—kicked at, spat on and berated—as they trudged through the group. As he watched, a few more sec men joined the crowd, hopping down from the roofs of the train cars and bringing the grand total up to perhaps ninety, an effective little army. All of the guards were armed, but there was no uniformity to them. Their weapons and clothing were individual. Many of them carried blasters, though some had simpler weapons such as knives and swords, Ryan saw, a scimitar glinting with the rays of the sun, a machete stained with coppery rust.

The sky was a bright shade of red above them, the rising sun blazing over the horizon, casting long shadows of the group and the train. Rain-heavy thunderheads blew through the sky, blotting the rays of the sun for brief moments as they drifted onward.

Ryan scanned the crowd but there was no sign of Jak.

"He's not here," J.B. confirmed as they took up a spot at the edge of the loose grouping.

A burly man wearing a dark-colored vest walked toward the crowd from a car near the front of the huge train and the haphazard, lively music ceased. Wide-shouldered, the man walked with a heavy, determined tread. He wore a blaster holstered low on his right hip, a leather tie securing it just above the knee. As he got closer, Ryan could see that the man had several white streak scars across his face and down one arm.

Behind the scar-faced man came three people—a man and woman in their thirties accompanied by a much older man with wispy white hair and spectacles perched on his nose.

Ryan had seen all four of them before, when he had watched the activities at the second tower. Scarface seemed to be some kind of foreman, giving out orders to the sec crew. The other three had been working at the tower when the firefight with the scalies had broken out, and Ryan recognized their type—whitecoats or similar, definitely brainy types.

When he reached the front of the crowd, the burly foreman began speaking in a barked shout. "We're at journey's end for the night, brothers." At this, a cheer came from the crowd before the man continued. "Anyone who needs sleep or company can take it. The bridge comes alive in two hours, and we'll cross Saka-kawea then and be on our way. Until then, day shift in place, construction crew with me, everyone else use the time wisely. We've got a lot of track to cover and I don't need anyone falling asleep."

"We're three stops behind schedule," a young white-coat said, raising his voice as several of the sec men guffawed and heckled him. The foreman chastised them with a single, shouted instruction, and they quieted. "We've made up a little ground from the previous night, but we've still a way to go, and it is critical that we get the circuit operational on time."

"Why?" someone called from the crowd, clearly meaning it as an insult.

"Well," the man told the crowd, "that's really not down to me…"

"The preliminary tests have been encouraging." The young woman butted in, taking the attention off her colleague. "If all goes to plan this should be the last go-round. Then the baron will be able to move on to phase four."

Ryan and J.B. couldn't help but notice the smiles and looks of relief on the faces of some of the sec crew at this news. J.B. also noticed several sec men pointing across in their direction and talking among themselves.

"Ryan," he murmured, tapping his friend with the back of his hand. "Time to go."

Ryan didn't question his colleague. He simply took two steps backward, as though trying to get a better view over the crowd of the speakers. Then he and J.B. turned and walked back toward the rear of the train. Behind them, the conference continued.

"Interesting," Ryan said to the Armorer, keeping his voice low as they walked briskly down the length of the train. "I don't know what it is we've stumbled into, but I'm thinking it looks mighty big, J.B."

"Agreed." J.B. pointed to an open door ahead on the side of a car and Ryan took the lead, jumping up onto the raised step and ducking through it. J.B. followed, trotting up the step and out of the sunlight.

The interior smelled of incense, heavy and cloying, and thick drapes hung over the windows, blocking out the dawn light.

A single table stood in the middle of the expanse, oval and big enough to seat four, a fat candle burning in its center. A lone figure sat at the table, a woman wearing a hood. She looked up at their entry, lit by the candle in front of her, and Ryan saw the deep lines of age crisscrossing her face. She was hunched in on herself, her hands hooked into claws through rheumatism, and there was something glistening on both of her cheeks.

"Come in, gentlemen," the woman said in a whispery voice.

As they stepped closer to the elderly woman, Ryan saw what it was that sparkled on her cheeks: twin tears of blood. And then he felt the world drop from beneath his feet.

DOC WATCHED as his companions ducked into one of the cars a little way down the gleaming length of train. He watched momentarily as three armed men followed them, then ducked back into the cool shadows between cars, knowing it wouldn't do to be caught out here. He holstered the LeMat, reached up to the metal bar at the side of the open car door and pulled himself up.

His head had barely eclipsed the sill of the step when he spotted the moving feet, padding along the corridor of the car away from him.

Damnation!

He ducked back, crouching beside the open door. If he stepped into the car now, the stranger would be immediately aware of him. And that wouldn't do. No, that that wouldn't do at all.

SITTING ON THE BUNK with Krysty, Mildred heard the sounds of movement in the adjacent cabin. Whoever was in there had woken up, and she heard a loud groan—a yawn—followed by the quiet, distinct sound of a belch.

She had quite forgotten that there were likely other people in the compartments around them. Ryan had listened at all the doors when they had staked out this car, she recalled, and he had decided that this compartment was the least dangerous. Mildred shook her head. Ryan and his instincts.

There were further sounds of movement, then she heard the door to the compartment ahead of them slide open, and the heavy tread as someone exited the room. With the train stationary, the walker's movements shook the car slightly, a light trembling that passed to Mildred's feet through the wooden floorboards.

"You awake, Scott?" a man's deep voice boomed from just outside the cabin. A moment later the man rapped three heavy blows on the sliding door, rattling its glass panels. As silent as a cat, Mildred stepped from the bunk and put a hand against the handle of the door, instinctively pulling her double action ZKR 551 revolver from the holster at her side.

"Come on, Scotty," the man's voice continued, "we gotta go. Day shift's on."

Mildred looked at the target revolver in her hand, thinking about the noise it would produce if she were forced to use it in this confined space. Krysty looked at her from the bunk, and Mildred pointed to her back-pack. Krysty winced as she pulled herself from the bunk, clearly in a lot of pain, and quietly passed the backpack to Mildred, exchanging it for the ZKR 551 in her hand.

At the door, her face inches from the glass, Mildred could hear the man cursing his sleeping friend. It wouldn't be long now, she realized, pulling a hypodermic syringe from her bag.

The man called Scotty again and Mildred felt the pressure on the door handle as his hand pulled at it. "If you've left without me, ya fink, so help me I'll skin ya alive!"

Mildred held the door handle with her left hand as she adjusted her grip on the syringe, deftly rolling it through rotating fingers.

"Nukin' door's stuck," the man outside growled, then he pulled at it again and Mildred let go.

The door slid back with a dull rattling on its treads, and a bearded, muscular man burst into the room, looking startled by his own swift entrance. Mildred jabbed the syringe into the man's neck the instant it cleared the door frame, and it stuck fast, translucent contents pouring into his thick, blue vein.

The man turned to look at her, his face red with anger. "What the hell? Who are you?" he bellowed. "What the hell'd you just do to me? Stuck somethin'..." He reached up, yanking the syringe from his neck and giving it a momentary look before tossing it aside. The syringe flew across the tiny cabin, droplets of translucent liquid splashing from its needle as it spun through the air before hitting the glass of the exterior window at the far side of the compartment.

He swung a punch at her, his heavy fist cleaving the air with an audible whoosh. Mildred ducked and the man's fist slammed into the cabin wall above her head, shaking the glass and frame of the sliding door. She pushed forward, driving a knee into his gut, knocking the wind out of him. He stumbled back a half step, arms reaching as he regained his breath in a short gasp.

"What have you done with Scotty, slut?" he snarled at her, his rank breath pouring from his mouth with the words. His hand reached forward in a blur and suddenly he had a hold of Mildred's plaits, painfully pulling her toward him by her hair.

Mildred punched at his chest, his sides, but she couldn't get any purchase while he held her like that, couldn't get any weight into the punches. And then a dark shadow whipped across the corner of her vision and something heavy slammed into the back of her attacker's head, knocking both of them to the cabin floor, Mildred underneath. Mildred expelled her breath with a loud grunt as she hit the hard floor.

On top of Mildred, the man struggled to get free, but something was holding him down, some weight pushing against him in the enclosed space of the cabin. Mildred squirmed beneath him and he seemed to remember his first objective. He couldn't seem to free his arms, but it didn't stop him. Opening his jaws wide, he lunged at her, hoping either to head butt or bite her, she didn't know which.

And then, as suddenly as it had begun, the man's head lolled to the left and he slumped on top of her, his eyes flickering until the lids closed. The sedative in the hypo had finally kicked in.

Mildred looked up, the heavy weight pushing at her ribs. She saw that Krysty stood by the door, her body closed up on itself like a tortoise trying to revert into its shell. She had pulled the sliding door closed, containing the noise of the fight from prying ears. Mildred saw now what had hit her assailant from behind—Krysty had to have rolled the corpse from the luggage rack overhead, letting it drop onto Mildred's attacker.

Struggling to drag in a breath with the weight of two

heavyset men atop her, Mildred called to Krysty. "A little help?"

Krysty pushed the bedraggled hair from her eyes and helped her friend push the two men away.

As they were wondering what to do with the dead man and the sleeper, Doc joined the women in the cabin, a secret knock confirming his identity. "By the Three Kennedys!" he exclaimed when he saw the two men lying on the floor caught up in the blanket that had fallen from the corpse. "What in the name of the Messiah did I miss?"

"We had a gentleman caller," Mildred explained, and she set to work wrapping the corpse back in the blanket while Doc tied the wrists of the intruder.

"And what did you do to him?" Doc asked, alarm in his voice.

Mildred smiled, but her expression seemed firm and serious. "I gave him a little sedative, just to make him sleep for a while," she said.

"Do you know how long it will be until that wears off?"

"I don't know how much went into his system before he pulled the needle out, but I'd say six hours," Mildred answered thoughtfully. "Call it five to be on the safe side, heavy bastard like this."

"We must find somewhere to place the gentleman, then," Doc stated, "unless you plan to chill the train personnel one by one."

Mildred shrugged. "I hit him with the sedative the second he burst through the door. He should have trouble remembering what he saw. We could probably put him back in his compartment."

"And what if he should awaken and decide to pay another visit to his late friend?" Doc asked.

"We could tie him up, then. Gag him," Mildred suggested.

From her position seated on the cot, Krysty spoke up in a quiet, strained voice. "Ryan would chill him," she told them. "Loose end, otherwise."

Doc and Mildred looked at each other in silence, knowing the truth behind Krysty's statement.

RYAN AND J.B. crashed to their knees, slumping to the floor like rag dolls. There was something about the room or the woman at the table or both that was affecting them.

Ryan looked around, dizziness making his vision blur, the sickly sweet aroma of the heavy incense suffocating his nostrils, clogging his mouth. He reached forward and his right hand slapped against the hardwood floor of the train car, barely propping himself upright. The elderly woman was smiling, the scarlet tears poised on her cheeks as she watched them both.

J.B.'s voice penetrated Ryan's thoughts like something hard and jagged thrust into his brain. "It's the air, Ryan. There's something in the air." His voice sounded far away, the words tumbling together like echoes in a cave.

Ryan felt his strength ebb, could feel his body falling forward, but he had no energy left to stop it. His face smashed hard into the floor, hitting on his left side, jarring his skull with resounding force. J.B. was right. The incense. There was something about the incense.

Kneeling beside Ryan, J.B. was struggling to stay upright. His body wavered and his clammy hands left watery trails of sweat as they slid on the polished floor. He noticed something then, his eyes caught by the glint of metal the way a magpie will focus on a mirror. Low down, beneath the surface of the table, was a chain, its links solid and newly fashioned, gleaming with the stuttering light of the candle flame. One end of the chain was attached to a solid metal ring that was sunk into the floor. The other end was attached to a clasp that was locked tight around the elderly woman's frail, bird-thin ankle.

As he swayed on the floor in front of the woman, J.B. heard the tramping feet as first one man and then a second and third entered the car through the same door he had used with Ryan a moment before. J.B. tried to turn his head, but it felt heavy and strangely unattached to the rest of him, as though it had gone numb like a slept-on limb. He felt himself falling and struggled to remain upright, but his sense of balance was gone and the demands of gravity too strong.

As he collapsed, he looked at the door through which he and Ryan had entered the strange car. The three sec men who had been following them stood there, sideways in his vision, kerchiefs pulled up over their mouths and noses. They were aiming heavy blasters at the Armorer and his companion.

Chapter Twelve

J.B. focused his eyes on the chain around the woman's ankle, trying to keep himself from sinking further into apathy. He breathed, shallow and fast.

"Who are you?" the muffled voice of one of the sec men called through the kerchief over his mouth. "Why haven't I seen you before?"

Ryan piped up, not a trace of fear or worry in his voice. "Construction crew," he answered. "Got on two stops back as per instructions." He still lay on the floor, struggling to get up, but the knock on the head had done him a surprising amount of good. He felt woolly headed from the incense, but he also felt the pain at the front of his skull from the swelling bruise. And that pain felt good, a throbbing beacon to focus his thoughts on.

"Never seen you around before," the lead sec man stated bluntly, pointing a well-maintained Smith & Wesson revolver at Ryan's flailing body.

"Con...construction crew," Ryan stuttered. He focused on the pain on the left of his skull, trying to keep his thoughts rock steady.

"Could be," one of the other two sec men suggested.

"Hmm." The lead man grunted, sounding doubtful. "Then why you come to see the *bruja* without a mask. You stupes, the both of you?"

"Forgot the rule," he said, raising his head very carefully from the floor. He looked at the sec men, their image swimming in front of his good eye.

One of the sec men spoke to the others. He had the same voice as the one who had said "could be" a moment before on hearing Ryan's lie. "Adam probably didn't even warn them. You know how he likes his jokes."

"I don't like it," the lead man replied. "This operation's too close to completion now to let anyone infiltrate it. I've given four years of my life over to Baron Burgess and his plan. I signed on right at the start. Gave him my daughter, too."

"Shut up about your daughter, for once." The third man spit. "They're construction guys. You're as paranoid as a one-armed mutie in a beauty contest." With that, the man stepped over and offered Ryan a hand.

His companion, the one who had mentioned Adam's jokes, came over and handed a spare kerchief to J.B. where he was sprawled on the floor. As he did so he murmured something to the Armorer confidentially. "I don't like having the *bruja* on here neither."

They sat in the dirt outside the car for a while, catching their breath and regaining their senses, and the three sec men finally left them alone.

"What the hell was that?" Ryan asked J.B. once they were sure they were out of the hearing range of any of the crew.

"Potent airborne drug," J.B. told him, still trying to shake off the feeling of drowsiness. "Crazy potent."

"Yet it doesn't seem to affect the woman in there," Ryan pointed out.

"The *bruja*," J.B. stated. He had heard the word through the muzziness of the assault on his senses.

"Mean anything to you?" Ryan asked. "*Bruja*, I mean. It's a new one on me."

"Means witch," J.B. said. "You see her ankle? She's chained in there."

"Breathing that crap all day?" Ryan said, incredulous. "Why would you need a witch on a train?"

"Why would you need a train?" J.B. grinned. "C'mon, Ryan, we're neck deep in mystery here, and we don't have clue one to what's going on."

Ryan looked off into the middle distance, letting his thoughts wend their own patterns while the soft breeze blew on his skin. He noticed that some of the sec men patrolling the perimeter seemed almost mindless, zombie-like in their trudging patterns. It struck him as more than simple boredom that was affecting them, something deeper, as though they were puppets, no longer in control of their actions. Just then, the cry went out, repeated down the line of the train, called to the guards at the perimeter. It was a single word. "Storm!"

As the rain hit, accompanied by vicious little hailstones, Ryan and J.B. ran alongside the train to the compartment where they had left Krysty, Mildred and Doc.

J.B. SPREAD OUT HIS MAP of the Dakotas on the tiny, molded desk once again, and Ryan, Mildred and Doc crowded around him in the small compartment. Krysty lay on her back on the bunk, pleased to finally be rid of the corpse of the previous occupant. Mildred and Doc had decided not to chill the second man, even though they agreed with Krysty's "loose end" argument. Instead they had followed Doc's suggestion, tying him to his bunk in the cabin next door by ankles and wrists, a gag in his mouth. They had tried to make it look like some fetishistic sex game, so that if anyone should stumble upon the man they might assume he had been left by his gaudy slut.

"We're here, Lake Sakakawea." J.B. pointed at the body of water labeled on the map. "Didn't see the lake ourselves, but the CO spoke of a bridge to cross it, naming it as he did so. Not sure where we are exactly, but I'd estimate we've traveled about sixty-five miles. That makes the towers about twenty, twenty-five miles apart."

"Any idea what they are?" Mildred asked.

"Not a clue," J.B. admitted.

Ryan sighed as he added, "They didn't say much about them, but a whitecoat spoke of the operation being a great success, though a little behind schedule."

"Did you see Jak?" Doc wondered.

Ryan shook his head. "No sign of him yet, but we didn't get much exploring done. Met someone, though," Ryan told them, and the tone of his voice was a warning in itself. "They call her the *bruja*. J.B. tells me that means witch."

"If she's Mexican," Doc stated, the amusement still clear in his voice, "then she's certainly a long way from home."

J.B. shot him a look. "So are you, Doc."

"Touché." Doc smiled, before falling silent.

"The *bruja* is on her own in a car, seven down from our location," Ryan told them. "J.B. says she's chained to the floor by an anklet, though I didn't see it myself. There's something about the car or about her, it hits you—*bang!*" He clapped his hands together. "Sec men followed us in wearing kerchiefs to breathe through, so we think it's the incense she's got pumping through the room. Thing is, it doesn't seem to affect her." Ryan looked at Mildred before adding, "You got any ideas on this?"

"Airborne hallucinogen, maybe?" she suggested. "If there's an antidote or counteragent then she could be dosed up on that, the crap in the air wouldn't affect her."

"Sounds reasonable," Ryan agreed. "Whatever, if you need to work through the train for any reason, be prepared. You walk in there without a filter over your nostrils and you won't make it three paces."

Doc was looking out the window, watching the violent rainstorm as it continued to pound into the ground, spotting the dirt with huge puddles like shallow lakes. "Why are they holding her?" he mused. "You said she was chained in place."

Ryan sighed. "The more we see, the less we know just now, Doc. Just keep your eyes open."

J.B. sat at the desk and studied his ancient map, trying to familiarize himself with the nearby territory so that he could recognize upcoming features. Assuming, of course, that said features still existed in the postnuclear world.

"So," Mildred asked, "what next?"

"CO says we'll move inside two hours," J.B. told her. "Guessing that's about 105 minutes now."

"They have to do something to the bridge," Ryan explained. "We didn't have an opportunity to find out what."

"Only bridge on the map would put us near Garrison," J.B. stated, his finger tracing the length of Lake Sakakawea, "unless they built themselves one."

"And how likely is that?" Doc asked.

Ryan pondered, his single eye watching the hail spatter against the car window, rapping on the glass. "They seem very organized," he said. "Lazy, mebbe, a little too trusting, bored of their routines. But this whole thing is heavily organized. It isn't something someone's whipped up on a whim."

"One of the sec men that found us with the *bruja* mentioned four years of work," J.B. added.

"But to do what?" Mildred asked, frustrated.

"Whatever it is," Ryan told them, "it's one big op."

The companions remained in silence for a long while after that, each pondering the ramifications in his or her own way. And, on the bunk, Krysty Wroth slipped in and out of a restless sleep.

IN THE CAGE inside the twelfth car of the train, eight sets of eyes were staring at the chalk-white boy. The prisoners were braver now, after Marc had established that whatever the gangly youth was, he wasn't a ghost. He had a solid body and his skin was warm to the touch. Marc had expressed his disappointment at that because, as he told it, he had always dreamed of eating a real-live ghost. It seemed kind of far-fetched, and Humblebee suspected that he had said that just for something to say, or mebbe trying to impress Maddie who had expressed precisely no interest in him.

It was Maddie who had rolled the boy over, with Marc's help, and looked at the wound on his chest where the sec man had shot him. Luckily they didn't touch the hidden razor blades in his jacket. His dark shirt was torn where the blast had penetrated, and an ugly bruise had formed on his skin. It didn't seem to matter that much—the boy's torso was covered in scars and bruises, old and new. He had to must be some kind of fighter, Maddie reasoned.

In the center of the ugly, purple bruise, a wicked color against his pallid flesh, was the end of a dart. Maddie told Marc and two of the smaller children to hold the chalk-white boy down, and she carefully pulled at the dart until she had plucked it from his flesh with a little, tearing sound.

A tiny spot of blood formed around the hole where the dart's nib had rested, and everyone was fascinated that it was red, just like their own. Humblebee had actually laughed, for about the first time since she had been snatched and put in this filthy cage. "See," she said, giggling, "no way is he a ghost now." Maddie had given her a stern look to silence her, then bent to take a closer look at the wound in the youth's chest.

The dart had clearly hit him hard, and the range was almost point-blank. He had taken the full impact between the lowest ribs on his left side. The skin had broken around the dart's sharp tip, but the hole it had made was negligible. It was whatever had been in the dart that had knocked the youth out.

Maddie looked at the youth's face, easing the mane of hair—just as white as his frighteningly alien body— from where it had stuck to his cheek. His face was angular, young and yet old-looking. He seemed somehow serene in sleep. And, yes, it was sleep. Now that she was closer she could discern the faint breathing coming from his nostrils in the dawn light that filtered in from the door and the cracks in the wood-plank walls. She wondered how old he was. At first glance he could pass for fifteen, but she noticed the start of white stubble on his cheeks, the long curls in his sideburns that only came about when a boy had turned into a man.

Francis-Frankie reached forward and tried to grab at a shiny object that seemed to be caught in the boy's coat. His hand snapped back, whip fast, and he looked at his finger. It was bleeding, runnels of red rushing down its length and making tracks across his little hand as he watched.

"Hand up—" Maddie demonstrated "—hold the wound."

Francis-Frankie did as he was told, tears silently streaming from his eyes as he sat there. "The ghost boy's coat bit me," he told them.

Maddie inspected the light camou jacket, keeping her hands clear of the shining objects that poked through its surface here and there. Razor blades, hunks of pointed metal and sharp shards of broken glass had been sewn into the fabric. Holding the chalk boy had to be like trying to hug a porcupine, she reasoned.

On Maddie's request, Humblebee passed her one of the three hessian sacks that the imprisoned children used as blankets. She brushed it with her hand, knocking off tiny, writhing bodies that had affixed themselves to the open weave. Then she rolled the sack-cloth in on itself, turning it over and over in her hands. Gently, Maddie raised the ghost boy's head, feeling the warmth of his skin through the ice-white hair. She placed the rolled-up cloth beneath his head, pushing the hair once more from his face and eyes.

Maddie turned to face the others. All of them were watching her with interest. She "walked" toward them on her knees, shooing them back with wide gestures of her hands. If the chalk boy had to sleep, he would at least be comfortable, she told herself.

"He's one of us now," she told the others firmly.

Chapter Thirteen

The vicious hailstorm continued its relentless assault on the ground as the train finally started moving again. Where the hailstones hit they left tiny smouldering craters in the soil, and the wisps of smoke formed a misty, foglike blanket over the first couple of inches of the surface after a while. The rainwater helped damp the blanket of toxic fumes down, but the air still took on the acrid stink of petroleum and made it unpleasant to breathe.

Despite the horrendous weather, the construction crew had continued to work at the front of the train. The bridge that spanned the eight-mile expanse of Lake Sakakawea beside the old Garrison Dam had been blocked off at both ends using the corpses of dead automobiles. The cars had long since lost their engines and been stripped of their contents. In place of the interiors, the vehicles had been filled with concrete or rocks, significantly adding to their weight. It took equipment and organization to shift the vehicles, and acted as a solid deterrent to any parties that may think of interfering with the train operation across the bridge. A similar, fenced-off bay at the far side of the bridge acted as another stopping point, so that the blockades could be erected again. It was a laborious operation, even using a portable crane that was stored in one of the cars, but it served to dissuade interference. Should another group get it into their minds to damage the bridge, it would have put a significant dent in the usability of the train. Slow and sure were the watchwords for the whole crew here, the bridge identified as a weak point on the trail.

The construction crew bent to its task slowly.

Ryan and J.B. had found what they described as a mess hall, just a few cars down from their unit. To get there they had walked through three cars devoted to bunks for the crew. Two of the cars were similar in design to the one they had left Krysty and the others in, old stock brought back into service with minimal repair work and a little brute force, although the farthest one included a compact, foul-smelling restroom at one end. Between these cars was a windowless truck, with double-stacked bunks lining both of the side walls. Some of the bunks were curtained off, but Ryan and J.B. had seen several sec men sleeping, one sitting on the top bunk field stripping a remade AK-47, and several empty beds. The man who worked at the AK-47 didn't bat an eyelid as the companions passed—bedroom or walkway, he couldn't care less.

The mess hall served boiled vegetables and meats of unknown species, their true tastes barely masked by the liberal use of strong spices. Hungry, the pair sat quietly at one of the makeshift tables, some kind of wooden bench. For a while they ate in silence, watching the other inhabitants of the car. There were more sec men here, looking exhausted from their night trip. Ryan realized that these men may well have been involved in the showdown with the scalies. If that was the case, it was little wonder that there was a general feeling of malaise about them. Night fighting muties took a lot out of a man.

Outside, the rain continued to pound against the windows, creating a shushing noise in the mess hall as it rattled through the countryside. One of the sec men had commented on it to Ryan, who sat resting his head on his left hand, elbow propped on the table and hand obscuring the distinctive, black eye patch he wore. Ryan had nodded, mumbling a vague agreement, not wishing to get involved in any conversation that might reveal him to the crew.

J.B.'s busy hands worked with scraps of the food, parceling it up and slipping it inside his pockets so that he could take it to Mildred, Doc and Krysty. Their instinct about leaving the other three in the compartment had been good—the crew was almost entirely male, with no one over forty. The women and Doc would have stood out and encouraged too many questions, where Ryan and J.B. managed to bluff their way through. Mildred possibly might have been able to pass for crew, but the female complement was so small that it seemed very risky.

"We're tempting fate here," J.B. whispered across the table, his eyes watching the far door of the mess hall as three construction workers entered. "We need to get Jak and get off."

Ryan chewed at a stringy piece of meat. "And what about Krysty?" Ryan whispered back, his eye never leaving the other entry door to the car.

"Use a gateway to leave the area." J.B. stated, "Mebbe it'll go."

"And what if it doesn't?" Ryan asked.

"Then we're off the train of horrors, at least."

Ryan sucked at a hollow tooth. "Let's find Jak."

"DID YOU NOTICE ANYTHING odd about those sec men back at the bridge stop?" Mildred asked, breaking the relative silence of the cabin.

Doc looked up from the map of the Dakotas that J.B. had left laid out on the tiny desk. "What's that, my dear?"

Mildred seemed deep in thought when she spoke again. "The sec men at the bridge stop, patrolling the fence. They seemed—" she clenched her eyes for a moment, her whole body tensing as she tried to find just the right word "—wrong," she concluded.

Doc thought back to the stopover at the fenced-in area. There had been a handful of armed men shuffling around the edges of the area, keeping a slow, steady patrol. He tried to picture them, but they all blurred in his mind, none of the features really affixed in his memory. "I'm not sure, my dear doctor," he stated, glancing across to the window as though for inspiration. He sat there, watching the green-tinted hail as it pelted the glass with a rattling tattoo. "The hail!" Doc exclaimed suddenly. "They didn't come in out of the hail, did they?"

"They didn't," Mildred agreed.

And that was odd. The hail out there could seriously hurt a man.

"Of course," Doc said, thinking out loud, "we do not know what their orders were. If they were told to stay outside then I would guess—"

"No," Mildred butted in. "Everyone came in when the rain started. J.B. said they shouted the instruction down the line, to make sure everyone knew."

"But the sentries remained," Doc muttered, his voice barely more than a whisper.

"Zombies," Mildred said, biting off the word through clenched teeth. "I think they're zombies."

Doc shook his head. "My knowledge of such subject matter is, I freely admit, somewhat limited, but——"

Mildred held up a hand to silence him. "I don't mean, like, undead, movie zombies. I mean they were, I don't know, mindless."

Doc nodded as he thought back. "I watched while our comrades joined in the salutation to the dawn baloney. I was watching as the construction hands peeled away from the others, going about their business. I was a long way away, but what I saw…well, it would seem to reinforce your viewpoint."

Wordlessly, Mildred encouraged the white-haired man to continue. "They were trudging in their movements, no life to them. They clearly followed the sec officer's orders, I can assure you of that, but they didn't seem to be thinking for themselves. They followed him in a line, Mildred. A line, do you see?"

Mildred glanced at the window, seeing the reflection of the oil lamp swinging to and fro above their heads. "They weren't soldiers, Doc, they weren't marching," she half asked, half stated the point.

"No," Doc assured her. "And yet they walked in a perfectly straight line."

Mildred and Doc looked at each other across the width of the tiny cabin, the ramifications of their realization only just beginning to sink in, its implications blossoming like the petals of a flower before them. And yet they walked in a perfectly straight line.

RYAN AND J.B. headed forward from the double mess hall.

The next car was another storeroom, this one containing a few dismantled weapons along with the usual sheets of steel, tins, jars and bottles of rivets, and strings of chain stretched across the ceiling. There were two small windows at the front of the car, one on either side of the unit. Ryan and J.B. checked the view through the windows simultaneously, J.B. taking the one to the right. It was the same on both sides—the train was speeding through fields of green plants and brown earth, the sand of the desert long since left behind.

Both of them had mentally calculated the journey to this point of the train, but they were reassured to see a large letter *B* painted across the door that led into the next car. *B* for *bruja*.

Ryan pulled a sweat-stained neckerchief from his pocket and tied it firmly around his throat. Beside him, J.B. was doing likewise with a piece of cloth he took from one of his pockets.

Ryan opened the door and they stepped through together, pushing open the second door and into the *bruja*'s darkened compartment.

There was a popping sound, and the train suddenly leaped, wheels clipping a badly soldered segment of the track. Tensed, Ryan felt his heart jump with the train, and for a moment he had a vision of the whole unit being derailed, tossing them across the fields. Then the train rolled on, wheels meeting track with the reassuring thrumming they had become used to.

A black curtain made of heavy velvet had been drawn across the doorway to the *bruja*'s car, and Ryan pushed his hand into its voluminous folds. The thing seemed to wrap around his arm like liquid.

As Ryan stood there, his left hand lost in the folds of black velvet, J.B. breathed his name through his cloth mask and pointed to the right. Ryan saw it, too—a thin walkway had been curtained off using the drapes of the room. The staff of the train could walk down this corridor without disturbing the witch. They hadn't noticed it when they had been in the compartment the first time, automatically assuming that the curtains covered the walls.

They walked swiftly down the curtained-off corridor, until it curved back inward at the far end, presenting the front door of the *bruja*'s car. As they walked, Ryan heard a soft laughter coming from the other side of the curtains. It was slow and somehow painful. He opened the far door and stepped across the gap into the next car, closing the door behind J.B.

The one-eyed man stood with his back against the door, pulling the neckerchief from his face but leaving it tied in place. He felt the relief pour through him like the heat of whiskey, and took a deep breath to steady himself.

"What is it about her?" Ryan asked.

In answer, J.B. simply shook his head. "Once bitten, twice shy, I guess," he concluded with a grim smile.

They were alone in a metal car filled, floor to ceiling, with tins of food. Old-fashioned, mil-prepped cans, a fortune in prenukecaust foodstuffs. J.B. picked up a can at random and looked at the illustration on the label. "Pineapple." He grunted before secreting the can in a voluminous pocket of his jacket.

They continued, making swift progress through two more cars of food stock until they reached a car guarded by a sec man. They were eighteen car from the rear of the train and at least forty from the front.

"Gonna need to see your orders," the sec man shouted,

even though Ryan and J.B. were no more than four feet in from of him.

Ryan looked at J.B., the barest hint of confusion on his face, before turning back to the sec man. He was something approaching six foot eight in height, and he had the shoulders to match. Biceps strained through his stained shirt, and his legs looked solid as the trunks of oaks. He was either a very large man or a very small ogre. Ryan wasn't one hundred percent certain which.

Behind the ogrelike man was an armory, shelves and shelves of blasters, grenade launchers, knives and swords, all lit by a low-hanging oil lamp like the one in the cabin they had secured for Krysty.

J.B.'s eyes widened as he took everything in. They had found the mother lode.

"Orders!" the giant shouted again, his right hand reaching for the blaster secured in his belt.

INSIDE HER MIND it felt like the ocean, where the ocean meets the shore.

The *bruja* sat there, in the darkened compartment, the blurred vision of her cataract-obscured eyes seeing the flickering candle as a light show, flashing and popping in front of her with all the wonderful colors of the spectrum. The woman sat there and she felt the ocean, washing up again, slapping against the folds of her medulla oblongata, right there at the back of her skull.

A woman, perhaps?

The *bruja* wasn't certain, not yet, but she thought it most probably a woman. In her heart, at least.

The *bruja* came from a whole family of women, of sisters young and old, sisters of different generations, each one schooled in the craft of the wise, each one a *bruja* like her. And so, quite naturally, she associated power with women, because that was as it had always been. Not blasters, not fists, not the ability to cause violence and pain. No, this was real power that she spoke of when she spoke at all.

And it was almost funny, she thought, that here she was, trapped and enslaved to a man, to Baron Burgess. His power was artificial, a slight thing, minuscule and irrelevant. But he had caught her, had trapped her and employed her services. And in return she was fed, sometimes.

Years ago, when she had begun the long trek from Sâo Paulo, when she had still been a young woman, she would never have believed that she would be captured and held like this, traveling across the Northlands in a mechanical thing shaped by the hands of man. Moreso, she would never have believed how little the incarceration being against her will would actually matter to her in the end. But that was more than seventy years ago, when the Deathlands was still being constructed from the ashes of the old United States, and she had been young and idealistic.

Now she sat there, her old eyes watching the flickering candle flame through a rheumy haze, and she felt for the mind that was like hers. It had joined the train not long past, already shrieking in its pain; in *her* pain. It felt like something burning as it washed up once more, the foam of the ocean searing the *bruja*'s brain. And then the burning ocean retreated once more, washing away and leaving trails from its smouldering foamy wash.

This one would hurt more, she knew, before the end.

THE FIRST THING that Jak saw when he slowly opened his eyes was a pretty girl, barely into her teens, with silky long black hair pouring like a waterfall over her neck and shoulders. The girl's skin was golden and her thin eyes were pools of hazel brown.

A box full of children? Was that it?

The girl was a few feet from him, and he could see the wire mesh of a cage behind her, its crisscross metalwork just barely twinkling in the little light of the shaking room. He closed his eyes, not wanting to alert her that he was awake until he was ready, and concentrated on reaching out to his surroundings using his other senses.

He was lying down, his right cheek resting against a coarse fabric, solid and hard-packed, a hard floor beneath his body. There was movement here, the continuous rocking of a ship or...

A train. They had brought him to a train and then they had—

He was lying on the hard floor of a train. The floor was warm, holding his body heat. But the room was cold, air whistling all around as the train shuddered onward to its destination.

He could hear voices, too, the giddy shrieking of children. Not the girl. He didn't think that she had moved from her vigil. But there were other children behind her, nearer his feet. Yes, that made sense. There had been children on the train. He had seen them.

And then someone had unholstered a blaster and they had pulled the trigger and...

He shifted his weight slightly, a minuscule movement, in time with the rocking of the boxcar. His arm twinged, pain running through it where he had taken a hit outside Fairburn. But there was more. His blaster was gone. His Colt Python. It should be there, resting at the small of his back, but its familiar weight was no longer there. Had he dropped it? He couldn't remember. He remembered a scuffle, brief and bloody, not really enough to it to call it an actual fight. The light had been bad, he was hurried, they had overwhelmed him, surrounded him.

And they had brought him to the train, and then they had shot him.

Jak's eyes flashed open with the memory and he leaped from the floor, his hands reaching for throat of the dark-haired girl beside him. She pulled away, even as he was reaching, a startled scream starting in her mouth, but she was too slow. Jak struck like lightning, pushing the girl—by the throat—to the floor. Her scream cut off, turning into an abbreviated squawk.

Behind him, at least two children were shouting incoherently, and he could hear the scrabbling of feet as they tried to find somewhere to run to in the stinking, enclosed space. A child's voice, could be boy or girl, Jak couldn't tell without looking, shrieked a single word. "Maddie!"

"Where?" Jak asked the girl as he held her head to the floor. "What happenin'?"

The Asian girl's eyes were wide; she was terrified. Her mouth opened but no noise came out. Jak loosened his grip on her throat and the girl made a squeaking noise, working her mouth painfully.

"Where?" Jak repeated, his voice a low growl.

The girl breathed rapidly, looking in his eyes, fear receding. "I don't know," she told him. "Please."

A boy's voice, cracking as he spoke, came to Jak

from over his left shoulder, where the kids were huddled. "Let her go, Ghost Face. You have to play nice."

Ghost face?

Slowly, warily, Jak looked over his shoulder. Seven children stood there, encompassing a variety of ages. The eldest was a boy, thin and wiry, like Jak had been as a lad, tousled dark hair on a dirt-streaked face. Jak guessed he was the same age as the girl, no older than fourteen. The boy stood in front of the younger children protectively, his arms stretched at his sides as though to stop anyone from passing. Jak admired him for that.

Slowly, making it clear just what he was doing, Jak pulled his hands from the girl's throat and held them out from his shoulders, palms visible. "Okay," he said, "mistake. Woke thinking chilled." None of these children could hurt him, he realized, and it was a given that none of them had anything to do with his imprisonment. They weren't a danger; they were cell mates.

Jak eased himself from the floor, leaving the girl where she lay as he faced the protector of the group. He heard her splutter, trying to clear the scratching sensation in her throat "Name Jak. You?" he asked.

"Marc," the boy said warily.

Making no sudden movements, Jak offered an open palm to the teen. The boy looked reticent to take it, but eventually he opted to shake.

"See?" Jak told him. "Gentlemen now. Just misunderstanding before."

Marc nodded. "You were almost chilled," he told Jak, a nervous smile crossing his lips. He wiped his mouth with the back of his wrist as though to hide the smile.

"Yeah," said another child, this one younger and

with wildly curling blond hair that could belong to a boy or a girl. "The big man shot you." The child sounded enthusiastic about the shooting. His blue eyes were wide with excitement at the memory.

"That's enough, Francis-Frankie," the girl said from behind Jak. She had a commanding voice, a natural leader, and he noticed that she had recovered from his attack very quickly. She stood behind him, fists bunched against her hips, and showed no fear when Jak turned to her. She looked at him, openly studying his face for a moment, before asking, "What's wrong with your eyes?"

"Eyes?" Jak replied, wondering what she meant. Had he been wounded? He reached up, but there was no dried blood, no cuts, no tears. Then he realized what she meant—his red eyes, the eyes of the albino. "Just that way," he told her. "Momma birthed me as seen. Red 'n' white, veins of blue, just like old flag."

"Are you a mutie?" the girl asked. There was no judgment in her tone, it was clearly just curiosity, a need to get all the facts in order.

"Nope." Jak shook his head. "No suntanning."

The girl stood still, looking Jak up and down for a long moment, considering all that he had told her. Despite her small frame, her dirt-smeared, torn smock, she had a quiet dignity about her, Jak thought. Then she nodded. "Okay," she said, holding her hand out to him. "I'm Maddie."

Jak took her hand and shook it once before looking around at the surroundings. He was in a cage in a wooden train car. There were small gaps in the walls where the planks didn't meet and where there were knots in the wood. Water seeped though the holes. Jak looked closer, poking his eye to one of the knotholes. It was daylight outside, daylight and raining. Heavy clouds sat across the sky, not interested in going anywhere.

"All prisoners, then?" Jak asked, turning back to the children in the cage. He knew the answer, of course, but he needed to break the ice, to make friends quickly with these children. They may be a crucial resource in his forming escape plan, and it was a definite that just one of them crying foul because they weren't on his side would scupper any chance he had of getting off without alerting the guards.

"Just like you," Marc told him.

"Mister?" A small girl child with long blond hair tied in dirty, uneven pigtails stepped forward. Jak guessed she was about eight years of age. "Are you really a ghost?"

Maddie laughed uncomfortably, the reaction of an adult to an embarrassing question, not that of a child. "Ignore Humblebee," she told Jak, "she has some silly ideas sometimes."

Jak bent, addressing the blond-haired girl at her own height. "Hi, Humblebee," he said gently. "Jak not ghost." He held his hand out in front of the girl, palm spread, fingers stretched outward. Humblebee reached across, mirroring Jak's movement, and placed her palm flush against his. "No ghost," he told her, smiling. "See?"

Humblebee laughed, a nervous twitter of a noise. And then she nodded, suddenly solemn. "Not a ghost," she agreed.

Chapter Fourteen

J.B. flicked his wrist and the Tekna blade flew through the air, landing with a solid thud in the sec man's throat, forcing him back.

Ryan had his SIG-Sauer in his hand now, leveling it over the man's shoulder toward the far end of the car. A noise from that end drew Ryan's attention. A tanned arm appeared, homemade tattoos running down its length in a scribbling of blues and greens. The tattooed arm ended in a tattooed hand and the tattooed hand ended in a cut off shotgun.

The sec man who had abruptly taken J.B.'s knife in his throat took another unsteady step backward, his teeth turning red as his mouth filled with blood. A river of scarlet dripped down the pale skin of his throat, and J.B. and Ryan could only guess how much more was going down the inside, drowning the unfortunate bastard as he struggled to comprehend what had gone wrong. He reached forward, trying to raise his blaster, but it fell from his grip, clattering to the metallic floor beside the low counter where the man had been stationed.

Twenty feet away, at the far end of the car, a woman's head appeared, popping out for just a fraction of a second from a shelving unit full of ammo, twitching like an inquisitive bird. Then the head disappeared behind the shelves. It didn't matter. Ryan had her height now. The rest was just waiting or flushing her out. She had to know that a stray shot in this car, filled floor-to-ceiling with ammunition, grenades, rockets and blasters, would be catastrophic. And Ryan could see the far door, she had to have realized that by now. If she made a move to escape he'd have her, so she had to stand and fight.

The huge sec officer finally dropped to his knees behind the counter, and then his heavy head fell forward. With a crash, the sec man slammed face-first into the metal flooring of the shuddering car.

"Phil?" the woman called. "Phil, you okay?"

Ryan stood still, his right arm raised, the SIG-Sauer steady, his left hand gripping between wrist and elbow to keep his aim absolutely firm.

"Phil?" the woman called again, and Ryan heard the familiar sound of the stock being pulled back and readied on a shotgun.

J.B. crouched, watching the far end of the car where Ryan had targeted. He reached forward, glancing down a fraction of a second to map the movements of his hand, and pulled the knife from the dying sec man's throat. There was a quiet squelching pop as the blade was drawn from the bloody hole, and then a rapid rush of blood spurted from the man's throat.

Ryan saw the gunmetal tip of the shotgun barrel appear between the shelving units, and suddenly the woman's head popped out as she took aim at the strangers. Ryan's single bullet hit her equidistant between her eyes before she had time to pull the trigger on her shotgun, and she fell backward, knocking into the shelves as she fell to the floor.

Ryan stood there a moment, listening to the sounds of the car until he was certain there were no more sec men to be taken care of. Then he turned to his companion.

J.B. was resheathing his knife in the wrist hideaway. "What happened to stealth?"

"You threw the knife," Ryan stated, walking away down the corridor between the metal shelves.

"But I threw it quietly," J.B. grumbled as he followed Ryan to the door at the far end. The Armorer scanned the shelves as he passed, grabbing a few clips of ammo that he knew would fit one or other of the companions' blasters. He passed twin clips of 9 mm bullets for the SIG-Sauer to Ryan as he reached the door. "Thought this was going to get easier," he asked.

"We're a hairsbreadth away the whole time," Ryan replied, shaking his head. "All we got is luck on our side and, damnation, but we don't often get much share of that. You want to do something with the bodies?"

J.B. nudged the woman's corpse under a low shelf with his foot. It was out of immediate sight, but if anyone looked down they would see her tattooed arm catching the overhead lamplight. Behind him, the huge sec man's corpse lay in its own blood behind the counter. "Nah, let's just keep moving," he said after a moment.

Warily, the pair made its way through the adjoining doors into the next car. This one was the same as its predecessor, an ordnance car stocked with more weaponry, though the emphasis was more on explosives—bundles of dynamite, some plas ex that could be molded by the user to suit the person's needs. Like the one before it, this ordnance car had two sec men on permanent duty, one at each end. The man nearer to the back door raised an eyebrow when J.B. and Ryan entered, then went back to the pack of cards he was dealing out in some interpretation of solitaire. He probably assumed that the strangers had been vetted in the previous car.

"Just passing through," Ryan said as he and J.B. walked past. The sec man turned over a black seven and placed it on the eight of diamonds that was showing in one of the stacks in front of him, making no acknowledgement whatsoever.

The sec man at the far end, dark-skinned with a handlebar mustache and a weeping, blind eye, nodded to the companions as they walked through the car. "You looking for anything, gentlemen?"

J.B.'s eyes drifted to the plas ex on one of the high shelves. "We're with construction," he said. "Might be needing some explosives soon."

The weeping man laughed. "Adam send you? You got orders?"

"We were *ordered*," Ryan said, stretching the last word, concerned that they were about to start another blasterfight that they could ill afford, "but he didn't give us anything to show you."

"We're both new to the crew," J.B. added hastily. "Got on three stops back."

The half-blind man shook his head, tutting. "You need to show me the coin, Adam will give you one. Didn't anyone explain this when you came aboard?"

Ryan sighed, clenching his hand into a fist. "Ah," he said, "you don't want to know."

The sec man laughed at that. "Yeah, sometimes it gets busy, everyone rushing around. You see the scalies? Heard that was some serious crazy right there."

J.B.'s glance flicked to the high shelf once again,

thinking. "We'll come back. Have everything in order. There's no rush."

The sec man smiled at them. "No problem," he said, "I'll see you when you're all sorted." He winked his good eye.

J.B. felt something instinctive then, he didn't know why, and he turned back to assess the card-playing guard at the other end of the car. The card player was oblivious to them. J.B. looked back to the one-eyed sec man, offering his hand. "John Dix," he said, "and my pal, Ryan."

The mustached man took the hand in a firm, two-handed grip. "Good to meetya, John."

Once the introductions were complete, the pair departed, heading onward through the train.

The next car was unmanned and seemed to be a storeroom for the oil lamps that they had seen lighting cabins and corridors. Ryan stopped as soon as they were through the door, closing it behind him and glaring at J.B. "What the hell was that?"

"Making friends," J.B. explained. "Might be handy later on, Ryan. We agreed to do this by stealth, remember. Sometimes stealth is just fitting in."

Angrily, Ryan shook his head. "One minute we're chilling people, the next we're playing baron's banquet."

"You seek out your own kind at the baron's banquet," J.B. reminded him, "so you have someone who'll step in front of the bullet when your enemy shoots."

Despite himself, Ryan felt a smile cross his lips. "You never cease to amaze me, J.B." They continued down the corridor between the shelves and pulled the sliding door at the far end aside.

As Ryan was about to step through, J.B. grabbed him

by the shoulder, and he turned back to look at the Armorer. "I would sure as hell like to get my hands on that plas ex, I can tell you," J.B. said seriously.

"You got ideas for it," Ryan asked, "or just feeling greedy?"

"I think we're all agreed," J.B. stated, "that whatever is going on here—the train, the scaffolds—it isn't going to benefit places like Fairburn."

"Does that matter?" Ryan asked. "To us, I mean."

"Putting a dent in an operation like this," J.B. said thoughtfully, "strikes me as mighty wise. Even if it's a temporary setback, I think we'd do well to halt proceedings if we can."

Ryan held the door open, looking at the windowless metal door of the next car. "Let's find Jak first, maybe he'll have some insights we could use."

J.B. followed his friend through into the next car, another crew quarters with triple bunks along the long walls.

The sound of loud snoring filled the room from a high bunk to the left. On one of the lower bunks, two men sat beside each other, one with his shirt off to display a web of blue ink down the right-hand side of his chest. Next to him, a sec man was holding a small knife blade in the flame of an open oil lamp that he had set beside the bunk, watching as the blade glowed from red to dazzling white at its tip. Suddenly he turned to the bare-chested man and carved further line work on the man's chest with the searing blade. The man clenched his eyes, expelling a slight gasp between gritted teeth as the hot knife touched his flesh. Ryan watched as the blade began to cool, its length turning an orange-red throughout. The man with the knife was adding ink to the new wounds, slowly drawing another tattoo on the chest of his companion.

As Ryan reached for the door to the next car, the train lurched, and he realized that the brakes were being applied once again. He entered the car, J.B. at his side, and they both looked around in wonder.

"WE'RE STOPPING AGAIN," Mildred said, looking across the claustrophobic compartment to Doc from her vigil over Krysty at the bunk.

Krysty had become more lucid in the past half hour or so.

Doc grunted a reply, like a man being woken from a dream, and looked at her with a befuddled expression. Mildred knew that sometimes Doc would drift off into his precious memories, enjoying the happier times with his wife and children before Operation Chronos had uprooted him from the time stream. Of all the companions, Mildred could sympathize with this trait the most, as she, too, had been uprooted from her place in chronology, albeit in a less abrupt manner. But she had become used to the philosophy of the Deathlands, that you lived in the present or you got chilled. She tried to restrict her moments of reverie to the quietest, safest times, when the companions had found safe harbor to sleep in, watch posted. Doc had been active here longer than Mildred, walking the grim paths of the postapocalypse, yet he still clung to those strong attachments of his previous life. He had been promised, not so long ago, that sticking with the one-eyed chiller would offer him the magical route back home, and he spoke of this in their quiet moments, the words of the old shaman's prediction still enticingly loud in his ears.

For a moment Mildred wondered if the white-haired

man had heard her, but he finally answered her with his infectious smile. "Indeed we are, Doctor."

"Krysty seems to be okay," Mildred said, looking at her companion who was sitting beside her on the bed, smiling to herself as she looked out the window.

"How are you feeling?" Doc asked Krysty. To him it seemed a remarkable change, but her health had been a back-and-forth pendulum since they had all stepped out of the Minot redoubt.

Krysty looked up at Doc and smiled, her green eyes bright and alive. "I feel okay. I feel kind of...normal." The surprise was clear in her tone.

"Her temperature's back to normal," Mildred confirmed after asking Krysty to hold a pocket thermometer in her mouth for a half minute. "It had skyrocketed when we got her to Fairburn, and it's been high ever since. But it's normal now."

"This is most peculiar," Doc stated. "Perhaps it really was the gateway jump, an adverse reaction to the matter transfer."

Mildred sealed the thermometer back in its covering plastic tube and replaced it in her backpack on the floor of the cabin. "Scuppers your theory about the towers," she said, but there was the trace of query in her voice.

"But you think, perhaps, that that hypothesis still holds some merit?" Doc asked.

Mildred reached a hand up to her brow, pushing hard against the points where her eyes met her nose as she thought. "It just doesn't ring true," she said. "There's something here, but every time we think we've got a handle on it, the rules change. First it was the bad gateway jump, but her health deteriorated so swiftly that we started to wonder if it was something else. Then we wondered if it was the ville, the tower outside, the train. And meanwhile, Krysty has been yo-yoing between off-color and near-catatonia. There's just no pattern."

The three companions looked out the window as the train pulled to a halt. Outside they could see rolling hills of green, beautifully tranquil. Suddenly, Doc piped up, struck by inspiration. "Eureka!" he exclaimed.

"What is it, Doc?" Krysty and Mildred blurted almost in unison.

The older man stood from the side desk in the cramped cabin, pacing a moment in the tiny area of floor. "A switch," he told them, raising his index finger upright from a clenched fist. Then he folded the finger back into the fist. "Turned on and off. Simplicity itself."

"A switch?" Mildred asked, the disappointment clear in her tone.

"Consider the prospect," Doc said, "if what is affecting Krysty is on some kind of switch mechanism, be it by timer or other factor, then until we know the pattern of the switch we will not recognize the pattern of its effect."

"A switch," Mildred said again, but this time there was more acceptance in her voice. "Something on the train, you think?"

Doc shook his head. "No, not the train. Forget the train. It's irrelevant. This is something—" he gestured sweepingly to the window "—out there."

"But what?" Krysty asked eagerly, swept up in Doc's wild theory now.

"The towers, of course," he told them both, "it has to be the towers. Whatever they are doing, they do not do it all the time. There is an off switch, just like on a lamp."

Mildred was dubious. "We didn't find an off switch at the one Ryan looked over at Fairburn."

"And we have no idea what they do," Doc agreed, "so how could we identify an off lever when we had not the slightest comprehension of what we were admiring?"

"He has a point." Krysty nodded.

Mildred peered through the window, looking up and down the tracks as far as she was able. "Then we need to find out what the towers are about."

"Of course," Krysty said gleefully. Doc's idea seemed to have lifted a weight from her mind.

But Mildred knew she had to dampen that elation. "Not you, Krysty," she said. "Too dangerous. You're the one who's reacting, I don't want you to go near these things, just in case." Though she saw the logic, Krysty still looked disappointed. "Doctor's orders," Mildred added firmly.

Doc spoke again, reaching for something on the tiny desk that J.B. had left along with his map of the territory: his minisextant. "Why do you think we have stopped?"

"I wouldn't be surprised if it's because of a tower," Mildred said, agreeing with Doc's unvoiced conclusion.

Doc held up J.B.'s minisextant, and took a single, long stride to the door. "Bring the rifle," he called back to Mildred as he stepped into the corridor.

Mildred did so, following Doc down the corridor once she had confirmed that Krysty would be all right on her own for the duration.

THE TRAIN had stopped moving, he knew.

Keeping their voices low, Jak quizzed Maddie and

the other children about the sec patrols. There didn't
seem to be any pattern to them, he learned—the sec men
simply came by when they felt like it, irregularly providing the prisoners with food. For the most part,
however, the children in the cage were left on their own,
to do as they wished. It was assumed, reasonably
enough, Jak thought, that they would not be able to
escape, so having a sec man watching them was a waste
of personnel. More so, Jak realized, thinking back to his
parade alongside the train to this car, when you took into
account that there was more than one cage.

"Sometimes, when the train stops," Marc told him,
"they put someone at the doors to make sure we don't
try anything."

"Which is stupe," Maddie whispered, "because
there's nothing we can do anyway."

Jak disagreed, but he chose to say nothing. He didn't
want to raise the hopes of this ragtag group of children.
He was older than them, and they were beginning to
adopt an attitude of subservience and obedience to him
as they would to any adult. Before Jak had arrived, they
had decided that Maddie and Marc were co-leaders by
virtue of their age and, hence, seniority. Children, it
seemed, followed the same patterns in pretty much any
situation, and Jak realized just how easy it was to prey
upon the innocent because of this.

At five foot five, he was taller than anyone else in the
car, the Asian girl Maddie's head just reaching to his
breastbone. Standing upright, he could stretch and touch
the wooden ceiling, but he needed something to stand
on if he was to put any pressure on the boards in the
hope that one of them might give. There was nothing
immediately at hand, but the children might be per-

suaded to form a human ladder if required. For now, however, he dismissed the idea and considered other avenues of opportunity.

The side walls were wooden boards, with gaps between that were wide enough to fit his thumb through. He tried shoving the hard part at the base of his hand against a few of the planks to see how much give the joins had in them. There was some, and he might break one of the boards away with a solid punch or kick. Though he had lost his Colt Python, the sec men hadn't bothered to check his jacket sleeves or his pockets, and he still had his sharp throwing knives secreted on his person and sheathed inside his boots. These might also be used to lever the boards apart, he realized, but he would need an extended period without the possibility of a sec man stumbling upon him. He would need to pick his time carefully for that, as opening a hole in the side of the car while the train was moving would be very dangerous for the children. While Jak's number-one priority was to save himself from this situation, he would help the children if he could.

Jak also checked the flooring of the boxcar, but he did so only briefly, unable to think of a safe way to exit in that direction, even if the train was stationary. He noted that the floor was alive with lice and tiny, wriggling silverfish, thriving on the damp wood.

Finally, with Maddie ushering the children away, Jak took a close look at the lock and hinges on the cage door. He instructed both Marc and the inquisitive girl, Humblebee, to watch both entrances to the car—he did not want to be seen tampering with the lock.

Silently, Maddie stood behind Jak as he examined

the bolt mechanism that held the gate closed. There was a corridor running along the front and one side of the cage, the same one he'd been brought in by; it was very narrow, someone of Ryan's build would have to shuffle sideways along it, he realized.

The mesh wall looked flimsy but the construction was solid and the material had an awkward malleability that meant it bent without snapping away from its attachments at floor and ceiling. Jak stopped putting pressure on it, looking again at the lock and hinges of the door. It would be hard to break the lock from inside, hard to get a good angle on it or a solid enough run up to add significant force.

The door's hinges were attached by flathead screws, however, and Jak placed his thumbnail into the groove of one and tried adding pressure there. The screw didn't move. It was wound absolutely tight, embedded in the metal. But with one of his throwing blades he might be able to twist the screws free, one by one.

He looked back at the children, all of them sitting quietly, watching the doors with his appointed sentries except for Maddie. The girl was watching him, her head tilted like a dog's with the effort of comprehension. "What do you see?" she asked him, a tight smile on her lips.

"Couple good escapes, but—" Jak gestured to the children "—plenty responsibilities, too."

Maddie couldn't disguise her happiness, her smile widening and her eyes creasing as she replied. "So, you would take us with you?"

Jak nodded, firmly and slowly. "Kids not belong," he said simply.

Chapter Fifteen

"Krysty's health is flip-flopping like a beached fish,"
Mildred griped to Doc in a taut whisper. "I'm not comfortable leaving her alone for too long."

She and Doc were lying on their bellies beneath their
train car, peeking out between the oily wheels. Up close,
the track was almost as haphazard as the train itself. By
necessity the gauge was precise, but there seemed to be
a hodgepodch of material in use to bring it into being.
Between the metal rails were struts of wood, though
none of the struts matched in color. Some of them had
licks of splintering paint across them, where they had
served a previous life as a door, windowsill or shelf.
Shingle was tossed between the tracks, its rough points
pressing into their torsos as they rested their weight on
the ground.

Mildred was to Doc's left, clutching Ryan's Steyr in
front of her as she hunkered in the shadows beneath the
train, hidden from view. Doc leaned forward, adjusting
J.B.'s minisextant where he had placed it upright on the
shingle in front of him. Satisfied, he leaned down and
looked though the spy hole once more, the device's tiny
telescope aimed toward the front port side of the train.

"Ah," Doc said, beaming, "there you are, my beauty."

Mildred glared fiercely at the old man, but her look
was wasted—he was absorbed in his work with the

minisextant. "Do you ever hear a word I say, Doc?" she growled.

"I heard," he replied, still looking through the telescopic attachment. "Our Krysty is in rude health right now, Doctor, and she will be fine, I am sure."

"*You're* sure," she scoffed, a harsh edge in her whispered voice.

"We have other, pressing matters to attend," Doc told her, twisting the focusing knob on the little device. "A mystery which may, in turn, be the root cause of Krysty's health problems, as you have already acknowledged."

"Yes, but I said that while I was still sitting where I could keep an eye on her," Mildred grumbled.

"Pish posh," Doc said, dismissing her. After a moment he added, "They are coming out now, take a look."

They had already observed a group of twelve, armed sec men trek away from the train, through the trees and off into nearby fields of cereal crops. Other sec men warily patrolled the terrain, blasters ready in their hands. Their position beneath the train was dangerous, but they both agreed that they needed to see what was happening with the towers, even if Mildred was starting to have second thoughts about leaving Krysty alone in the car above them.

Mildred tilted the Steyr to look through the scope, panning hurriedly across the field of vision until she found the point where Doc was looking.

"See them?" he asked quietly.

"Mmm-hmm," Mildred acknowledged. "What are they doing?" She was looking at two technician types who appeared to be in deep discussion with a muscular man in a dark vest. She adjusted the scope, bringing the figures into tight focus—Vest Top had several white scar lines down his arm and across his face, while the technician types were the two thirty-somethings that Ryan had told her about.

"To the left," Doc whispered, "a little way out from the tracks."

Mildred shifted the weapon slightly and the view through the scope shuddered for a moment until she located the tower. It was a twin to the one they had found on the outskirts of Fairburn, a scaffold structure built into a thin pyramidal shape like an obelisk. From this distance, with no sense of scale, it reminded her a little of the old Washington Monument, towering proudly into the blue sky, oblivious to all that went on in its shadow.

As she watched, another technician or whitecoat came into view, older with wispy white hair, his round spectacles catching the sunlight. He patted the side of the tower with one hand, perhaps to assure himself of its structural integrity but just as likely to keep his own bent frame balanced on the rough terrain.

"This is it, huh?" Mildred whispered. "The whole magilla."

Doc watched silently through the telescope attachment of the minisextant. He had seen this process once before, during the long night while his companions were sleeping, but he wanted Mildred's opinion before they came to any conclusions. His theory about their being a switch felt viable, but they needed evidence to go further in acting on it.

They both watched as the man in the dark vest walked over to the tower, followed by the younger whitecoats, and spoke to the elderly man. Then, entering their tight viewpoints from the right of frame, from somewhere on the train, Mildred realized, two men carried a large, cylindrical canister to the tower's base. They walked slowly, legs spread wide to hold the weight of the object. The canister was about four feet in height, painted the deep orange color of paprika, a yellow hazmat label affixed to its side.

"What is that?" Mildred muttered, all thought of the sharp stones beneath her now forgotten, dismissed from her mind.

The man with the scarred arm ducked down, dropping himself inside the base of the tower between the skeletal legs. Once there he worked his fingers into the ground, grasping something that was buried there. Mildred thought back to the tower at Fairburn, remembering the metallic disk that was sunken in the sand at its base. With visible effort, the man began to twist something, his arms spread wide as though he was turning the steering wheel of an eighteen-wheeler truck. The older whitecoat leaned in, pointing at something on the ground there.

"What are they doing?" Mildred asked quietly.

"That is what we are here to find out," Doc whispered back. Though he had witnessed this operation once before, he hadn't known what to look for then, and it had been at night. This time, in the bright, midmorning light, he was ready and had instructed Mildred on where to look.

A large steel cap, like a trash can lid or a manhole cover, was lifted from the ground by the man in the dark vest. He balanced it on its rim before rolling it along the ground, away from the tower's base.

The female whitecoat stepped over, a measuring stick in her hands, and knelt in the grass beside the tower. Leaning down, she popped her measuring stick into the ground—presumably into whatever the metal disk had been covering—and reached forward so that her arm disappeared beneath the surface up to the elbow. When her hand reappeared, the dipstick was glistening with some sort of liquid. Mildred tightened the focus on the scope but she was not quick enough to see what mark the liquid had left.

"Do you see it?" Doc whispered.

"Yes," Mildred breathed. "Liquid. Couldn't see what."

"Do not worry," Doc told her, "there's more."

Mildred watched as the three whitecoats discussed the dipstick at some length before settling on a decision. It took almost three minutes until there was any further activity, and Mildred began to wonder what spectacular feat Doc was expecting her to witness. Then they reached a consensus, and the man in the dark vest who had removed the metal cover stepped over to address the two men with the heavy cylinder, explaining some operation with hurried hand movements as well as words.

Slowly the canister bearers "walked" it to an area beneath the tower, half stepping, half turning the heavy item in the grass until it was in place. Then they unscrewed a small black plug near the top of the orange cylinder, revealing a round opening a little off center. Together, following the shouted orders of Dark Vest, they tipped the canister very gradually until a thin drool of liquid began pouring from the hole.

Mildred adjusted the focus on the rifle scope again,

trying to get as close a view as possible. Doc may have said "This is it" right then, but she wasn't really listening anymore.

As she looked, a dark shape blotted her view, like a lunar eclipse across the crosshairs of the scope, as one of the patrolling sec men wandered across her field of vision. She cursed inside her mind, her lips moving but no sound coming out. Get out of the damn way, she thought, as though thoughts might have an effect. Then, just as abruptly, her field of vision was clear again and she watched as gray drool was poured into the space beneath the legs of the tower, disappearing into whatever the removed lid had revealed.

The gray liquid poured slowly over the lipped opening in the orange cylinder, its passage uneven where it contained small, solid lumps. Whatever it was, it was viscous, like mucus, the consistency reminding her of the old fruit smoothies she used to drink at college in her days before cryo sleep. Could it be organic? Refined liquids didn't pour like that. This was more a paste than a liquid. It could be animal, more likely, really, but Mildred was a doctor not a vet—when she thought organic she extrapolated from her knowledge of the human body. She watched, thinking of the gunk that man produced: blood, saliva, urine, sweat, feces, semen, mucus, breast milk, perilymph… There were others, she knew, things hidden in the flesh, sebaceous glands and their ilk.

She felt Doc shift beside her, and suddenly the old man was moving with urgency. She took her eye from the scope, looked to her right and saw him rapidly crawling backward out of the hidey hole beneath the car using his elbows, off to the starboard side of the train— the opposite side to all the activity at the tower.

"What is it?" Mildred asked, her voice low.

Doc's head poked beneath the train to look at her. "Stay put," he instructed her, and then he was gone. She watched his feet stride along beside the car, heading toward the rear of the train.

There was no time for this, Mildred realized. Doc could take care of himself and whatever urgent business he had. She placed her right eye against the scope once more, watching the activity at the scaffold tower. The female whitecoat was back now, extending her dipstick into the hole in the ground while the two men with the canister held it upright in the same spot, no longer pouring liquid from its innards.

Suddenly a shot rang out just behind her and Mildred flinched. Doc? she wondered.

SITTING A LITTLE WAY back from the cool surface of the window glass, Krysty looked out at the area around the train. Propped in the chair by the tiny desk, she focused on some movements she had noticed in a flank of trees about seven hundred yards from the stationary train.

She watched eight men stalking through the shadow of the trees. Dressed in dark clothes with wool caps pulled over their hair, the men drew heavy blasters as they approached the train. One of them held a pair of binocs to his eyes, his head turning as he panned the monstrous length of the train, his expression grim. He lowered the binoculars, turned to his comrades and flashed a hand signal at them that Krysty didn't recognize.

A moment later two men from the rear of the group stepped forward. The first had what looked like a long pipe slung over his shoulders, like an old-fashioned milk maid, his head bent forward, his hands holding the weight in place. The diameter of the pipe was roughly that of a man's leg. As Krysty watched, the man swung the pipe from his shoulders and, after further discussion with the leader holding the binocs, knelt and rested the pipe over one shoulder. His partner rooted through a leather satchel and produced three identical items: three-feet-long tubes with pointed ends. Rockets.

Krysty unconsciously flinched as she saw the satchel bearer load the first rocket into the homemade launcher and light the fuse.

RYAN AND J.B. stepped warily into the new car, looking left and right, automatically scanning their surroundings for possible attack. But the area appeared to be empty of personnel.

The room was quite dark; the only lighting came from the walkway that ran down its center, indirectly splaying from the edges of the raised, metal grating. One wall was lined with pressurized canisters standing upright in the confines of a metal unit, and these were painted the burnt-orange color of paprika and displayed the familiar hazmat symbol on their sides. The holding unit clunked and hummed to itself, its groans echoing through the chamber. To the right side of the car was a jumble of intricate pipework, running over and under a long desk that ran almost the car's full length. It reminded Ryan of the moonshine stills he'd seen from time to time in villes throughout the Deathlands.

The car featured large, rounded sides, bloating outward beyond the standard width of the train. This was one of the three fatter cars they had seen during their walk along its side beside Lake Sakakawea.

There was a definite clinical feel to the setup, and, as they walked slowly through the car, J.B. pointed out the pivoting spotlights that were arrayed above the desk on a long rail. A thick cable attached to the far end of the rail ran to a worn-looking gasoline generator, and a chimney hose ran from the genny to the ceiling, disgorging waste products as required. Currently the genny and the spotlights were switched off.

Automatically, J.B. checked the rad counter on his lapel. "Radiation's at normal levels," he told Ryan.

"Any idea what all this stuff is?" Ryan asked, peering around the unmanned car.

J.B. reached across and warily placed the back of his knuckles against one of the canisters lining the wall. "Cold," he stated.

Up close they could see that a sheen of water droplets had formed on the shelved canisters like morning dew, and the humming unit they sat within exuded cold air.

Ryan walked to the far end of the car and found a second generator hidden from view by the bulky cooling unit. The gasoline genny was jumping up and down in place, chugging away as it powered the refrigeration unit. A hose system took the waste products out through the ceiling, in the same way as the one that powered the desk spotlights. The car didn't smell of gasoline, though there was the faint whiff of alcohol, implying that the ancient gennys had been converted to run on the more plentiful fuel source.

Ryan strode across to the door at the far end of the car. It was wider than any they had stepped through up to now, and featured a level board of metal that ran directly into the next car, thus forming a flat walkway between the two. A small, square window with reinforced glass, the familiar crisscross pattern of wirework within it, was in the center of the door, and Ryan peeked through. The next car was also empty, and featured a similar long desk with spotlights along one side of the room. The other side held five parked carts, and Ryan could see that the wall featured a large set of double doors that would open at the left-hand side of the train. At the far end he could see light coming through another square window like the one he was looking through. A dark shape obscured the light in the far window for a moment as someone passed. "Next one's empty," Ryan called to J.B., "but I can see movement in the next but one."

J.B. grunted in acknowledgment. He was busy checking the burnt-orange canisters, reading the details on the hazmat labels and examining the dark, coglike seals that were found near the top of each unit. The labels told him very little. They were standard instructions about storage and he couldn't be certain that they even referred to the contents now in these canisters—after all, so much of the material in the Deathlands had been acquired for new lives long after its original purpose was forgotten. A rough square of paint had been chipped away on each canister on the rounded top and an alphanumeric code had been written there in a clear, bold hand using a black marker. In earlier times this information might have been added using printed labels and barcodes, but such luxuries were rarely found in this new world. J.B. couldn't attach any special significance to the numbers, but concluded that they were probably just a storage code rather than a clue to the contents.

He reached forward and carefully unscrewed one of

the dark caps that sealed a canister, before propping his spectacles on his brow and putting his naked eye to the opening. He shifted his head this way and that as he tried to get some light on what he was looking at, but it was very difficult with only the underfloor lighting of the car.

"What do you see?" Ryan asked, keeping his voice low.

"There's some kind of liquid in there," J.B. replied, "I can see the shimmer of reflections. Can't tell what it is, though." He sniffed at the contents, which gave off very little smell, just something faintly acidic. If J.B. recognized the odor, he certainly couldn't place it.

"What'd it smell like?" Ryan asked as J.B. resealed the canister.

J.B. sighed, trying to gather his thoughts and overcome an uncomfortable nagging he had in the back of his mind. "Death," he answered after a moment, "and I can't place why."

As the pair walked toward the door into the next car there was a loud explosion and the whole train shook. Ryan staggered, reaching his hand out to the wall to steady himself as J.B. stumbled backward into one of the generators.

"Fireblast!" Ryan growled, looking around the car. "Something hit us!"

MILDRED HEARD THE FIZZING noise coming from ahead of her as it passed from left to right, but she continued to watch the process at the tower through the powerful rifle scope. A second later the car above her shook, and a shower of dust fell over her bare arms and shoulders as the noise of an explosion filled her ears. Doc had disappeared just five seconds before, and she had heard the report of a blaster just prior to the explosion. She realized what it meant—the train was under attack. No wonder Doc had rushed off when he did. While she had been watching the work at the tower through her scope Doc had to have been scanning for hostiles in the area around them and spotted the attack a split second before the rocket was launched. He'd trusted Mildred would be safe beneath the train while he guarded her from attack.

Whatever had hit had done so farther along the train, somewhere much closer to the engine. Unless someone targeted her car, she should be safe for now; Doc would see to that.

She dragged Ryan's longblaster across the ground, keeping her eye to the scope as she tried to locate their attackers. A squad of sec men charged from the train toward a clutch of trees on the horizon, and shots whizzed over their heads as the roof guards set up cover fire. The group at the tower had ducked, the dark, vested leader crouching in a classic protective stance as he reeled off a volley of shots from a heavy blaster into the nearby shrubbery. With naked eye, Mildred glanced back at the tower, leaving the scope focused on the action in the trees, and watched the three technicians hurry for the armored protection of the train.

Something crossed her field of vision as she watched, a thin object moving at high velocity, and there was a second explosion. A cloud of dust kicked up near the tower and the train rocked once more.

Mildred put her eye back to the scope on the SSG-70 and watched flashes of light in the trees as the sec men reeled off shot after shot from their blasters, trying to locate their hidden attackers.

SOME SIXTH SENSE had told Doc to look around the train a few seconds before the attack had begun. That was all he could attribute it to as he rushed along the starboard exterior of the vehicle, hugging the side and sticking to the shadows there. He had his LeMat blaster in his hand, loaded and ready, as he dashed toward the back of the train.

Above him, he could hear gunshots as the roof gunners took aim at their assailants. Beside him, the train shook as it took a rocket to its midsection, and Doc looked behind him and watched as the rocket exited on his side of the train, having blown a hole clean through one of the cars near the front of the long vehicle from port to starboard.

He looked to his left, his eyes roving the patchy forest for signs of more attackers, and suddenly he saw another rocket burn through the air out of the trees, heading straight toward him. Doc threw himself to the ground and the rocket zipped overhead before slamming into the train car just behind him.

The explosion rang in his ears, and he looked back to see the extent of the damage. A wide hole had been created in the side of the car to his right, barely ten feet behind him. The edges of the hole glowed hot, and flames could be seen bursting from the interior. Several dented sheets of metal tumbled through the hole where they had been freed from the shelves in the storage car.

He struggled back to his feet as multiple shots rang out. The rooftop gunners had spotted the glint of metal in the trees and were peppering the area with a spray of bullets.

Doc stepped back into the shadows, dodging into the space between two storage cars near the rear of the monstrous train. He watched from his hiding place as sec men rushed past, calling to one another about the fire in the nearby car.

A series of shots rang out from the trees, chipping at the wet ground around the train as a team of sec men rushed into the woods, trying to get a bead on their attackers. Suddenly, Doc spotted the movement in the branches above them, and a skinny man in homemade camouflage clothing appeared with a blaster in each hand, firing at the train guards. Three sec men fell at his devastating attack, and Doc heard the whoosh of air as another rocket launched from somewhere in the same clutch of trees.

As the rocket blasted through the air, its tail aflame with propulsion, Doc swung the LeMat and reeled off a single, devastating shot. Three of the upper branches of the trees disintegrated as the large ball slammed into them, and the skinny man fell to the ground in a whirl of limbs. It was a curious position that he found himself in, Doc realized, defending the prison that held his colleague. But right now there was no other option if they were to have a chance of rescuing Jak.

Then the rocket hit, smashing into the sheet-metal wall of the last car, shaking the structure of the whole train. Doc blinked back the dust from his eyes, shook his head to try to clear the ringing noise that gripped his ears, and peeked out from his hiding place. The rocket had slapped into the wall of the final car, denting the side but not piercing the sturdy boxcar. As J.B. had surmised, the last unit of the train had been toughened to withstand attack, and its heavy contents added to its shielding.

Doc glanced around, realizing that no further noise was coming from the trees to his left. Four sec men were trudging back to the train, weariness replacing the adrenaline that had motivated them just moments before. Two of them carried one of their colleagues, bearing his weight on their shoulders. The man they held stumbled, hopping on one foot, afraid to put weight on the other leg. Blood poured from a wound in his left leg, glistening in the morning sun.

Men from the train rushed all around, sliding back the large side panels of several of the storage cars at the back of the vehicle and removing sheets of steel, rivets and welding equipment. They organized themselves quickly to make swift repairs where the train had been holed. Doc dropped farther back into the shadows between the cars, wondering what to do next.

JAK HAD BEEN examining the lock on the cage door when the train shook with the explosion. He spun automatically, looking toward the rear of the train as though he could peer through the wall and see where the explosion had come from.

The train rocked in place for a few seconds before settling once again. Some of the younger children began to wail then, and everyone voiced the same question: what was that?

"'Splosion," Jak told them, urging everyone to be quiet as he walked across the small cage and put his ear against the back wall. He could hear lots of shouting and the crackling sound of flames. And there was screaming—the high voices of children, scared and hurt. "Everybody on floor," Jak instructed firmly, pointing to the wooden boards of the floor. "Lie down."

The children looked at him quizzically, several of the younger ones like Francis-Frankie shrieking in terror, their faces red. Maddie reached out, gently touching the shoulders of several of the children as she repeated Jak's instruction. "We all need to lie down, like we're going to sleep. Come on, quietly, lie down."

It took a few moments, and Maddie had to pull one of the younger children—a dark-haired five-year-old called Allison—gently to the floor, but eventually the children were lying down, leaving only Jak standing. He heard the tinkling of a bell, two urgent rings, echoing along the train cars—some kind of alarm system, he guessed. He stepped away from the back wall, imagining he could feel the heat of flames but also certain that it had to be his imagination. The dull ache was still playing at his left arm, and he rubbed it through his jacket as he stepped across the car, looking all around.

With no warning, there was the sound of a second explosion, coming from the port side of the train, and Jak looked across at the wooden wall past the wire mesh of the cage wall. He heard something hit the side of the car there, a shower of rocks and dirt, he guessed. The shells were getting closer.

His eyes swept around the little box of the room, his brain working urgently to try to find a way out. On the floor, some of the children had taken fetal positions, curling in on themselves as the car shook all around them. Others hugged each other, glistening tears streaming down their cheeks. Marc looked scared, his own cheeks damp with tears, but he held tight to two of the smaller children, promising them they would be safe. Jak was conscious that three sets of eyes were watching him, including Maddie. When she caught his eyes she mouthed a question. "Are we going to be okay?"

Jak shrugged, his gaze sweeping across the roof, this way and that, as he heard the gunshots all around. Then he looked down at Maddie on the floor once more and he realized what he had to do. He crouched in front of her, knees bent, balancing on the toes of his worn boots. "We be fine," he told her firmly, locking his eyes on hers.

There was another explosion, far back in the train but still enough to shake their car, and Jak leaned down, resting his body beside Maddie and the other children. He gazed at the wooden slats of the roof, listening to the stuttering song of automatic weapons from all sides.

THE SEC MEN HAD EXITED from the third of the bloated cars as soon as the explosions began, and Ryan and J.B. rushed into it the second they were sure it was empty. They had discussed going outside, finding out what was causing all the damage, but the urgency to find Jak had become paramount now as the situation on the train became more perilous.

They were stopped in their tracks by what they saw in the third car, though it affected Ryan more deeply than J.B. Like the previous two, this car featured what looked to be distillation equipment along one wall, coupled with a bloodied bone saw, and half of the opposing wall was taken up with another refrigerated unit full of the tall, burnt-orange cylinders. But the remainder of that wall, beside a grumbling gasoline genny, featured four little, square cages stacked two atop two. Three of the cages were empty, but the final one featured the body of a naked boy, lying in the tight space, curled up on himself. The child's skin was dirty, and there was evidence of dried blood around his face and neck. His skin was lusterless, and bony ribs stuck out from his chest. The boy was about eight years old and he appeared to be sleeping.

J.B. had noticed Ryan's discomfort. "You okay?" he asked, keeping his voice low.

Ryan shook his head, his single eye still looking at the child in the cage. "Just made me think for a moment," he stated. There were things in Ryan's past, a child of his own now lost somewhere in the Death-lands, his own childhood so abruptly cut short by his murderous brother... Ryan didn't dwell, but, all the same, there were old wounds that would never heal, not completely. "The sec man back in the car, the one I iced, he said something about children—about how they would take, would steal children."

"He explain why?" J.B. asked.

Ryan shook his head. "We didn't talk extensively. I'm thinking of Jak, wiry little runt that he is. It was pretty badly lit where they picked him up. Reckon they thought he was a kid?"

J.B. laughed in spite of himself. "That's rich." He smiled. "Jak would just love that."

Ryan reached for the bolt mechanism on the exterior of the cage, but J.B. put a hand out to stop him. "Not our problem, Ryan," the Armorer stated firmly. "But you open that cage, he'll become our problem. One we can't afford."

Muttering a curse, Ryan withdrew his hand and the two of them headed to the door and into the next car.

IT TOOK ALMOST twenty minutes, but finally the sec men rounded up the few remaining stragglers of the rebel party that had attacked them. There were three survivors in all. The party of sec men that had been dispatched into the fields as soon as the train stopped had eventually attacked them from the rear, culling them in swift order. The three remaining attackers, still dressed in their dark clothes and wool caps, were made to kneel in the dirt close to the tower, and their hands were tied behind their backs.

Adam, the commanding officer of the train crew, wearing his dark vest to better show the ghastly scarification running down his arms to match his misshapen, abused face, pulled the .44 Magnum blaster from his hip holster once more and held it at the head of the first of the three living attackers.

"Why did you attack the train?" he asked.

"Screw you, outlander." The man spit, looking firmly at the ground.

"Look at me," Adam growled, "not the ground. Look at me, brave man, and say that again."

The man grunted and slowly raised his head. In less than a second the top of his head disappeared in a cloud of blood as Adam's blaster fired a shell through his skull.

"The next one won't be so lucky," he explained. "The next one, I shoot in the gut and leave for the burrowers."

The two kneeling men looked at Adam as he swung the blaster toward them. "Now," he told them, "I want to know why you attacked my train."

The man to the left spoke through clenched teeth, venom in his voice. "You came here nine months ago," he told Adam. "You came in the night and you stole our crops and you took my only son. And not just him—

other children from the ville. For eight months we asked the same question. Why? Why did they take our sons and our daughters? Why?"

Adam grinned maliciously as he looked at the man. "Nine months is long enough to produce another son," he told him. "Think of the boy as your tribute to the baron."

Anger welled in the man's expression and he lunged at Adam, launching himself from his knees, head down, toward the larger man. Adam sidestepped, and the man fell facefirst into the mud behind him. Slowly, almost casually, Adam aimed his blaster at the man's torso and blasted a hole below his rib cage. The man howled in agony, crumpling on himself where he lay.

The third man, still kneeling in front of Adam and the tower, found his voice at last. "We answer to no one here—Hazel has always been a free ville."

Adam walked away from the kneeling man, instructing his men to follow him back to the train. The engine was warming up now, snuffling like an animal woken from hibernation, as it got ready to continue its journey along the metal tracks. The sec men who patrolled the grounds fell in line, making their way back to the train, as well. The fires had been extinguished and temporary plates had been added to the sides of the train where the rockets had hit; it was ramshackle, but it would do for now, until they could find a safer stopover point.

Adam barked out a single laugh. "A free ville," he shouted. "You hear that, men? A free ville is what Hazel is." And he laughed again, a humorless, mocking bray.

FROM HER WINDOW, Krysty felt her stomach drop as she watched the two sec men approach the kneeling man where he struggled by the skeletal tower. These sec men wore large, sturdy backpacks that glinted with the sheen of metal, and they each held a long pipe in their hands. The pipes were attached to their backpacks with a short length of hose.

The sec men stood eight feet from their kneeling victim, three or four paces between them, and leveled the pipe nozzles. Krysty turned away but she could see the man's fate in her mind's eye as he began to burn under the ghastly power of the flamethrowers.

THE BURNING MAN'S agonized scream was cut short almost as soon as it started as the flames engulfed his mouth and tongue.

Watching from her position under the train, Mildred heard the familiar hum as the engine warmed up, felt the car above her begin to vibrate as thrumming power began to pull at the heavy burden.

Ahead and above her she could hear the call going down the tracks as each sentry repeated the instruction. "All aboard!" When it reached the sec man who was standing three feet in front of her, she hoped he might jump onto the train, but he just stood there, his dirt-streaked boots directly in front of her.

She felt the thrum of movement on the tracks where she rested as the train began to pull slowly away, and watched as the wheels began to gradually roll. Mildred pulled herself tighter under the train between the tracks, watching the wheels pass her. The length of the car above her was eighteen feet, she had that long to come up with a way to roll out from under its moving body, kill the sec man and get back onto the train—not necessarily in that order.

She hugged Ryan's blaster closer to her body as the train chugged along the tracks, gathering speed.

Chapter Sixteen

A wall of moving wheels blocked her exit and the sec man was still there. Why hadn't he boarded? Mildred reminded herself that the speed of the train was negligible just now, barely three or four miles per hour. Outside, standing by the tracks, the guard could probably stroll beside the train and grab the rung of a passing ladder without a second thought while it traveled at this pace. Meanwhile, she was stuck below the moving behemoth as the space beneath became tighter and tighter.

From underneath, Mildred looked toward the rear of the train as it began to pick up speed. The clearance above her was about fifteen inches, and she could see that at least one of the ramshackle units rested lower to the ground than that. She pushed her chest and the side of her face to the shingle between the tracks, clutching the weapon to her side as the train trudged over her, clattering loudly on the tracks.

She shifted her head uncomfortably to the left, watching as a thin, sunny gap between the cars approached. The next car would follow, the storage unit with the windshield walls that she had walked through less than twelve hours before. Its bed fell lower and there were thin, spiky shafts hanging below where the pipework of the structure had been rudely finished. The struts were pencil-thin and various lengths, one almost reaching to the ground, and each was marked with the grime it had picked up on the journey.

As the sliver of light between the cars passed overhead, Mildred took a deep breath and closed her eyes, pressing her nose down into the pebbly surface between the rungs of the tracks. She felt the spikes drag across her back and shoulders, snagging runs of her skin and wrenching them painfully away. Farther down her body, she felt a tug at the seat of her combat pants and she pressed herself harder into the ground, willing the ordeal to be over. The sound of the train was almost deafening against the tracks beside her, the loud rumbling of its passage like an underground waterfall. She felt something tangle in her hair and the skin of her scalp burned as something pulled at it until, with a painful snap, a braid of her plaited hair was yanked from her head.

Over the racket of the moving cars she heard a sudden crash right in front of her, out of sync with the rhythm of the train. She rolled her head carefully, the shingle biting into her left cheek, and looked out from under the train.

The dark, oil-smeared wheels passed just two inches from her face, and then came the gap between them and Mildred saw the dark shape of the sec man lying there, his mouth wide open, his eyes blank in death. A bloody line was drawn across the bottom of his shirt, and his guts sprawled across the muddy ground where a blade had slashed a horizontal streak across his torso.

"Come on, my dear doctor," the familiar voice of Doc called. "You have a patient to treat." She looked farther to her left where the voice had called from. She could see Doc's swordstick hanging in the space between the cars and she ducked down beneath it as it passed overhead.

She timed the movement of the passing wheels on the next car, saw the gap between the large sets of wheels, and scrambled out from beneath the train, still holding Ryan's Steyr. From the gap between the car ahead of her, Mildred saw Doc's smiling face poking out, and he beckoned her with his hand as he stood on the lip of the door. "Quickly now," he encouraged, and she darted forward and grabbed his outstretched arm, using it to pull herself up between the cars beside him.

"Thanks, Doc," Mildred said breathlessly, relief in her eyes. She was covered in mud and beige dust from the shingle, and there were tiny traces of cuts all over her face and bare arms.

Doc opened the door to the next car and pushed her, somewhat less than gently, inside before following her. Once inside, Mildred dropped the blaster to one side and folded over, placing her hands behind her calves as she gathered her breath.

"Close," Doc's voice said behind her as she sucked in deep breaths. "You almost missed your train and the good Lord alone knows when the next one's due."

Despite herself, Mildred smiled.

MILDRED AND DOC WERE back in the compartment with Krysty, though now it was Mildred who sat in the bed while Krysty tended to her wounds, dabbing them with a piece of rag doused in the antiseptic mouthwash that Mildred had picked up for her med kit somewhere on her travels. It wasn't the antiseptic she would have chosen, and it stung like hell when Krysty applied it to the abrasions on her face, but Mildred knew she needed to clean the wounds and the small alcoholic content of the mouthwash would do that just as well as anything marketed for the job.

"I've been trying to place where I've seen those towers before," Mildred told the others while Krysty dabbed at her cheek, "it was there all along, in the back of my mind." She looked at Doc as she addressed him. "Doc, you spent some time in the twentieth century, didn't you?"

Sitting at the desk, the blade of his sword now hidden once more in the sheath of the ebony walking cane, Doc nodded. "Some, but, alack-a-day, it is sometimes a very blurred period in my memory."

"Did you ever see one of those old RKO movies?" Mildred asked. Then she put on the deep, clipped voice of the typical 1930s newsreel announcer. "'An RKO Radio Picture.' Do you remember that?"

Doc shook his head slowly, a weary apology on his face.

"There was a tower," Mildred continued, unfazed, "just like the ones we've seen out there. A radio broadcast tower that spanned half the globe." She gestured with her hands, drawing it in the air for them both. "An illustration, showing how the RKO company was able to send their information through the airwaves."

"Perhaps I saw something of its ilk," Doc said hesitantly. "It strikes a vague chord with me, to be sure."

"This tower stood proud over the world," Mildred explained, "and little bolts of lightning or something, the signal I guess, zapped off its highest point like so..." She snapped her hands open and closed a few times, as though she were playing a set of invisible maracas.

Krysty watched Mildred's pumping hands and smiled. "This 'Arko' used to flash lightning bolts over the world, in the days before the megacall?"

"No," Mildred told her patiently, "it was an illustration. An animated way of bringing the idea of broadcast to life."

"Like a radio," Krysty concluded as understanding dawned.

"I think that those towers out there are radio transmitters," Mildred stated, looking from Krysty to Doc.

"But there is no wiring," Doc said, shaking his head, "nothing visible at least."

"The wires are underground," Mildred told him. "That thing we saw, that big metal plate—that opens into the lower part, beneath the broadcast tower. That's where the workings are."

"And what are they transmitting?" Doc asked, clearly dubious. "Classic show tunes? Or perhaps they are sending telegrams to each other?"

"Except," Mildred stated slowly, "I don't think it's a radio. That liquid they were using to fuel the cells, that was something organic, I'd swear it was. It had the sort of consistency you don't get in refined material."

"What does the fuel matter?" Krysty wanted to know.

"I think it's the fuel that's making you ill," Mildred said confidently.

The three of them sat quietly, considering what Mildred had just said, wondering at its implications. Krysty moistened her rag again and sat behind Mildred to work on the cuts across her back and shoulders.

"If that is true," Doc wondered out loud, "then why doesn't being aboard the train seem to have any direct effect on Krysty? The fuel is stored here, after all. I saw them remove it from one of the forward cabins."

"Proximity," Mildred said, enunciating the words slowly, "and pulse."

"Meaning?" Krysty asked.

"Predark we had mobile phones," Mildred stated. "A cell phone signal is not one continuous stream. It broadcasts in waves. If you put a cell phone beside a radio, you can hear the pulse affecting the reception, crackle-crackle, clear signal, crackle-crackle, clear signal again." Mildred's words were coming quicker now, saying them out loud was helping to form the theory she had been slowly working on in the back of her mind. "Now, like anything automated, that pulse would work to a set rhythm. What if our towers out there are doing the same, working to a set rhythm?"

"But if this signal is what is affecting Krysty's fluctuating health, would not we have noticed the pattern of the broadcasts?" Doc asked.

"Proximity," Mildred stated again, and Doc nodded, suddenly understanding her theory.

"We have been traveling all over North Dakota," he answered, "at varying distances from the towers. If they are broadcasting in waves, in pulses, and we have varied our distance from them, then the pattern would be almost impossible to recognize without studying all of the factors and amassing a significant amount of empirical data. Perhaps with study and a map of the towers' locations…" He was nodding to himself now, seeing the point that Mildred had begun to explain. "Am I right?" he asked her.

"Am *I* right?" she echoed. "That's the sixty-four-thousand-dollar question."

HUMBLEBEE WAS LAUGHING as she and several of the other children tried to copy the trick that the ghost boy, Jak, had shown them. He had produced a pocketknife, its blade gleaming in the indifferent light from the open door, and let the children carefully handle it, proving that it was as solid and real as they were. Then, with a flurry of his hands, the white-skinned youth had somehow made the knife disappear, apparently into thin air.

The children had applauded and several of them had squealed in delight, insisting he show them again. Jak had talked them through the trick, repeating the mantra "Eye slow, hand quicker" at several points as he whipped his arm around and tucked the leaf-shaped blade into his sleeve.

Then Jak used the pocketknife to carve away two small, rigid strips from the wooden walls of the car and passed them to the children, under Maddie's silent sufferance. The wood strips were roughly the size and shape of his knife, and were, according to Jak, "good practice not getting hurt." Maddie had pointed out that the wood was splintering and its ends were sharp, but Jak had just shrugged. "Splinter never chilled," he assured her.

The knife trick had been more than entertainment. Jak had wanted to get the children used to carrying shivs, working them in their hands. He wanted them armed, however crudely, for when he broke them free from the cage.

As the children practiced with the wooden spikes, Jak went back to his own task, working away at the tight screws that held the hinges to the cage door. The screws were embedded deeply into the metal, but Jak had worked the thin point of a knife into the circular holding and slowly twisted. The knife had slipped numerous times, unable to hold in place against the tight screw, but he had silently endured, replaying the process until he finally got the right angle to use a torque action to loosen the fastener. He gradually rotated the knife by the leather-bound handle, careful not to lose the grip he'd found on the screw, and, slowly, the head of the screw pulled away from its grounding.

The light was poor for this work, streaming through the far door open to the moving countryside beyond and dazzling Jak while putting the hinges in shadow. But Jak worked carefully, feeling as much as seeing, shielding his eyes now and again to check on his progress. He wanted the screw just free of the lip of its hole, enough that he could work it free easily, in a matter of seconds, when the moment came, but not so much that the door would fall off if a sec man knocked into it.

Satisfied with his progress, Jak left the screw in place and began the process on the second screw in the hinge. There were four screws in each hinge, eight in total, and he intended to loosen them all. He had nothing but time.

As he sat cross-legged, working his knife at the second screw, Jak became aware of the grumbling in his stomach. It had been hours since he had eaten, the spiced ribs in Fairburn were almost eighteen hours in the past now. He would survive for a while, but without food he would become weak for the final assault. "When eat?" he asked, turning to look at Maddie who was, once again, sitting close to him, watching his busy hands at work.

Maddie shrugged, a resigned smile on her face. "When they remember to feed us, I think," she told him.

Jak bent, looking closely at the screw he was loosening. It was coming away from its slot nicely. "Often?" he asked.

"Can be," she replied. "Other times it will be almost a day. But sometimes we get two or three dishes, good food even, if it's a nice man."

Jak's head turned and his scarlet glare pierced her, frightening Maddie. "None nice," he told her. "Remember and stay alive."

Maddie tugged at her bottom lip with her teeth and nodded. "I'm sorry, Jak. I'll remember."

"Don't be sorry," he stated, his voice softening again. "Be alive. Best type Maddie ever is."

She nodded again, but Jak had turned his face back to his task. Maddie looked at his busy hands, fascinating in their whiteness as though dipped in paint, the long fingers with their protruding knuckles so delicate, despite the traces of old scars that covered the pale skin. She looked at his face in profile, the concentration absolute in his expression, taking shallow breaths through his barely opened mouth. His face was all angles, the high scarred cheeks planed like a statue, and his alabaster skin only added to that impression. His long, straight hair was white like the rest of him. She thought back, remembering the warmth that his skin gave off as she had touched his face as she had moved his head onto the blanket-pillow.

"Maddie, Maddie, look!" That was Humblebee, excited as she called across the tiny cage. Maddie looked up, seeing that Marc had one of the wooden shards. "Look what Marc did!" Humblebee cried, her face glowing with excitement. Maddie watched, her face impassive, as Marc palmed the wooden shank just as Jak had shown them.

"Good," Jak told him. He had glanced up without Maddie realizing. "Show others."

Marc smiled. "If I can remember."

RYAN AND J.B. continued to make their hurried way through the train. The cars were busier now, as they got ever closer to the engine that drove the beast. There were more sec men, the small construction team they had seen at the towers, and at one point they passed the three whitecoats in the tight corridor of another bunk room, heading in the opposite direction. They passed through another double mess hall, busy with hungry sec men who watched the gyrations of a dancing, jolt-high slut as they ate.

There were two more rooms of food similar to the one where J.B. had found the pineapple chunks, though the side of the foremost one had been damaged. The right-hand wall was peppered with holes like buckshot, and J.B. and Ryan took a closer look. The Armorer poked his index finger through a hole, feeling the rush of air outside with the train's rapid passage across the Dakotan fields.

"Took a hit from a home-made shotgun," Ryan suggested.

"No," J.B. said. "Look at the way the wounds wept." He pointed to the melted metal remains that ran beneath the holes like tears. "This is acid. Probably from a toxic rainstorm."

"Avoided most of the shelling but I guess this part of the state couldn't escape everything," Ryan commented.

His words were borne out shortly after when the train thundered through the rad lands of the far south. They had walked through another pair of acid-damaged cars, both filled with repair supplies like those at the rear of the train, and one of them showed some evidence of attempts to patch up the holes in its side since, when J.B. nudged a steel plate aside, they saw the holes were larger on this unit. A third car full of stock equipment was undamaged, however, and it wasn't until they reached a car full of bunks that they could look through windows into the outside world again. What they saw was depressing.

Since they had left the redoubt in Minot, North Dakota had proved to be a changeable mishmash of territory. The bland desert around Fairburn had given way rapidly to greener areas and so to farmland that produced the richness of foods that had been sold in the walled ville. Fairburn had seemed isolated, but it was perhaps fifteen miles from farmland. But that patch of rich, fertile land had proved brief, and as they had crossed the lake they had seen evidence of poisoned terrain, destroyed by toxins in the air. Here, far to the south of the old territory, they saw the rank devastation of radiation. The land that the train traveled over was bare and pitted; no plants or greenery of any sort existed, not even moss or lichen. The soil was burned a dark shade of brown, almost black, in fact, looking more like charcoal than earth. Large cracks crisscrossed the land, digging deep into the lifeless soil like scars on a man's flesh.

The air stank, an awful, putrid smell like rotting meat. Carrion birds flew across the sky, their vast wingspans mutated to grotesque proportions. They swooped through the air, flying parallel to the train until Ryan and J.B. heard shots from above as the rooftop gunners took aim. One of the sec men was unlucky, and they watched as he was dragged away in the colossal claws of one of the vulturelike birds, screaming as blood spurted from where the talons had pierced him. The booming report of a heavy cannon cut through the air over the shuddering racket of the train, and J.B. watched in fascination as a heavy shell blasted through the air from the front of the train. The shell failed to hit any of the fast-moving, enormous birds, but it served to scatter them and they swooped away toward the horizon.

The ground here was sloped, evidence of earthflow, and the train traveled at a lurched angle, its port side noticeably lower than starboard for almost three miles. The tracks followed a perfectly straight line for the duration of the slope, any curves would have likely derailed the train.

As the ground began to level out once again, the squeal of brakes being applied rang through the train, and Ryan spotted another scaffold tower in the distance from the window of the third crew bunk car in succession. They were forty-one cars from the back of the train, closing on Jak's position fast.

WITH NO WARNING, Krysty fell to the floor, stretching her hands out before her to cushion her fall.

Doc leaped up from the lone chair in the tiny compartment and Mildred jumped from her seated position on the bed, crouching beside their companion. "Are you all right? Krysty? Krysty?"

Krysty worked her swollen tongue in her mouth, swallowed against a suddenly dry throat and mumbled the words "I'm fine," even though she wasn't. The pain had started again, appearing from nowhere, an ax wound to her skull. Her muscles ached with cramp, her arms and legs heavy, and her heart was pounding in her chest as though thumping at her ribs to break free.

Mildred and Doc helped lift her from the floor, pulling her across to the bunk and stretching her out there. Mildred placed her hand gently on Krysty's forehead, feeling for a moment in silence. "She's burning up," she told Doc.

"This is madness," he replied, "sheer madness. She was fine, absolutely fine, not ten seconds ago. It is impossible."

"It's happening," Mildred confirmed, "so it can't be impossible. Whatever it is, it's happening again—" she looked at the beautiful redheaded woman on the bed, watched in horror as blood began streaming from her nose and around her gum line "—only worse."

Doc walked to the window, looking out across the bleak landscape. "We are coming up on a tower," he stated, a strange sense of satisfaction in his voice.

"You think the theory stands?" Mildred asked.

"Though hardly the proof we wanted," he decided, "I would say that this is, at the very least, a good signifier of our perceived correlation, would not you?"

Mildred nodded. "Hell, yeah."

ADAM HAD HOPPED BACK onto the train at the rearmost mess hall car when they had pulled away from the Hazel tower. He had sat alone, consuming a late breakfast as the train trudged on to its next, inevitable stop. He knew the route so well now, having traveled with the train on every one of its bimonthly journeys, and he had grown to hate this section of the route—the burned grounds south of Jamestown, where the fallout from the nukes had stretched its withering hand. It was a hot zone, the air itself still poisonous even after a century of supposed recovery, and he could feel the poisons burying themselves into the scars that crossed his arms, his face, eating into the muscles and tendons. Thus, he chose to eat on this section of the loop on every go-round, so that he never need see the awful, barren landscape.

Adam had been with the train crew from the very start, when Baron Burgess had assembled his team and proposed the project. Just another sec man in Burgess's army, Adam had climbed the ranks in the subsequent four years, and now held the position of commanding officer, Burgess's trusted right-hand man. The baron couldn't travel with the train any longer, though he had been with it in the early days as the monstrosity had shuddered along the tracks, placing towers and creating new rail routes where they required, the old whitecoat at his side. These days, Baron Burgess couldn't leave his citadel. Like many of his men, Burgess had had to make sacrifices for the Grand Project, and the worst of them had been his own mobility.

And so, Adam had taken the position of train commander. While the train was traveling, Adam was a demibaron and these people were his to command.

After he had eaten, he got up and made his way toward the engine. They would be stopping at the next tower shortly, and he knew from experience that without a supervisor the crew was likely to forget something. Messing up things was not an option any longer. The project was at final stage, they could no longer afford mistakes. He had asked both the whitecoats and the baron himself how the project fared, and they had all made agreeable noises: the tests, it transpired, had proved very encouraging.

Adam had made his way through the cars, passing the store car and the curtained car of the *bruja*. Adam did not approve of carrying the witch aboard, but Baron Burgess had felt she provided a service they could not get in any other manner. Adam was uncomfortable around the *bruja*. He disliked the old woman, and he respected her mystical abilities the way one might respect a dog with sharp teeth. Fear and distrust.

After three more cars stocked full of foodstuffs, Adam felt the familiar thrum through the soles of his boots as the driver pumped the brakes. They would be stopping at the tower in a couple of minutes, he knew. The drawn-out braking procedure of the train was etched into the back of Adam's brain after all this time, as natural to him as blinking.

He stepped into the ordnance car and stopped, looking around him. The metal-sided car appeared empty. "Hey!" he called loudly, then repeated it five seconds later when no one had answered.

There was no one here, no guards. This was a weapons car, and he had posted guards. His men weren't known for disobeying his orders; he was the baron as far as they were concerned. None of them had even expressed the slightest hint of mutiny. So there should be two sec men here, keeping watch, checking orders whenever anyone requisitioned a blaster. He had insisted, right from the start, that they keep tight tabs on the weapons. No good having a train if you couldn't defend it. Every shot was accounted for, every blaster numbered and tracked.

He stepped farther into the car, looking back and forth, a growing sense of unease welling within him. Where were the guards?

At the low counter he found the giant, Phil Billion, who appeared at first to be sleeping on the job. "Wake up, you worthless half-wit," Adam shouted at the huge man, but Phil didn't move. Adam bent closer, looking at the reclining body, spotting the dried stain on the metal floor beneath his face, his neck. Crouching, Adam prodded his ring finger into the dark stain, feeling the liquid that pooled there. The blood had congealed. It was almost dried now and had taken on the dirt brown color old blood. There was a wound in Phil's neck, a small hole piercing the cartilage of his trachea, maybe an inch across.

Adam looked at the blood on his fingertip, looked at the corpse, then stood once more. "You got aced, you lazy simp," he muttered as he stalked down the car, flicking the catch on his hip holster and drawing his .44 Magnum blaster. Jen worked here, too, always the shift with Phil. He had drawn up that rota; the two always asked to work together.

"Jen?" Adam asked tentatively, his voice barely audible over the squealing of the brakes. "Jen, you here? You hid, girl? You hid yourself?"

Adam walked in a semicrouch, heading for the front of the car, checking carefully between the shelving units for Jen or intruders. When he reached the far end, he stood by the door to the next car, his breathing even and quiet. He turned, looking back down the length of the car he had just walked, seeing Phil's corpse lying there in its own blood. He couldn't see Jen, couldn't see anyone else.

Holding the blaster in one hand, Adam lowered himself, bending at the knees to drop to the floor. Someone could hide under one of these shelving units, some thin bastard come to chill his men. He lowered his head, stretching his body flat to the floor, the blaster close to his face, tracking the floor with eyes and blaster in unison. There was no one under there. The car was empty bar himself and the corpse.

Then, at the very last moment, he saw the hand hidden in the shadows beneath the shelving unit immediately beside him. There was a tiny tattoo of a rose, its petals proudly flowering in a burst of red within the jumble of greens and blues that covered the hand. Jen.

Adam pulled the woman's corpse out by the arm, bringing her from beneath the shelving unit until he saw the puncture in her forehead where the bullet had gone straight through her brain. Reaching forward, he closed her shocked eyes. Then, he stood and made his way to the horizontal cord that ran high along the left-hand edge of every car. He reached for the cord and pulled at it once, twice, thrice.

A bell rang, a merry little tinkling, completely at odds with Adam's mood. Three rings: alert.

They had intruders.

Chapter Seventeen

Jak had loosened five of the screws that held the gate's hinges to the frame of the cage. He was working at the sixth when Humblebee rushed over to him and said, "There's a man coming." She whispered it in that way that children will, awkward, loud and showy, making a performance of its being a whisper. Jak pulled his knife from the groove of the sixth screw and palmed the blade as a sec man trudged in from the rear of the car, shuffling sideways along the narrow route that ran by the side of the cage.

The train had stopped a few minutes before, and they had heard shouting from outside, the rumbling movements of heavy equipment over the rumble of the idling steam engine.

Jak remained cross-legged by the cage door and watched the sec man from the corner of his eye. The sec man had a curly mop of dark hair, long sideburns and the signs of several days' beard darkening his chin. He carried a large longblaster held on a strap that rested on his left shoulder crosswise over his body, hanging below the level of his groin. The longlaster looked homemade, spliced together from old parts, but it took a standard ammo clip of 9 mm slugs in an awkward-looking top-loader. The man was dressed in muted greens and browns, a passing effort at camouflage should he find himself in the woods. As he stepped in front of Jak, the albino flicked his wrist as though swatting away one of the flies that hung around the little mound of feces in the corner of the cage. The movement pushed his leaf-bladed knife from its hiding place in his hand down his sleeve, the sec man none the wiser.

"What you doin' there, Whitey?" Curly Hair demanded, the smell of rotgut on his breath as he leaned down to address Jak.

Jak's ruby eyes flicked up, locking with the sec man's, showing no fear. He remained silent, however, considering possibilities in his mind. There were five loose screws on the hinges, with a good kick or shoulder slam, the door would buckle and fall open, flattening the sec man in the process. While he was trapped beneath the cage door, Jak could use the shiv in his sleeve to cut the man's throat, or he could do him without any need of a weapon if the man couldn't get his blaster in place, snap the man's neck with a twist of his ankles or the thrust of an outstretched hand.

"I asked you a question, boy," the curly haired man growled. "You a simp as well as a snow-skin freak?"

Jak continued to look at the sec man, his glaring eyes locked.

Maddie's voice broke the stalemate. "Did you bring us any food?" she asked.

The man looked up at her. The second he stopped looking at Jak, the albino youth began to examine his home-made longblaster, analyzing details, wondering about its rate of fire, what kind of recoil it would produce. The thing was scratched all over, and initials— R.H.—were carved in the black metal of the butt.

"Brats want to eat?" the man grumbled. "And what you gonna do for it? How you gonna earn your dinner? What? You gonna sing for it? Put on a striptease, maybe, little piece like you?"

Maddie stood still, looking at the man, watching as his eyes played over her thin frame. She didn't like the way he looked at her. She wanted to cower, to hide from his gaze, but she stood there and concentrated on her breathing, steady in, steady out. An amused sneer had formed on the man's lips, sharp, yellow teeth showing between his curled lips. Seeing that sneer appear, Jak became suddenly conscious, more than ever, of the weight of the blade hidden in his sleeve.

"Leave her alone," Marc piped up, stepping in front of Maddie, trying to hide her from the man's gaze. "She's just hungry. We're all hungry."

There was a shout outside the car and the sec man turned, looking through the open doorway. Men were walking around outside, Jak could see them busying themselves as they patrolled the area around the stalled train, blasters ready. Curly Hair shouted something, just an acknowledging grunt really, and looked back at the children in the cage. His blue eyes pierced Maddie where she stood behind Marc, and he held her gaze for a moment.

"Be back for you, sweetmeat," he promised, an ugly smile on his face. Then he spit on the floor of the car before turning and striding to the exit door. He walked down the steep steps and exited the car, Jak's glowering eyes following every movement.

J.B. HAD SPECULATED that the triple burst of bells was some kind of warning system, and Ryan agreed, feeling deep in his gut that they had been discovered. The companions continued along the train, keeping their heads low as they walked through two more cars stocked with repair equipment and demolition explosives. J.B. paused at the demolition material, picking up a few items and judging their weight and flexibility. Old-fashioned dynamite stood there in sticks like thick candles, but there were also some combustible liquids, some accelerant and a small slab of plas ex. Unlike the weapons store, this area remained unguarded, though the explosives were of the same type and caliber. It was interesting how the context changed the security protocols; while the train pirates didn't concern themselves with guarding this storeroom, J.B. saw it as a wealth of armament opportunities.

There were two more cars full of food stock, a few old mil rations sitting side by side with cured meats and preserves.

The train began moving again as they entered the next car. They had walked into a wooden box featuring a ladder that led up to a raised portion of ceiling in the middle of the room. Built into the roof, an ex-military rail blaster had been mounted on a swiveling pedestal, and a gunner sat there, scanning the landscape with a pair of binoculars. The sides of the car featured arrow slits, holes big enough to shoot a blaster from while still keeping the occupants well protected. There were five sec men in the car, including the upside gunner, and they were all on high alert. As Ryan and J.B. stepped through the door they found themselves facing a selection of blaster barrels.

"Easy, brother, easy," Ryan said calmly, his hands raised to shoulder height, open and empty.

"He one of them?" a bearded man in the rear of the car asked, training a Heckler & Koch longblaster on the strangers.

"Don't recognize either of them," one of the others replied, looking Ryan and J.B. up and down, a blaster with an ugly, sawed-off snout ready in his hand.

J.B. kept his hands held loosely at his sides as he stood behind Ryan, feeling the folds of his coat sway around him.

"What's going on?" Ryan asked.

"You heard the alarm," the sec man with the broken-snouted blaster replied. "Adam says there's intruders on the train. Found two dead in the ordnance cars."

"That's too bad," Ryan stated sincerely. "Who was it?" He tried to remember the name the woman had shouted. "Phil? They get Phil?"

"Yeah, I heard it was Phil and his missus," the sec man stated, lowering his blaster slightly but still holding it trained on Ryan.

"Phil," Ryan said, moving to look over his shoulder at the Armorer. "You hear that, J.B.? Didn't he owe you some jack?"

"He had only two left to pay," J.B. stated. "It ain't right." It was code and he hoped Ryan would pick up on it. J.B. could take the two on the left but he didn't have a clear shot for the others; Ryan would need to deal with them.

"I got some. I can cover your debts," Ryan answered, looking ahead once more to scan the men to his right. "Think I could make things right."

The sec man in the rear, the one who had initially failed to recognize them, spoke up again, his Heckler & Koch still targeted at Ryan's head. "You fellas knew

Phil?" he asked warily. "I don't remember you. You got names?"

"Ryan and John," Ryan said, slowly lowering his hands. "We were with one of the construction crews. Jumped on last night, just outside Fairburn."

The sec man in the rear pondered. "Is that—?"

He was cut off abruptly as bullets flew through the air. Ryan had shouted the word "Now!" as he skated across the wooden boards of the floor of the car, pulling his SIG-Sauer from its holster as he moved and firing off shots from the hip. J.B.'s hand was already beneath his coat, firing a burst from the Uzi he had stashed there out of sight, clipping holes in the wooden side of the train as he wasted the two sec men to his left.

Ryan fired five shots. The first took out the farther of the two men to the right, mashing into his bearded cheek and obliterating the bone on one side of his face. The man stepped in place unsteadily, the force of the bullet drilling his head back, snapping his neck as he was whipped backward. He managed to get off a single shot from the Heckler & Koch, firing wildly into the ceiling as he fell to the floorboards, but two more bullets from the SIG-Sauer slammed into his chest, finishing him with certainty.

The second man leaped aside as Ryan reeled off shot after shot at him, tracking his movements as the man sprinted across the car from right to left, ducking behind the thick, metal rungs of the ladder. He watched as his two colleagues slumped to the floor under the barrage of bullets that J.B. had loosed from the Uzi, its sounds loud in the tightly enclosed space.

The man at the overhead rail blaster peeked down the ladder, a silver-plated .38 shining in his hand. Ryan reeled off a shot in his direction and the man ducked back into his cubbyhole.

There was a pause then, the car falling silent. Ryan swiftly reloaded the SIG-Sauer, the spent cartridges clattering to the floor while J.B. covered him.

A stream of bullets came at Ryan and J.B. from behind the ladder as the surviving sec man fired blindly in their direction. The blasts from the ugly, flared snout of the blaster dug chunks of wood from the wall behind them, and Ryan and J.B. scurried to the right, out of their attacker's potential arc of fire. Ryan watched him through the rungs of the ladder while J.B. trained his Uzi at the top of the ladder, ready for the overhead gunner.

Suddenly the train lurched around a sharp bend in the track and all three of the men on the ground level staggered, losing their positions. The sec man behind the ladder recovered, aiming his blaster at J.B.'s chest, firing three rapid shots. Two of them missed, whizzing past J.B. as his finger gently squeezed the trigger on his Uzi, unleashing a stream of bullets at the man, spraying him over the upper legs, chest and face as he fell backward with their impact. J.B. staggered as the sec man's third bullet took him low in the torso, and his breath blurted out of him with the bullet's impact.

Ryan looked at the Armorer, seeing the flash of pain that crossed his face, and his single eye moved down to J.B.'s gut where the bullet had hit. A dark stain was forming on his shirt. The Armorer looked down as he regained his composure, pulled back one side of his jacket, reached into an interior pocket and pulled out the can of pineapple chunks. There was a dent in the can and syrupy liquid was trickling from the far side, creating the stain. The can had deflected the bullet, just enough for it to miss the Armorer, glancing off into one of the walls somewhere. J.B. looked at it, a grim smile crossing his lips, and tossed the leaking tin to one side of the boxcar with a clatter.

An eerie silence had descended on the car once J.B. stopped firing and the fallen sec man stopped moving. The companions waited, their breathing hard as the adrenaline pumped through them, waiting for the upside gunner to reappear. There was a sudden report from his blaster, and they watched as a bullet embedded in the floor beneath the ladder. Then a second and third followed, hitting different points in the floor, but none of them hit near Ryan or J.B.

The two companions walked carefully forward, edging around the area beneath the circular hole in the roof, watching more bullets pump into the floor from above. It was clear that the sec man wasn't aiming, just hoping a stray shot might catch the intruders.

Across the other side of the ladder, J.B. gestured to Ryan, miming the pumping of a shotgun barrel and making a querulous face. J.B. was right—the man could have a whole stack of weapons up there besides the .38 blaster. It wouldn't do to just rush up there while he appeared to be reloading.

J.B. took careful aim with the Uzi and blasted off several rounds up the ladder and into the cavity above. They heard the man curse violently as the bullets whizzed around him in the enclosed space, and he reeled off four more shots in reply, the bullets embedding themselves in the scratched wooden boards at the foot of the ladder.

Ryan edged closer to the ladder, silently instructing J.B. to fire again. The Armorer did so, and they heard the man scream in pain. One of the bullets had hit him, maybe off a ricochet. A stream of profanity accompanied bullets from the .38 as the man blasted shots down the ladder, several of them close to where Ryan stood.

Ryan reached up, the SIG-Sauer handblaster steady in his grip, and pushed the nose of the blaster against the car's wooden roof. He pulled the trigger, and reeled off three shots through the rotting wood and into the space above. With the second shot they heard the man scream once more, then heard him slump to the roof above with a heavy thud accompanied by the sound of a blaster shot but no sign of the bullet. Ryan continued to hold the SIG-Sauer to the ceiling, shifting it slightly to where he thought the thud had come from and firing off three more shots. He pulled the blaster away as three thin streams of red began to drip through the bullet holes in the ceiling.

Without looking back, Ryan and J.B. reloaded their weapons and continued onward.

MILDRED HAD HELD Krysty's head, pulling her hair back while the woman spluttered blood into the washbowl that Doc had passed her. After a while, Krysty had turned to spluttering pink drools of saliva, dry heaving but producing nothing else from her stomach. Her whole body shook, and she had cried pitifully with the explosive force of her vomiting, but it had finally passed and she now lay back on the bunk, her eyes closed as Mildred and Doc watched over her. The vomiting spell had lasted almost fifteen minutes, pretty much the whole time that the train remained stationary at the tower in the wastelands. Doc had kept one eye on the comings and goings outside the window, but remained disinclined to investigate further, genuinely fearing for Krysty's life now. Again he had had to remind himself of how wrong this all was, that Krysty's destiny was not to die by the hand of some rogue, unseen infection, whatever the cause.

"Curse those blasted towers," he suddenly exhorted, pumping a fist into his open palm with a loud slap.

"Doc," Mildred said, trying to calm him, "There's nothing we can do but keep her safe." She looked at the old man, seeing the anger that had finally broken through his calm exterior, and held her gaze on him as he wrestled with the situation in his mind.

"I hate to see her hurting like this," Doc said, his voice still tense.

"It hurts us all, Doc," Mildred insisted, keeping her voice level.

Doc sat quietly for a few seconds, looking at the shapely redheaded woman on the bed, at the dried blood smeared across her chin and throat. "Ryan should be here now," Doc said firmly but quietly.

Mildred looked at the floor, shaking her head slowly. "This whole situation has been impossible since the second we got here," she said quietly, almost as though she spoke only to herself. "We're stretched thin, vulnerable and Krysty's..." She stopped herself, looking at the still body of the woman lying on the bed, hands folded across her chest as though lying in state.

"Krysty's what?" Doc encouraged, not from spite but from a need to hear the truth.

"Krysty's in a lot of trouble," was all Mildred would

tell him with any certainty. She didn't want to say the other thing, the word that was looming at the forefront of both their minds.

RYAN AND J.B. FOUND themselves in an unlit, cold car that stank of human waste. To their right was a cage and inside were six children along with the corpse of a seventh. The children huddled together under a sack that had been split to make a blanket, remaining as far from the rotting corpse as they were able in the tight confines of the cage. Ryan and J.B. were both relieved and disappointed to find that Jak was not among them.

The cage was an add-on, the unit they were in looked like some kind of cattle truck or maybe a horse box with a gaping hole along the wall of the corridor, opposite the cage itself. The cage had been constructed using some kind of sturdy mesh, and Ryan pushed his hand against the grille wall with some force before concluding it was solidly built. The mesh bent under pressure, but seemed to have enough give in it to simply bounce back when he let go.

J.B. stood with his Uzi ready, watching through the open slit of the car as the tortured landscape hurtled past. The children ignored both men, clearly used to armed adults intruding on their tiny world, assuming them to be part of the force of their captors.

"We should free them," Ryan said to J.B., keeping his voice low.

J.B. agreed, nodding a definite yes as he thought through the angles of such an operation. "Need to have somewhere to put them, a way off the train, way to keep the crew off our backs and theirs." He pointed to the horizontal slit that ran the length of the car, gesturing to the dead landscape outside the train. "It's rad hot out there, no place to take children."

Automatically, Ryan checked his lapel pin rad counter, saw the tiny display had turned orange: a hot zone, but not immediately lethal. Run around in it for three or four days on the trot and you'd start to see sores on your body that wouldn't heal, though, and the immune system of malnourished kids like this, well, it would be game over.

"Hey," Ryan said, offering the children a friendly smile as he approached the door to the cage. "I need you to help me." None of the children reacted. They just watched Ryan blankly, their eyes wide in fear. "I'm looking for a friend of mine, a man with white skin, anyone seen him?"

The children continued to look at Ryan, remaining absolutely still and silent.

J.B. reached across, skimming Ryan's arm with his knuckles. "They're scared, Ryan. They're terrified."

"I know," Ryan said quietly, his jaw set as he looked at the children in the cage. He crouched on his haunches, looking at the group of children for a moment. "We're friends," Ryan told them. "We'll get you out. We'll come back and we'll get you out. I promise." Then he and J.B. departed, stepping through the door into the next car.

RYAN AND J.B. STEPPED through the remains of a cage, parts of the grille work still dangling from the holed roof. There was blood and body parts all over the car, and a gaping hole in the exterior walls on either side bore witness to where the rocket had passed straight through. The body parts were small, the little legs and arms of children. One of the bodies was almost intact, just missing a hand, but it was charred, black where the flesh had burned in the ensuing fire after the rocket had hit.

Maybe some had escaped during the confusion. Ryan clung to that thought as he walked across the blood-smeared wooden boards of the car, his SIG-Sauer still in his hand. J.B. disturbed his thoughts then, stooping and prodding at some body parts with the muzzle of his Uzi. "Find something?" Ryan asked.

"No one I recognize," J.B. stated, his face set, fury burning behind his eyes.

Ryan looked at the body parts, thinking about how these children had died, their last days spent in terror, captives to the psychopaths running this hellish train until one of them was taken off, stripped naked and used in whatever foul experiments they had stumbled on in the bloated cars farther down the train.

J.B. rose from his sifting on the floor, his expression equal parts weariness, anger and determination. "Jak's a survivor," the Armorer reminded his friend. "He'll be right as rain."

They walked through the ashes that covered the floor and opened the door into the next car.

"MEN COMING," Humblebee and Marc called across the cage to Jak from their vigil watching the rear door of the car. Jak palmed the knife in his hand and rolled back from the cage door. Marc was holding one of the makeshift daggers that Jak had carved from the wall, and he copied the albino's move as best he could, palming the weapon in a half second.

The rear door opened and two men walked in, blasters in their hands. The one in the lead had to crab-walk through the narrow corridor alongside the cage, just as Jak had imagined.

"Ryan," he said, beaming when he saw his old friend. "And J.B." He stood and walked with them as they both rounded the cage to stand in the larger gap in front of the bolted door.

"Dark night, it's good to see you!" J.B. exclaimed, looking through the mesh at his imprisoned friend.

"How they been treating you?" Ryan asked, looking past Jak to the children that filled the cage.

Jak pulled open the top few buttons of his dark shirt, showing Ryan the purple bruise that had been generated when he had been hit with the tranq dart. "Dart gun," he explained. "See again, chill shooter."

Ryan laughed. It was a relief to see his friend in such high spirits after all that had happened in the last, terribly long half day.

"Krysty?" Jak asked, not sure how he should broach the subject. "Better yet?"

Ryan looked wistful, his mouth a thin line. "Hard to say, Jak. She's been out of it half the time. Mildred was none the wiser when we left them. They're both on the train with us, along with Doc, keeping a low profile in a secure cabin."

J.B. spoke up then, his tone faintly amused. "Surprised to see you in here. Thought you'd have come up with six escape routes by the time we caught up with you."

Jak held him in a steady gaze. "Got seven, deciding when for."

"That's my boy." Ryan laughed.

Jak felt a presence at his side and turned to see that Maddie was standing there, holding Humblebee's little hand in her own, with Marc and Allison just behind. They were all looking at Ryan and J.B.

"Introduce friends," Jak told Maddie and the others, "Ryan and J.B. Hundred percent loyal." He gestured to the children, went through them, telling Ryan and J.B. their names.

It was uncomfortable, making small talk with children when they all knew they were on a tight schedule, but Ryan spoke to the children, doing his best to put them at their ease while J.B. kept close watch on the closed doors at either end of the car.

Francis-Frankie pointed to Ryan's face. "What happened to your eye?" he asked, not a trace of malice in his voice.

Ryan put a hand to the patch, running his fingers around the edge where it met his scarred flesh. "I had a fight with my brother, a long time ago, and it ended up that he took my eye out."

Several of the children gasped, imagining how it had to have happened. Marc stepped forward, speaking quickly. "Didja chill 'im?"

Ryan nodded. "Had to in the end."

Just then, the door at the front of the car opened and the curly haired sec man burst in. "I'm ready for your little dance, sweetheart," he said with a laugh as he stepped into the car, blaster in hand. He stopped in mid-stride, looking at the two armed strangers in shock.

Chapter Eighteen

Adam had called together his troops when the train had halted at the tower in the poisonous wastelands, telling them of his discovery in the weapons car and advising them to pass the information along. He wouldn't entertain the idea that this might have been a domestic dispute of some kind, either between Phil Billion and his lady Jen or perhaps with another crewman. He ran a tight team here, ragtag mercs but ones good at obeying orders. A lot of the crew had been with the project right from the start, and many of them had a vested interest in seeing Baron Burgess's plans come to fruition after such a long investment of their time. Internal squabbles, while not unheard of, had never escalated into chilling like this.

When he explained the situation to the dozen men who had joined him during the tower repairs, one of them had piped up with an interesting point. The man's name was Boran, a sour-tempered individual with a hook in place of his left hand, but still a dead aim with his right. "Anyone seen anything o' Sean Givin?" he asked. "He was rearguard and I was meant to relieve him this morning, but when I got there there weren't no sign of him."

"Givin," Adam muttered out loud, trying to place the name. He knew every man's shift, the patterns etched into his brain after so many journeys. "Why didn't you bring this to me earlier?" he asked.

Boran shrugged. "I di'n't think it meant anything. Mebbe he just slipped and fell off, what do I know?"

"Yeah," Adam agreed, "could have been. We've lost men before, I'll accept that. You weren't to know better."

"So what do we do now?" another sec man asked, tossing a scimitar idly in one hand like some perverse circus act.

"Get the word out," Adam told them, "we got us some intruders aboard. Mebbe one, mebbe more. You see anyone you don't recognize and you challenge 'em, bring 'em to me if you think it's necessary. We're a big crew, I know, and there's mebbe people on side you don't know. Use your brains, stay alert. Don't chill one o' our own."

"This is mayhem," one of the sec men called, "anarchy. We go around challenging everybody? What about the project, man. What about that?"

Adam looked at the tower, where work repairing one of the struts had just finished. "I'll make sure the project stays on target. You just let me worry about that."

As the train pulled away, the men went about distributing the alert. Adam paced the length of the train as it trudged slowly past him to his left. When the forty-seventh car had reached him, the red *B* sloppily painted on its side, he leaped aboard, a dark kerchief pulled over his mouth and nose. It was time to consult the *bruja*.

RAY HAD KNOWN the second he entered the prison car, before he had even seen the two men who stood there.

It was the change in atmosphere; the heavy taint of fear wasn't there any longer.

There was a man standing at the door to the cage. He was tall and powerfully built, with the sure stance of an arena fighter. His unruly dark hair was long and curly, and he wore a holster at his hip. The man held a blaster.

"I'm ready for your little dance, sweetheart." Ray had laughed as he entered the car, tormenting the little Asian girl with his words as a prelude to what he planned to do with her slim little body. But when he opened the door, the tall man had turned his head to look over his right shoulder, the fiery blue of his eye cutting through Ray as he stood there, door handle still gripped in his hand. There was a black line across the man's forehead where a leather patch was strung to cover his left eye.

Ray heard a noise off to his right, and he looked across to see the second stranger. Ray couldn't claim to know every person on the train, as he'd only been with the operation for two months. This was only his second go-round the loop. But he was sure he had never seen these two before. The second man stood, covering the room while the man with the eye patch spoke to the prisoners. This one was shorter, his eyes watching behind steel-rimmed spectacles, a battered fedora on his head and a heavy jacket wrapped around his wiry frame. The coat was bulky in places, stained and scuffed with spatters of ash and oil. The shorter man was holding a compact Uzi machine blaster, the long handle cutting the barrel to create a T shape. Ray watched the man raise the Uzi in his direction; the expression on the shorter man's face was the familiar look of a seasoned chiller.

It was automatic, an ingrained survival instinct. Ray pulled the door back toward him, leaping backward and slamming it as a spray of bullets thudded into it. His footing slipped as he rushed through the next car, another cage unit full of stinking, filthy brats, a narrow walkway along the left side. Recovering his footing as he heard the door open again behind him, Ray dashed ahead, reaching for the wooden door at the front of the car, the sounds of children's screams filling the rocking room. He dived through the door and into the next car as a burst of gunfire spurted from the Uzi.

"DAMN!" J.B. GRUNTED as he followed the curly haired sec man into the next car. The man had stumbled as he ran down the narrow corridor beside the cage, but by the time J.B. was clear of the door, the man had recovered and managed to reach the far door, placing the cage of children between himself and the Armorer.

J.B. rushed forward, sweeping the Uzi in a tight arc as he blasted shots at the receding figure of the sec man. To his right, the caged children began screaming. "We got a live one, Ryan," J.B. shouted, hearing his heavy footsteps as Ryan bounced into the car behind him.

Together, Ryan and J.B. dashed through the car and reached for the exit door into the next unit.

J.B. went through the door first, keeping his head low as a volley of shots from the sec man's blaster split the air above him, thudding into the wall to his left.

Ryan dived through the door behind him and they found themselves in another storage unit, half-empty but stocked with food. The dark-haired sec man was scrambling through the tight corridor between the wooden shelves, blasting off shots behind him without taking aim. In this enclosed space and with the rate of fire his blaster achieved, the sec man had concluded that aiming didn't much matter.

Ryan and J.B. weaved between the half-empty shelves, using them as cover. A bullet plowed into the shelf just by Ryan's face, splintering the wood as he turned from the scattering debris. J.B. pumped off two short bursts from the Uzi, the shots splitting food packages on the shelves, tossing frost-blackened vegetables and clouds of powdered egg into the air. At the far end of the car, the sec man had reached the next door. He turned, firing a stream of bullets behind him before jumping across the gap between moving cars and into the next unit. Ryan's back slapped into the wall, making as small a target as he could as the bullets streaked past. He looked across the car, seeing J.B. doing the exact same thing. The bullets raced into the far wall, bursting several more food parcels as they went.

"We do not need this," J.B. growled.

"Agreed," Ryan said, rushing through the car toward the door in the front. "Let's shut the runner up and get back to Jak."

They ran between the shelves, and Ryan took the lead as they prepared to enter the next car. A continuous tolling bell echoed through the train.

With J.B. standing across from him, Ryan's hand reached out to turn the handle of the door when the air was split with the noise of a shotgun. A volley of buckshot thudded into the metal door, chunks of lead burst through and shook it in its frame.

Ryan dived backward, spinning as he dropped to the floor. J.B. leaped back as well, slamming himself into the wall behind him. A second round slammed into the door, and it teetered in its frame again, hunks of the metal plating disintegrating and clattering to the floor. Ryan brought up the SIG-Sauer to cover the door as it caved inward under the force of a mighty kick. He reeled off a succession of shots at the open doorway. There was a cry as one of his bullets met a target, and urgent voices called for calm.

"How many of them?" Ryan asked as he scrambled back to his feet.

J.B. was skirting along the side wall, skipping backward on light feet as he moved away from the open door. "Not sure, but it's more than just the runner."

"Fireblast!" Ryan spit.

"WHAT IS IT, OLD WITCH?" Adam asked, as the *bruja* drew back from noisy pain that was calling behind her. He stood in front of her in the incense-thick car, a dark kerchief over the lower half of his face, his breath steady.

The *bruja*'s head rose heavily, her dim eyes ineffectually piercing the gloomy car to see the commanding officer standing there, three paces from her table. He was so close that she might reach out and grab him, she realized, and a thin smile crossed her lips.

"Speak," Adam urged her forcefully. He was a man of little patience, and it was clear that being around the old witch made him nervous. "Is it the project?"

The *bruja* inhaled deeply, taking in the incense-filled atmosphere of her car prison, feeling its dulling effect blur her senses, making the pain something different and far away. "The project, yes," she said, her voice a screech, a whisper.

"But there's more," Adam said in realization, taking a step closer. He wore a large blaster in the holster at his hip, and he deluded himself that it equated to power. But, like many things in the world of man, this was but a fleeting power, easily dismissed. The *bruja*'s wandering gaze stroked at the weapon before moving up his body, watching his mouth form the words. "Speak, old witch. I won't ask you over and over."

Suddenly a continuous ringing split the air, and Adam looked at the ceiling where the noise came from before biting off a muffled curse beneath the kerchief. The *bruja* considered the space between them, insignificant now, close enough that she could grab him, rend his throat with sharp teeth and nails. And he, distracted, was more concerned with the tolling bell than the dangerous prisoner in front of him.

"Later," he blurted, turning from the crone and striding back toward the doorway at the front of the car.

"Another," she replied, her voice a whisper. But Adam had left and was jogging along the train's length.

The *bruja* closed her ancient, rheumy eyes and concentrated on the pain that was emanating from the other, the woman who, like her, could feel the stab of the broadcast.

RYAN AND J.B. WEAVED through the food storage car as a rain of bullets split the air. Behind them, three sec men had rushed through the door from the far car, including the curly haired man with the homemade longblaster.

J.B. ducked down behind a wooden shelving unit and peppered the car with a burst from his Uzi. The sec men took cover as the bullets rent the air.

Through the smoking hole of the open doorway, J.B.

saw more figures approaching, bursts of light as they fired rounds into the car.

Ryan had the near door open and turned back to put up some covering fire. He blasted several shots in quick order and felt a grim satisfaction when he saw one of the sec men's shoulders explode in a cloud of blood and bone.

"Come on," Ryan ordered, waiting for J.B. to cross the threshold into the next car.

J.B. leaped through the open door and sped down the narrow corridor by the side of the cage full of children with Ryan at his heels. "The doors are the weak spots," the Armorer observed. "We could pick them off, one by one."

Ryan started to respond, but his reply was cut short as a burst of buckshot exploded through the air. To their left, Ryan and J.B. watched helplessly as two of the caged children were struck with the deadly burst, dropping to the floor with blood streaming over their small bodies.

"Not here," Ryan stated. This was no place for a showdown. They needed to get clear of the sequence of cages that ran through the train, get to somewhere where they didn't have to worry about the children getting hurt or chilled.

Jak watched as the door burst open and Ryan and J.B. came hurtling through.

"We've got a wagload of trouble following us," Ryan told him urgently. "Keep the kids down or they're liable to get shot."

"Need help?" Jak asked.

Ryan nodded. "Whatever you can do."

"Door come off if pushed," Jak told him. "Been offing screws."

"Good work," Ryan said as he and J.B. rushed down the narrow corridor by the cage. "Choose your moment wisely. We probably won't get a second chance now." With that, he and J.B. disappeared into the next car.

Moments later, eight sec men filed through the car, and Jak instructed the children to stay low as the armed men passed. One of the rearmost sec men was the curly haired one who had taunted Maddie, and Jak slipped his knife from his sleeve as the man followed his colleagues along the narrow corridor and into the next car.

A moment later a ninth sec man, a straggler with blood on his shirt by his left shoulder, staggered into the car accompanied by a tenth man holding a Smith & Wesson revolver low to his body. Jak stood near the back of the cage, watching these men enter, and he hunkered low into himself, the knife hidden in his hand.

As the man with the wounded shoulder stepped in front of the cage, Jak ran at the door. He jumped off the floor, slamming high into the hinged side with shoulder and hip simultaneously. The hinges popped from their sockets, the loosened screws flying in all directions as Jak crashed into the door. The mesh gate fell forward, spinning on the bolt. The cage door toppled into the wounded sec man, the top of the door hitting his forehead with a loud crack. The sec man's legs gave way as the door and Jak's weight barreled into him.

As the wounded sec man stumbled backward, falling to the floor, Jak was already using his momentum to push him into the second man, the one brandishing the revolver. The albino youth's boots raced across the falling gate as he propelled himself at the other man, and he plunged the knife in his right hand into the man's body just beneath his sternum.

Smith & Wesson Man was pushed upward with the blow, his feet leaving the floor as the full force of Jak's attack slammed into him. The man toppled over on the pivot of the knife, and Jak spun aside, yanking the blade free as he went. The man crashed to the ground, knocking the breath out of him as he hit the wood floor, his weapon trapped beneath him. He lurched, trying to free his blaster as Jak leaped at him again, the blooded knife in his outstretched hand.

The blade's sharp point penetrated the man's back, cutting through his shirt and his skin and deeply into his body, puncturing his lung from behind. Jak's weight rested on the man's body, holding him down as he pulled his blade free and yanked the man's head backward by the hair. He drew the bloody blade across the man's exposed throat, slicing deep into the flesh and ending the unfortunate sec man's life in a horrifying second of fury.

The other sec man, the one with the wounded shoulder, was struggling to free himself of the collapsed gate, but Marc and Francis-Frankie were standing on top of it, holding the man down. Marc held one of the wooden shivs that Jak had carved, watching the man below his feet.

Jak had taken the Smith & Wesson from the dead man, and he turned it on the man beneath the cage door before loosing a single bullet into the man's skull. "We go," he told the terrified children in the cage, pointing to the rear door at the end of the narrow corridor.

In Maddie's mind, a mixture of revulsion and admiration warred for attention as she watched the albino youth lead the way to freedom.

THEY WERE IN the shattered car that had been rent open by the rocket attack. Ryan was already at the far end, pulling open the sliding door. J.B. ran through the ash and charred bodies of the dead children, ducking the broken remains of the cage.

Sec men charged through the door, the shotgun blasting yet again.

J.B. crouched low as he ran, the burst of buckshot whizzing over his head. Ahead of him, Ryan was firing 9 mm slugs from the SIG-Sauer, weaving his body as the smoke cleared and the sec men took aim.

As he ran, J.B.'s heel slipped in the ash on the floor, and suddenly he felt himself skidding forward, overbalanced and falling to his left. A rush of air slammed into his face as he stumbled through the gaping hole that had been left in the rocket's wake, and suddenly the Armorer was falling through space with nothing beneath his feet.

Ryan watched in horror as J.B. slid and disappeared from view. There was no time to do anything to save his friend. The primary mission now was to keep himself alive and he knew it.

As the sec men filled the air with bullets, Ryan dived through the open door behind him and rolled across the floor of the next car. He reached back and slammed the door shut as bullets whizzed through the open gap. The noise of the blasts continued as the shots slammed against the wooden door.

Breathing heavily, Ryan looked up into the faces of six startled and very frightened children.

Seven sec men ran through the car that Ryan had just exited. The eighth member of the crew had caught a face full of lead from Ryan's SIG-Sauer and was lying in a pool of his own blood, struggling to remain conscious as his heart slowed. The felled sec man bleated in pain as someone stepped on his torso, rushing in from the preceding car unit. Looking up from the floor he saw the white-skinned specter and was certain that this was Father Death come to take him. He closed his eyes, his lips fluttering as he mumbled a prayer.

Jak launched himself into the room, stepping on the wounded man and blasting five swift shots at the retreating sec men before they even realized he was there. Two of the men fell to the floor under his hail of bullets and a cloud of blood sprayed from the torso of a third man who staggered into the wall beside the door. The other sec men were already gone, but Jak had wounded three in less than five seconds and a fourth had stopped and spun to face him.

The Smith & Wesson in his hand was empty. Jak pulled the trigger twice more as the unhurt sec man turned, then he tossed the blaster at the man's forehead. The man ducked and Jak saw that it was the arrogant, dark-haired man who had taunted Maddie earlier. The sadistic sec man's face broke into a vicious smile when he saw the albino and the children who followed him. He raised his homemade blaster, laughing at his would-be attackers.

"You brung them kids out to chill me, Whitey?" the sec man asked as he leveled the gun at Jak.

"No," Jak responded, "pleasure to do myself."

Jak's arms whipped out and the sec man saw the glint of metal as something raced through the air toward him. He felt the pain immediately, like a kick to the crotch, and he spluttered his breath out in an urgent gasp. He looked down, burning fire racking over the top of his legs, and saw the handle of the leaf-shaped throwing knife where it had embedded in his groin to the hilt.

The sec man remembered the blaster in his hand, and looked up to target the freak who had thrown the knife, only to find that—in the scant second he had taken to acknowledge the knife protruding from his body—the albino had crossed half the length of the car and was leaping at him, another blade already in his hand. As the sec man pulled the trigger on his blaster, Jak's flying fist connected with his left temple, and the knife ripped the skin there.

The curly haired sec man fell backward with the force of the attack, Jak's weight pushing him down. Shots rang out from his longblaster, but the albino youth was well within the circle of fire, the blasts going wildly around the shuddering car.

Jak saw the other man by the door pull a bloody hand away from the wound in his side and turn around to face the unexpected attack. He held a scimitar, rust dappled along its lethal-looking blade, and he gritted his teeth fiercely against the pain as he took a step toward the entangled bodies of Jak and the curly haired sec man.

The albino teen flicked his hand, tossing the knife he held in a flat, spinning arc at the wounded man, then turned back to the curly haired guard and started to pound at his face with his fists. The knife spun through the air before hitting the man with the torso wound between his lowest ribs. The blade failed to stick, falling to the wood floorboards with a clatter, but the man staggered backward with the force of the impact. As he regained his senses, he turned and saw the wooden shank stabbing toward his left eye, held point down by one of the children from the cage. Then his vision went red and he felt a tremendous, unspeakable pain as the spike was driven through his eye and into the brain behind.

As Marc face-stabbed the wounded sec man, Jak drove the knuckles of his powerful fist into the throat of his curly haired compatriot. When he pulled his fist back, he could see the unnatural dent in the man's throat that hadn't been there a second before, and he slammed his fist into it again and again, making sure the man stayed down. Finally, Jak stepped back from the felled sec man, stretching the taut muscles in his hand as he clenched and unclenched his aching fist. The curly haired lech was chilled.

Jak looked behind him, seeing the children who were watching him in awe, and nodded his approval to Marc as the lad pulled the rusty scimitar from the hand of the sec man he had chilled. Jak gathered his throwing blades, dismissing the homemade longblaster as an unreliable burden for himself but instructing all of the children to take the weapons and arm themselves. Maddie, he noticed, chose not to take anything, even pushing the proffered wooden knife aside when Marc tried to hand it to her.

The train continued to hurtle along the tracks as Jak led the way into the next car.

J.B. TUMBLED ACROSS the cracked, poisoned soil of the irradiated terrain beside the rushing behemoth of chrome and steel, rolling bodily along the ground until he came finally to a halt. He shook his head as he raised himself from the soil, resting on all fours as he struggled to get back into a standing position. He removed his spectacles for a moment and wiped the debris of muddy soil from the lenses before replacing them on his nose. He looked across to his right, his head held low, and watched as the train rushed along beside him.

He pulled himself up and looked back down the tracks, considering how long he might have until the train was gone completely. There was a chance he could get back on, just grab one of the side ladders the same way he and Ryan and Mildred had originally boarded this monstrosity, but that window was finite and he would need to move swiftly. He looked around the cracked terrain at his feet until he spotted his compact Uzi, caked with filth, and next to it his battered fedora. Still unsteady on his feet, J.B. stepped across to them and plucked the weapon and hat from the ground before turning back to face the train.

The bloated cars had passed, and he had perhaps fifteen more cars until the last unit went by. He looked up, spotting three rooftop gunners. Raising the Uzi, he took aim at the nearest gunner and squeezed the trigger.

The roof guard staggered, his ankles buckling as the bullets cut through them, and he fell from the train with an agonized cry.

J.B. swept the Uzi in an arc, cutting through the next two roof guards in quick succession, his attack so swift that the complacent sec men had no chance to retaliate. He left them hurt but mostly alive, and he felt the pang of conscience at having to wound them. But the bottom line was that he had no time to deal with a blasterfight as the rear end of the train thundered along the railroad tracks toward him. There was still a roof man on the final car, but J.B. sprinted into the shadow cast by the train—he running in one direction as the train journeyed in the other—and trusted it was cover enough.

J.B. had spotted the metal rungs of a side ladder four cars from the back, just past the car with the windshield windows, and he steadied himself as he prepared to grab for it. He swapped the Uzi to his left hand as he waited for the ladder rungs to come to him, unwilling to be weaponless for even a second. This whole operation had been a disaster right from the get-go and it felt to J.B.—hardly a superstitious man at the best of times—that it was tempting fate to pocket the weapon even for a second.

The ladder sped toward him, and J.B. grabbed it as it passed, his feet scrabbling up the side of the train the second he had hold of it. His right arm burned in its socket but his grip held. He hung there, calming his racing thoughts as the spoiled terrain raced past.

His slip had left Ryan alone at the front of the train, facing more than a half dozen armed sec men who were all out for blood. And there wasn't a damn thing J.B. could do about it.

IT TOOK RYAN a moment to realize that he wasn't alone in this firefight. Only three men had followed him through the door into the car with the second level where he and J.B. had slaughtered the guards. He had rushed through the last car with the children in it, determined not to let them get hurt any more than they already had been. But he knew that at least six men had been chasing him when he had entered the last cage car, and yet there were only three now.

Buckshot peppered the car, tinkling as it hit the thick, metal bars of the ladder that stretched up to the second-story rail blaster. Ryan found a sheltered cranny by one of the arrow slits, and used his blaster to keep his attackers at bay. From where he was he couldn't get a clear shot but neither could they. Trouble was, the second he tried to escape the car they would have him. And they knew it.

Ryan's head flitted out from cover for a split second as he sized up the enemy. Three sec men, one armed with a shotgun, the others with automatic weapons. A hail of bullets greeted the appearance of his head, drilling into the metal plate that sheltered Ryan's face.

Once the shots had ceased, one of the men at the far end of the car shouted, "Nowhere left to run, son. You gotta know that."

Ryan's head appeared again, low now where he had adopted a crouch, and he unleashed two 9 mm slugs into a sec man who was creeping toward him along the right-hand wall. The sec man fell with an anguished cry, hurt but still breathing.

"Who says I'm going to run?" Ryan called back. Silence followed, and he swiftly reloaded his SIG-Sauer once more with one of the magazines that J.B. had handed him in the storage car.

The sec man shouted to Ryan again, arrogance in his tone. "You put down your weapon," he called, "and we'll let you live."

Ryan was standing now, his back flush to the metal panel that offered scant protection from the sec men. He held his blaster at shoulder height, listening carefully to the sec man's voice, pinpointing his location in his mind.

"You hear me, boy?" the man called. "We let you live. You chilled a coupla my guys here. I can't offer better than that."

Ryan swung out from his hiding place and fired six shots in a continuous stream at the voice. Two went wild, but four of the bullets drilled into the sec man, cutting through his left-hand side. The man staggered, splashes of blood bursting from the exit wounds. Next to him, the sec man with the shotgun brought it to bear on Ryan and pulled at the trigger. At the same second, the door behind the sec man slid open and Ryan saw Jak's pure white arm reach through in a swift flip as though pitching a baseball.

The man with the shotgun collapsed to the floor, never managing to get the shot off. Ryan looked at the body. Jak's leaf-bladed throwing knife protruded from high on the man's back, just below the neck, severing his spinal column.

Jak dashed into the car, looking left and right to check for further enemies but finding none. He was followed by the group of filthy-looking children that he had been caged with.

"Thanks, Jak," Ryan told him. "That's one I owe you."

Jak shrugged. "You came rescue. We 'bout even."

The two men gripped hands firmly for a long moment, their unspoken bond being ratified once more. Ryan saw that the children were armed now. Two of them held blasters while the adolescent boy had a wicked-looking scimitar in his hand, streaks of brown rust along its length. Two of the younger children held wooden stakes.

Jak crouched by the shotgun-wielding sec man's corpse and plucked his blade from the man's back. "Where now?" he asked, looking up at Ryan as he hid the knife back in the sheath in his sleeve.

"Back to Krysty and the others," Ryan stated. "Get everyone together and see if we can find J.B."

"Missed what?" Jak asked.

"J.B. avoided getting his brains splattered all over one of the cars by falling through a hole in the wall," Ryan told the albino. "Kept him alive, but not the choicest option."

"Alive's alive," Jak stated firmly.

Ryan nodded, a wry smile on his lips. "There is that, and I suspect J.B. would agree with you."

They turned toward the rear door, leading the way into the next car with the children behind them. Ryan had taken two steps into the food store when he felt the cold metal of a gun barrel crack into the back of his skull.

Jak saw Ryan fall in the poorly lit room before him and he made to turn, ushering the children back. As he turned, he found himself facing the end of a .44 Magnum blaster, similar to his own missing weapon. Adam, the commanding officer on the train, smiled as he cocked the hammer. "Your move, White Skin," he growled.

Chapter Nineteen

The first thing that Ryan felt when he awoke was the rushing wind slapping into his face and the burning pain in his limbs. It felt for all the world like he was falling, plummeting toward the ground in the way you will in a dream, that sick feeling in your stomach as you drop with nowhere to land. But he had woken up now, and he was still falling, still plummeting without end.

Warily, Ryan opened his good eye. Two parallel steel lines stretched off into the distance, and to either side he saw the forbidding landscape of the scarred and poisoned earth. Above, the sky was dark with fierce, toxin-heavy clouds, and Ryan could see the land rushing past him.

He had been bow-spritted, tied to the carved figurehead of the mutie bitch with the bare breasts and the snake's tail that stretched out in front of the massive engine of the train. Beneath him, the steel tracks glinted in the afternoon sunlight, just two feet below his hanging body.

The pressure on his arms was almost intolerable. Ropes had been tied around his wrists and ankles, securing him to the figurehead at a forty-five-degree angle, his head thrust forward and the full weight of his body dangling from those ties. The coarse fibers of the ropes chafed at him, but already his limbs were falling into a blessed numbness, all sensation leaving them.

And so he hung there, buffeted by the wind as the mighty engine dragged the train across the cancerous terrain, dust and bugs peppering his naked face as they were caught up in the draft created by the train's passing.

JAK HAD BEEN FORCED to watch as Adam's men hoisted Ryan's body up and tied it to the figurehead at the very front of the train.

Jak's own hands had been bound using a leather belt and there were fifteen sec men, including Adam, standing nearby, each of them armed and wary of the lethal albino.

"One-Eye here'll be hung there till he dies of thirst or starvation," Adam explained, "a warning to anyone who disobeys the baron's will." Jak looked at the scarred face of the CO, identifying the grim satisfaction he took from his cruel work. "What you think of that, Whitey?"

Jak sniffed, wondering if he was next. Behind him, he could hear several of the children crying, and one of the sec men walked passed him shouting abuse at them to shut up.

"What? Cat got your tongue?" Adam asked Jak, yanking him by his mane of white hair and forcing him to look at the tied figure of Ryan. "You ain't a mute, I know that, boy."

That was it. That was the key, Jak realized suddenly. "Boy." The horrifically scarred commanding officer of the train had called him "boy." Like the trick with the knife that he had shown the children, Jak knew that people would believe what they thought they saw. And Adam saw him as a boy, a child. As such, Adam would underestimate him, and therein lay his chance. Tied like this, unable to free his hands, cunning was the only weapon he had left.

"Stop!" Jak cried out. "Not hurt Pa."

Adam looked at him, a wicked smile crossing his lips. "This man's your pa, that right?"

"Not hurt Pa," Jak replied.

Adam turned his head to one side and spit a thick gob of phlegm to the bare ground before addressing Jak again. "You and your pa caused a lot of trouble back there, Whitey, chilled a lot of my men." He sighed, shaking his head. "How old are you, boy?"

Jak kept his mouth shut, his scarlet eyes looking fiercely at Adam. He knew that everything he told them now would be a lie, but he didn't want it to be easy. He wanted them to be convinced. If he convinced them that Ryan had come alone, a doting father come to save his wayward son, they might not look for the others. It was a long shot, but he would play it for what it was worth.

Adam backhanded Jak across the face, and the albino teen staggered two steps before tumbling to the hard-packed soil. Unable to put his hands out to cushion the fall, Jak hit hard and Adam sneered as he looked down at him.

"You start answering me, boy, or I'll put a bullet in your tongue," Adam growled at him. Then he checked himself, looking across to the blood-streaked children that his men had rounded up, Jak's cell mates and fellow rebels. "Better yet," Adam began, striding over to the sniveling children and pulling his blaster free. From his place on the ground, Jak watched as the hulking foreman eyed the children, his breath coming hard.

Finally, Adam reached out for the unruly mop of blond curls atop Francis-Frankie's head. The boy howled in pain as he was pulled off the ground by his hair. The .44 Magnum blaster was in Adam's hand now, and Jak knew what would happen next.

"Wait," Jak called.

Holding the child in the air in his left hand, the blaster in his right, Adam turned to look at Jak. He wore a thin smile on his lips and his eyes shone with challenge. Francis-Frankie was crying, and not for the first time, as he struggled to reach the powerfully corded arm of the man who held him.

"Don't," Jak insisted, unable to take his eyes off the hanging boy.

There was a sudden explosion and Francis-Frankie no longer had a jaw. Instead, there was just red.

It seemed almost casual, the way that Adam tossed the child's body aside. Jak watched, distantly aware of the sounds of crying coming from the other children, unable to take his eyes off Francis-Frankie as he fell to the soil. His tiny body jerked and spasmed, his arms reaching about him, reaching for his face. He was alive, at least.

Then Adam stepped up to Jak and nudged him in the chest with his booted foot. "So?" he growled.

"Thirteen," Jak mumbled, looking at the ground.

"What's that?" Adam bellowed at him. "What d'you say?"

Jak looked at him, warily eyeing the blaster in his hand. "Thirteen. Am thirteen."

"And what's wrong with you? What's wrong with your skin?" Jak didn't answer immediately and Adam punctuated his question after a moment with a sharp kick to his ribs. "You see what I done to your daddy up there and you saw what I did to your playmate. You better start answering or I'll be doing a damn sight worse to you. Now, what is it? You a mutie?"

"Not mutie," Jak said, shaking his head. "Just no sun in me. Won't stick."

One of the other sec men stepped over, pointing to his wrist chron. "Pa's up, we should get going. The schedule—"

"Let me worry about the schedule," Adam barked.

Jak looked up at Ryan, hanging at the front of the chrome-and-steel monstrosity. They had even left his SIG-Sauer in its hip holster, such was the contempt they had for the one-eyed warrior now. Jak could understand that. Ryan posed no threat to them any longer. Of course, they didn't know Ryan Cawdor like he did. Jak had learned, time and again, never to underestimate the man's abilities or the depth of his single-minded determination.

"So," Adam asked, turning his attention once more to Jak's fallen figure, "what you doing on my train? We picked you up spying on us, that right?"

Jak nodded. "Black gold," he said firmly, "on train." The capacity to drill for oil in the Deathlands had been almost forgotten, the technology simply no longer existed, having long since been bombed out of existence with the first volleys in the war a hundred years before. But the legacy of a society built around the use of oil as fuel remained, and anyone with access to it could command almost any price...if he could defend it.

"Oil?" Adam looked incredulous. "You think we got oil on this here beastie? Where you hear that?"

"Man tol' Pa," Jak said.

Adam laughed at that. "Man told him wrong then. The only oil we got is in the lamps, and that's from vegetables." Adam laughed again. "You was suckered here, boy."

Jak bared his teeth as he watched the man laugh. It had been a series of quick lies, and the fool had filled in all the gaps for him. Oil poachers sounded plausible, and it pleased the arrogant man to think that the whole thing had been a trick, a misunderstanding.

"So," Adam said finally, "how come he chilled so many?"

"How many *I* chill?" Jak asked.

Adam considered that a moment, realization dawning. "A family of assassins, that it?"

Jak nodded. "Whatever work," he grunted.

"So my men manage to pick up some hit man's son and stick him in a cage." Adam laughed bitterly. "No wonder your daddy came aboard mad and gunning." He shook his head, cursing under his breath as he looked at the unconscious figure of Ryan that now hung from the front of the engine. "You got a name? Your pa?"

"Thursby," Jak replied from his position in the dirt. "Floyd." He nodded toward Ryan's hanging body. "Junior," and he smiled, indicating himself.

"Well, I'm Adam," the scarred man told him, "and I'm gonna be the person who chills you, Junior Thursby."

Adam stepped back, making as if to walk away from the albino, then he took a short run and kicked Jak hard in the ribs. Jak groaned, expelling his breath in a painful rush. "You alone, Junior?" Adam shouted at him as Jak struggled to get his breath back. "You alone or I got to hunt every car of my train to find Mamma Thursby and the Thursby brothers?"

Jak blinked hard, stifling the cough he knew wanted to come. He looked across the dirt again at Francis-Frankie. The boy had stopped moving, the mess of red where half his face had been oozed blood over the ground. No one had gone to look at him, to check on him. "Alone," Jak whispered, "Just us, Pa and me."

Adam leaned down and pulled Jak's head off the ground by his hair. "You better be telling the truth, Junior," he snarled. Then he pulled back his fist and punched the tied teenager in the face before standing up.

Jak's head reeled and his vision swam; he flirted in and out of consciousness for a few seconds, unable to get his bearings. He heard Adam saying something, an instruction to his men. Search every car, every compartment. Jak's deception to hide the companions had failed. And somehow, without even realizing it, he'd gotten a five-year-old child chilled.

"THEY'RE GOING TO BE coming for us," J.B. assured the companions in the tiny compartment, standing with his back to the curtained door, "and they won't be sparing any bullets now, not after the show me and Ryan put on for them."

Doc was standing with his back to the window. Mildred sat in the chair, her backpack propped open on the tiny desk. Krysty lay on the bloodied sheets on the bunk, her breathing slow but regular, her eyes open.

"I seem to recall an agreement that stealth was to be the order of the day," Doc reminded J.B.

"We were put in a situation where stealth wasn't going to cut it," J.B. told him bitterly. "But we might still save our asses with it now, if we act smart."

"What are you thinking?" Mildred asked, her dark eyes wide with concern.

"No train tracks go on forever," J.B. said. "Sooner or later this thing has to stop, get refueled. We'll hang out, heads down, till then. Might be a better opportunity to free Jak, too."

"And what about Ryan?" Krysty asked, concern making her voice louder than it needed to be in the small room.

"Burns me up to leave him," J.B. admitted, "but I don't know where he is or if he's still alive or even on the train anymore. Sorry to say it, but the odds aren't good." Despite the bluntness of his words, J.B. was concerned. Deep down, the years of traveling together had made all of the companions close, and Ryan and J.B. were closest of all. They had been together since the days of Trader and War Wag One, a whole lifetime of trying to eke out a survival in the pitiable remains of the world. They had become brothers, bonded by experience.

"He's not dead," Krysty said firmly, sitting up on the bed. "I'd know if he'd been chilled."

Doc let out a sigh, part despair and part contempt, and Mildred left her chair and sat beside Krysty, wrapping an arm around the red-haired woman. "Let's be practical," Mildred said quietly. "We all need to keep our feet firmly on the ground right now, Krysty."

Krysty's green eyes pierced Mildred, and her lips tightened before she spoke. "They have cages, don't they? Ryan could be in one of those."

"Those are just for kids," J.B. told her. "I didn't see any caged adults. I'm just being honest now," he added after a moment.

"Screw honesty," Krysty shouted. "He's alive, I know it."

Doc rushed across from the window and stood in front of Krysty, reminding her to keep her voice low. "Let us not go throwing the baby out with the bathwater here, Krysty, my dear. Mayhap Ryan is alive, no one said he's not. But shouting up a storm and getting us detected would be an indubitable way of losing any opportunity of finding him, would it not?"

Krysty's expression softened and she looked from Doc to J.B. to Mildred in turn. "I'm sorry," she said, her voice level once more. "I just... I'd know, okay? I'd know."

J.B. swept the comment aside, focused on the main objective. "Unless anyone's got a better plan, I say we go into hiding until the train stops."

Doc agreed. "I hardly think we can take on a whole train of reprobates as we are."

"I'll take on the whole lot of them if it saves Ryan," Krysty told them quietly.

"We all would," Mildred told her, "but we have to play things smart."

"I USED TO THINK my daddy would come to save me," Maddie admitted to Jak as they sat together in the cage once more. She was sitting beside him, her knees tucked close to her chest, gazing off into the distance at nothing in particular.

Jak sat cross-legged, holding a piece of rag to the cut that had opened up just above his eye when Adam had punched him. His ribs ached where he had been kicked, and the throbbing was back in his left arm where he had strained the wound there during the brief rebellion. In his mind's eye, all he could see was the struggling body of Francis-Frankie as the bullet took half his face away.

Tight-lipped, Maddie looked at him, her eyes wide and scared.

After Jak's vicious interrogation, all the children had been returned to the cattle truck that held their cage. Jak had been stripped of the throwing knife he had hidden in one sleeve and other secret places, as well as the one he'd had held in his hand when he had been captured by Adam. The sec men had patted him down, but they had failed to check his boots and so had missed the two additional leaf-bladed knives he had hidden there. The other children had been stripped of their weapons, the blasters they had acquired as well as the knifelike stakes that Jak had hewn from the wooden wall of their prison. They sat around quietly, dejected and resenting Jak for the flash of hope he had shown them that had amounted to nothing. But mostly, he knew, the children were in shock at what had happened to one of their own, Francis-Frankie. Every last one of them knew that that was Jak's fault, too.

The door had been replaced, and the screws in the hinges hastily welded in place by a sec man with an acetylene welding torch.

"The first day I was here," Maddie said, turning to look at Jak for a second before turning back to gaze off at nothing, "I thought, sooner or later, Daddy will come aboard and rescue me and I can go back home and everything will be the same again." She shrugged. "Then they took Hugo. An old grandpa and a pretty lady with a notebook came and they opened the cage door and they took Hugo. She said he had a really important job to do for them."

"Hugo?" Jak asked, having never heard the name

before. In his mind he still thought of Francis-Frankie, his shuddering body lying in the dirt, not yet ready to die. The sec men had left him there, in the massing puddle of his own blood.

"He's nine years old, Jak," Maddie said. "I don't think he was even scared. He just went with them and I heard him tell the lady how pretty her hair was. And that was the last time we saw him. He didn't come back." Maddie's expression had hardened, a sort of determination in her dark eyes. "Three days ago, if you want to know. That's when Hugo left."

"Say where?" Jak asked.

"No." Maddie shook her head. "Just for the really important job. Don't know what." She looked at him, then her eyes swept the room, taking in the other prisoners. "Back on the farm, my mom would give me really important jobs, too, like picking the sweet cherries from the tree and taking Rufus, he's our dog, out to play so he wasn't 'cluttering up the house,' that's what Mom would say. Did you ever eat cherries, Jak?"

TWO MEN WERE assigned to search each batch of ten cars, checking for possible interlopers aboard Adam's train. In the last ten cars, the sec men assigned were Barry Jackson and Horse McGintey, who figured they had an easy job. Most of the cars were dedicated to supplies, so they had only four cars of people to worry about. "Sure, could be that an interloper would hide himself in the storage car but, really, how hard is that neg-wit gonna be to spot?" Horse had asked. To Barry, it seemed kind of ironic him saying that.

By the time they had worked their way through to car fifty-four, they had gotten the thing down to a routine. Check each compartment, poke their heads in, ask if everyone was okay and who they were meant to be, then move on. Jackson had heard the freaky boy explain it had been him and his pa alone, and he was inclined to believe him. The boy looked wiry, but not much against the full brunt of Adam's anger.

This car was split into four cabins along the port-side wall, with a corridor stretching along the starboard side toward the door that opened onto the first of the storage units. The sliding door to the first cabin was open, rattling in its frame as the train trundled along the tracks. The compartment was empty, an unmade bed to the right and a tiny desk with the remains of a meal on it to the left. The cabin stank of rotgut, and insects had gathered in a sticky patch on the wood floor.

The next door was closed, and Horse knocked firmly on the glass panel before sliding it aside. "Whoa, boy!" Horse said at the sight as he pulled back the door.

There was a sec man lying in the bed, a tough guy by the name of Blake whom Horse knew from a spate of rustling for the baron a while back. Blake's hands were tied together and secured to a wooden pole built into the wall above him, and, as far as Horse could tell, he was naked, a sheet granting him little modesty down below. Next to him a dark-skinned gaudy slut wearing an olive-green bra was snuggled up to him, a hand on Blake's hairy chest, smiling with a dazed expression on her stupe face. On the other side of Blake was another gaudy, this one a pale-looking redhead with curves in all the right places, naked as the day she was born, the sheet tossed indifferently over her legs. The redhead was asleep, her face beside Blake's chest. The room smelled fiercely of body odor.

"'Scuse us, ma'am," Horse grumbled, tipping a finger to his brow as he stepped out of the room.

Barry held the door a moment as Horse tried to slide it closed. "It's okay," Horse told him, "that's Blake, I know him from a ways back."

Barry snickered, looking at the gaudies dozing in the tiny bunk. "It ain't Blake I were looking at," he said. "Greedy SOB!" and he slammed the door back in its frame.

THE SECOND the door closed, Krysty lifted her head out of the sedated sec man's armpit and drew a desperate breath of air. "This is disgusting," she muttered in a harsh whisper.

Mildred looked across at her, her eyes wide open now. "I've sedated him three times in the past twelve hours. I think he's become a little sweaty."

"Whose idea was this again?" Krysty asked, swinging from the bunk and putting her arms back in her jumpsuit before zipping up the front. She had kept the legs on beneath the sheet, along with her beautifully tooled boots.

"They bought it, didn't they?" J.B. asked as he dropped down from the overhead rack where the dead body of the piggy-eyed sec man still lay. "At least you didn't have to turn tricks with corpse-boy up there."

"How is he?" Mildred asked, pulling her dark vest top over her head and tucking it into her combat pants as she stood. She winced as the light material scraped against the cuts she had sustained on her back from her brief excursion beneath the train.

"Decomposing," J.B. admitted with a sour look. "You should have got rid of him while I was gone."

"It's on my to-do list," Mildred grumbled, "right after distracting the guards with my tits."

J.B. smiled, shaking his head as though vindicated. "I knew they'd fall for it."

IN THE NEXT CABIN, Barry and Horse found an old, white-haired man neither of them recognized. The old man lay asleep in the bed, snoring loudly.

"You know this old duffer?" Barry asked quietly.

Horse shook his head. "He one of the whitecoats?"

"Nah, don't think so."

"Reckon we'll show him to Adam then?" Horse whispered.

"Old guy like this?" Barry pondered. "I dunno, how did he get aboard otherwise?"

"Mebbe he is with the whitecoats then," Horse considered.

Lying in the bed listening to their hushed conversation, Doc decided it was time to "wake up." He ceased snoring, his bright eyes popped open and he shrieked a single word. "Eureka!"

The two sec men were standing in the open doorway to the cabin, and both jumped back in astonishment.

Still fully clothed, Doc swung his long legs over the side of the bunk and reached across for his ebony, lion's-head cane. "May I help you, gentlemen?" he asked, smiling as he looked at the visitors.

"We were just discussing whether you belong here or not, old man," the younger of the sec men explained, a nasty leer on his face.

"Whether I belong here?" Doc asked, incredulity in his tone. "And who, might I ask, are you?"

"Barry Jackson," the younger man said, "and this here is Horse."

"Yes," Doc said patronizingly, "I know Horse already. I asked who you were, young man."

Horse was confused. He looked the old man up and down, then a smile crossed his lips. "We work together somewhere? I can't think."

Doc's mind flashed back to the map on the classroom wall and he tried to remember the name of one of the large North Dakota towns. "Moorhead, I do believe it was," he said, offering the man a bright smile.

Horse nodded, though he looked a little unsure. "Yeah," he muttered, "that must have been it."

Barry pointed at his partner and went cross-eyed. "Since his accident, Horse don't remember so good sometimes. Sorry, fella."

Doc nodded, understanding on his face. "Now, if you'll both excuse me, I do have important work to be getting on with."

"Sure," Barry said, "sure thing."

As the sec men pulled the sliding door closed, Doc twisted the handle of his swordstick back into place. That had been close. He thought for a moment he had been caught out, but once more it seemed that fortune favored the brave. A little bluff work went a long way, he knew, it was all in the delivery. He sat on the bunk and waited for J.B. and the others to reappear so that they could plan their next move.

THE REPORTS CAME IN, one by one, as though his men were paying him tribute, until Adam had heard from all the teams. There was no one else on the train, no one who shouldn't be there.

He sat in his Spartan cabin near the front of the train and pondered that. Why had they come out with this monstrous train again? When they started the operation, years before, it had made sense to carry all the equipment, the materials to build the towers and sometimes the very tracks that they traveled on. As Baron Burgess had refined the system, they had had to lay more track, and still the hulking workshops of the train had been required. But now? The supplies were barely required anymore, the men had become lazy and inefficient. They hadn't trimmed the train down to a more manageable length because of Adam's paranoia that they might need something from the old storage units.

Traveling across the dead terrain of North Dakota, the fear had always gripped him. What if they stalled? What if a rail broke, a point snapped or become stuck? What if? What if? What if? And so he had insisted, despite what Burgess and his whitecoats had said, that they were to travel with everything, with all the supplies. A ville in miniature, traveling on oiled wheels.

For the first time ever, someone had come aboard his train and instigated a massacre. Men had been chilled, good men, men he trusted and, moreover, he liked.

But there was no one else aboard now. Just himself, his sec force, the three whitecoats and a smattering of imprisoned children who were essential to the Grand Project. And the *bruja*.

Yes, the *bruja*. The more distance he could put between himself and that creepy old woman the happier Adam was. Maybe, subconsciously, that was why he had kept the train at this impractical length. There was a buffer zone between them of more than forty cars, and even then he felt her sometimes, picking through his dreams while he slept, her dry, brittle hands and talon-like nails sifting through his thoughts.

He sat there, in the darkness of his cabin, the curtains drawn against the rich afternoon sunlight, and he picked at his teeth. This would be the last go-round, this was the last mission before the project went to the final phase. Once that happened, they wouldn't need protection to travel the rails. No one would be left to challenge Baron Burgess and his loyal followers. They would be masters of all that they surveyed.

Chapter Twenty

"You have to eat," Maddie said.

Jak's head moved lethargically as he looked up at her across the cage.

"You have to eat," she said again, "or you'll get weak."

He nodded, almost imperceptibly, the movement so slight. A sec man had come by sometime earlier and passed the children several platefuls of some unrecognizable meat. The children in the cell had devoured it eagerly, but Jak hadn't moved. He just sat there, his knees pulled close to his chest, his arms wrapped around them, staring off into space. Maddie had watched him, concerned at what he had to be thinking, at what his mind was dwelling on.

Jak could see the boy's face—Francis-Frankie—in those hunks of meat. The boy, lying there in the poisonous soil, half his face gone and his life oozing away into the toxin-spoiled dirt. If he had just said something, just spoken up quicker, worked out his lie more swiftly...

Jak could hear the tinkling laughter of the boy even now, could hear that whiny quality of voice when he wanted something, when he didn't understand. Jak had spent perhaps twenty hours in the boy's company, half of those asleep thanks to the tranq dart he had taken to the chest. He had barely said five words to the boy, barely even acknowledged him except as a soldier in his failed little uprising. And now the boy was dead, thanks to Jak.

"Come on, Jak," Maddie said. She knelt beside him and proffered the scraps on the grease-streaked plate. "It's good. It tastes good."

He looked at the hunk of bloody red meat in her hand, a steak carved from the flank of a longhorn or maybe a mule, cooked and seasoned but still red beneath its dusting of charcoal. Red like Francis-Frankie's face at the end.

Maddie held the steak to his hand, pried his limp fingers away from his knees, forcing him to clutch the sparse meal. "I want you to eat," she told him firmly, her hand over his, holding it closed around the meat.

Jak looked at her again, but in his mind's eye he saw the explosion of sound and light as the child's jaw disappeared, and then he saw Maddie jawless. He blinked hard, scrunching his eyes closed as if to block out the images, then he looked at her again.

"It wasn't your fault," Maddie told him.

"Chilled plenty," Jak muttered. "Never this way."

Maddie shook her head firmly. "That man did it, the man with the scars," she said. Jak was surprised that there was no pleading to her voice, no question. She was telling him the facts as she saw them. "They had you tied up, and there was nothing you could have done. I loved Francis-Frankie, we all did, but there was nothing you could have done, Jak."

He saw the boy lying there, shaking as the blood streamed from his broken face. "Shoulda," he said. "Shoulda stopped."

"No, Jak," Maddie said. "Do you know why everyone's

so quiet now, why we're all sitting scared and sad and no one's really talking?"

"'Cause of me," he muttered. "Shoulda…"

"No," Maddie said firmly. "Everyone is sad because there was nothing we could do, either." Maddie's grip on his hand tightened then, ensuring he wouldn't drop the precious food.

Slowly, Jak's gaze swept the cage, looking at the inhabitants who sat or lay on the hard floor. They all looked drained, as though none of them had slept. Finally he looked at Maddie once more, her open face, the tentative, serious smile on her lips, and he nodded. Next time they had a chance for freedom, Jak would make sure none of them got so much as a scratch. It wasn't over yet.

ONCE THE SEARCH TEAM had departed, J.B., Krysty, Mildred and Doc regrouped in the tiny compartment they had used as their base for the duration of the train's passage.

"I want us out of here," J.B. told them. "If Ryan's still among the living, we'll find him and free him, that's for certain. But I don't want anyone going off half-cocked, thinking they can take on the whole train."

Krysty shifted uncomfortably on the bunk where she sat with Mildred, but she said nothing.

"And when are we to help Ryan?" Doc asked. "Come to that, when are we to help Jak, as well?"

"We'll work on the assumption that they're still onboard," J.B. told them. "When the opportunity arises, we'll know."

"So," Mildred stated, "basically do nothing."

"No train tracks go on forever," J.B. repeated firmly,

as though that put an end to the discussion. He stretched his muscles from his cramped position by the sliding door, stood and began gathering his maps and the mini-sextant from the tiny desk beside Doc.

Mildred shook her head, clearly deciding whether to challenge J.B. on this point. Krysty, whose health had continued to improve, reached across and placed her hand on Mildred's arm, locking eyes with her. The silent instruction was clear: J.B. is the leader now, his decision stands or we'll all get chilled.

Having packed away his materials, J.B. stood by the compartment's door. "We're going to bed down in the storage units," he told them. "Less chance of being disturbed, more chance to defend ourselves if someone comes knocking." He looked querulously at Krysty. "You up to this?"

The Titian-haired beauty nodded, a tight smile on her face. "I feel much better, thank you."

"Any problems," J.B. said to her, "you call. Anything—headaches, cramps—anything at all. You're our number-one priority till we can get to Ryan and Jak. Anything else?"

Doc spoke up, pressing a hand to his forehead. "I do believe I am suffering a little from a headache myself," he told J.B.

"Yeah," Mildred chipped in. "Stress is getting to us all. Let's wrap this one up quick and get off this ghost train."

Together, the four of them made their way through the cars until they reached a unit full of metal sheets and jars of rivets. Despite Mildred's plea, they would be on the monstrous train for a further three days before they reached their ultimate destination.

THE TRAIN STOPPED at regular intervals and the crew would examine the strange towers that had been constructed close to the tracks. Sometimes, Mildred, Doc or J.B. would sneak out and watch, and once, when she was feeling well, Krysty took up a post by the roof hatch of their car and watched the operation at the front of the train under the waning moon of the night sky.

The operation never varied. The whitecoats would examine the odd towers, compare their readings and decide whether the balance of grayish liquid feeding the structures from beneath needed to be altered. Doc and Mildred proposed various possibilities to explain what that liquid was, and J.B. used his own field of expertise to run through possible mechanical oils, pastes and unguents, but the actual nature of the liquid remained frustratingly elusive. J.B. told the others about his encounter with the canisters up close, and how the naked boy had been kept in a cage near to them. "The two may not be related," he stated before they ran away on a flight of fancy about why a child was needed in this process, but it left everyone feeling even more unsettled about the operation they were witnessing.

In the storage car, just one from the back, J.B. constructed a shelter within the masses of metal plating that was stored there. With the help of the others, he shifted sheet steel so that they had a small burrow to retreat to, and a place where Krysty could remain during the frequent periods when her health seemed to dip. The structure looked to be part of the storage system, a casual arrangement of the stocks held onboard the train. J.B. spent several hours viewing it from various angles to ensure it looked camouflaged, hidden as it was in plain sight.

On several occasions the companions had heard the

door in the preceding car being yanked aside, and they had scrambled to hide in the tiny shelter while sec men stomped through. One time, several men had stopped and had an extended conversation about the value of a particular type of rivet over another, and the companions spent an awkward forty-five minutes waiting for the men to leave. The whole time, J.B. had his M-4000 shotgun trained on the conversing men through a hidden gap in the shelter. Eventually, the men had left, and the companions had felt relief. However, it was a stark reminder that they were far from safe even here, sheltering in the darkness of the unmanned car.

Krysty had argued repeatedly for forming a search party to locate Ryan, telling them that every second they left him was a second he could be being chilled or worse.

"There's just four of us now," J.B. reminded her. "We need to pick our moment."

Tears glistened in Krysty's eyes, the frustration of the situation coupling with the pain she continued to suffer at frequent intervals. "When will that be?" she insisted.

"Soon, I promise," J.B. assured her.

In his own mind, the Armorer became increasingly unhappy with the situation he had led them into. Their food supplies were dwindling, and he had insisted they not raid the food stores—which were ten cars away—unless they absolutely needed to. It wouldn't do to put themselves in any unnecessary danger this late in the game. Still, by hiding the companions in the shadows it felt like he was failing to take charge. During their quieter moments, Mildred reassured him that he would know when it was time to act; she could sense his turmoil as much as any of them.

"We're two men down," she reminded him while Doc and Krysty slept, "and Krysty isn't in a reliable condition to help us. You're doing the right thing."

"It feels wrong," he replied quietly as the darkened car hurtled along the tracks.

"Sometimes deciding to do nothing can be the hardest choice of all," Mildred told him.

As time went on, and their third day on the locomotive turned into a fourth, J.B. admitted he had lost track of their passage. He tossed his map aside in disgust, and plowed a clenched fist into the hard metallic casing of the car with a resounding crash. Being cooped up in the windowless car for so long had not agreed well with J.B.'s temperament. Doc bent to pick up the map, while Mildred and Krysty watched them in the faint glow that seeped beneath the side door panels of the car.

"How far?" Doc asked, placing a hand on J.B.'s shoulder.

"I don't know," J.B. snapped, frustration in his voice.

"Yes, you do," Doc told him genially. "You started making the calculations as soon as you stepped onboard, I know you did. And you have checked and triple-checked them ever since."

J.B. sighed wearily as he looked at the old man. "Six hundred and forty miles," he told him. "That's how far we've traveled, assuming an average speed of twelve miles an hour, which roughly takes into account the stops."

"And we know we shall be heading to Grand Forks," Doc reminded him, his voice calm, "sooner or later, do we not?"

J.B. nodded.

"Well?" Doc said.

"If we continue to follow the loop I plotted out," J.B. said, "we'll get there in about a half day."

Doc smiled. "You have never yet given me reason to doubt your calculation abilities, J.B.," he said. "A half day it shall be. I will stake my cane on it."

The flash of a smile crossed J.B.'s face for just a split second, then it was gone. "Thanks, Doc," he whispered.

THE WAY JAK saw it, he couldn't free Ryan. He had spent two sleepless days mulling over the problem, approaching it from every angle. How do you untie a man from the front of a moving train without getting him chilled? Jak didn't even consider his own safety in these scenarios, he just worked out the possible ways in which to free Ryan and promised to worry about himself once a viable solution came to him.

The reality was this: as far as he knew, Ryan had been hanging there for more than two days, buffeted by the winds and assaulted by the elements. His arms and legs had to feel like jelly, no sensation left in them. If he was untied he would simply drop, no strength left to save himself. And, from where he was hung, any drop would result in him falling under the wheels of the massive engine.

Jak would require some kind of winch or hoist to free Ryan, so that he could both untie him and hold the man in place. But then where would he take Ryan, assuming he could construct some kind of makeshift hoist?

This all ignored the very real problem of getting there in the first place. Following the failed bust-out, a sec man had been charged with checking on the children every hour, leaving Jak with little time to work at an escape. The bravado he had shown J.B. when the Armorer had found him in the cage had long since evaporated. There was simply no easy way out of the jail he had been placed in, and any escape would likely result in the execution of another child by way of punishment, something that Jak had promised he would not let happen again.

Maddie continued to force him to eat, though not because Jak was in the thrall of depression as he had been when they were recaged. Now, Jak's mind was frantically working solutions, working through every scenario in meticulous detail before discarding it. His father had taught him the importance of planning, and ultimately it hadn't saved the man from the depredations of the cruel baron who ruled over them. But planning, Jak knew, took time. Which made it all the more frustrating when, after two days, he had no solution to the myriad problems he was faced with.

IT WAS LATE into the night when the train ushered around the curving tracks and lumbered the last few miles to the Forks. Adam had joined the driver at the rattling front engine as they came to the end of their journey. The driver was a stout man called Rhett who never slept and was permanently wired up to some liquid form of jolt stim that pumped straight into his veins. His cabin was painted completely black, and only the lights of his equipment, the dials and gauges that allowed him to monitor the locomotive's progress, provided any illumination. Adam considered Rhett the single most reliable member of his squad.

It never ceased to amaze him, that long approach to the Forks base. Years before, way back before the megacall, the unit had been a U.S. Air Force base. Like most of the military facilities, the base had been destroyed, and whole sections were reduced to rubble. But Burgess, in the days when he was just a gang master himself, before he'd assumed the title of "baron," had seen value in sifting through the ruins and uncovering the old base's secrets.

Baron Burgess had built his ville on the ruins of the military base, utilizing the underground facilities that had survived the attacks as an infrastructure to his grand design. They called it a ville, but really, beside several single-story outbuildings, it was one vast building, segmented to ensure it could stand, but stretching a half mile across the tortured landscape. It lurked on the horizon, a flat, low building so huge that it was unavoidable, even in the semidark of the waning moon. Lights glowed in its windows, the flickering of fires, gleaming like stars trapped in the vast structure. Towers and posts and minarets jutted from the low roof, bristling into the indigo sky as though jabbing at a heaven that looked down and mocked the man within.

The death train powered toward it, the brakes squealing as Rhett applied them, pulling at the three levers that applied the scattered friction brakes throughout the colossal beast. It would have been impossible to try to stop the train from just the engine alone. Other brakes were linked to its controls, slowing the wheels in unison when they were applied.

As they got closer, Adam spotted the sec men who patrolled around Forks ville, striding through the fouled earth or eyeing the approaching train from their posts along the roof of the massive building.

THE TRAIN HAD SLOWED to four miles per hour, little more than walking speed, and it followed the tracks into the open tunnel that ran the building's length. Inside, the vast cavern was lit by flickering oil lamps strung along the ceiling. As the train trundled inside, sec men watched it enter, blasters at the ready. A few of them saluted in the direction of the towing engine, presuming Adam would be in there even though it was impossible to see within.

Adam reached across, flicking the switch that sounded the bell along the whole of the train, letting everyone know that they had arrived at their final destination.

"Welcome home," he murmured.

Chapter Twenty-One

Doc shoved Jak's Colt Python into his waistband and smoothed his frock coat back in place to hide the weapon before joining the growing throng outside the train. He watched Krysty walking ahead of him, seeing her weave a little as she stepped into the vast, low-ceilinged cavern that housed the train. Krysty was still battling with ill health, more than four days after they had left the redoubt in Minot, and the pattern was still hard to predict. Before the companions had left the train, Krysty had assured them that she felt fine, but it was clear that she was struggling, that the sickness had left her weak.

Krysty wore her hair up, tucked beneath the battered brown fedora that J.B. had loaned her for the infiltration of the train pirate camp, and had the hessian blanket that she had retrieved when they left the sleeping cabin tossed over her shoulders. It would be difficult to disguise Krysty's curvaceous, female form, but wearing the shapeless blanket and hiding her vibrant hair helped draw attention away from her.

J.B. and Mildred walked a few steps ahead of Krysty, discussing their surroundings in low, urgent tones. Mildred's backpack disguised her a little, and she was hardly the statuesque beauty that Krysty was. When the train stopped, the four of them had agreed to look outside and, once they confirmed that they were in a vast, roofed stopover, they had decided to take their chances outside among the mass of train people and other men and women who strolled through the huge, cavernous space.

The cavern was man-made, its flat sides curving inward toward the top as though domed. The ceiling was about three stories above the ground, and lighting was attached to catwalks and metal struts. The ceiling lamps were dim, their weak glow unable to penetrate the gloom of the huge room, and they were supplemented by portable lighting rigs dotted around the room, powered by chugging generators like the one they had seen used on occasion to light the work at the scaffold towers. As they walked past one, Doc glanced over it and noticed the olive-green paint and the large, white-stenciled lettering along the side. It was clearly military, a period piece from predark. The whole, vast room had an indefinable military essence about it, Doc thought; parts of the walls were patched together from old mil matériel. Chickens and a few dogs ran through the crowds, fresh meals when the crew needed them, he guessed.

The area was large enough to hold the obscene length of the train, sixty cars stretching along one side of the room. The remainder was given over to a large, flat space, a meeting room sufficient for a vast crowd in the hundreds or even thousands, with a few doors leading off the sides here and there, presumably into separate, smaller rooms. Doc estimated there were perhaps three hundred men and women here, milling around, the majority of them armed. A raised dais was located in the center of the huge room where a hooded, cloaked figure silently watched the proceedings as the three whitecoats and the commanding officer of the train trailed up the steps to the platform. A bank of lights surrounded the dais, their glow soft like the embers of a fire, a bubbling liquid visible within through the transparent windows. The crowd—made up of hard-faced men and women, sec men, mercies and gaudies like the ones the companions had seen aboard the train—made their way toward the raised dais.

There was a party atmosphere here; people were laughing and dancing, loud. Echoing music tried and failed to fill the cavernous room. It reminded Mildred of rock concerts from the late twentieth century, except that everyone seemed to be armed and proud to show it. Barrel fires burned here and there as food was cooked and distributed to the returning crew.

J.B. turned to face the others, walking slowly backward as he spoke, his voice low. "Me and Mildred are going to do a recce on the train, see if we can find Ryan and Jak."

"I'd like to look, too," Krysty started, but J.B. held up a hand for silence.

"Stick with Doc," he told her. "You're our backup, and we might just need some friends hidden in the crowd before too long."

Just then there was a harsh, whistling sound from the central platform of the room. J.B. glanced over his shoulder, watching as the glowing lights around the dais grew in intensity then faded again. He saw two further figures had joined the others on the dais, and a chill went down his spine: the *bruja,* accompanied by a sec man. The frail old woman sat in a wheelchair, a skeletal-looking device with large wheels to each side.

She sat silently, wrapped in a shawl, her arthritic hands shaking incessantly, as a brawny sec man pushed her to join the others on the raised platform.

"Gonna get that plas ex," J.B. whispered, turning to Mildred and leading the way back the train.

He pointed subtly toward the front of the train. "I want you to find Jak and Ryan if they're still aboard. Most likely near the front of the train—that's where the cages are, and that's where we found Jak the first time out. Both of them may need medical attention."

Mildred hefted her backpack. "What about you, J.B.?"

"I'll join you as soon as I can," the Armorer told her, "but I've got a few things I want to do first."

"And what if I bump into sec men guarding these cages?" Mildred asked.

"I reckon most of them got off to stretch their legs and enjoy a taste of home cooking." J.B. smiled. "Probably won't be more than a half dozen onboard now."

Mildred flipped the catch on the holster that held her ZKR 551 target revolver. "Great," she muttered, looking over the vast beast of chrome and steel that stood on the silver rails.

A man brandishing a heavy longblaster appeared in one of the cars near the front of the train, and J.B. and Mildred quickly moved on, heading ever nearer the mighty engine that pulled the colossus. Mildred heard a familiar voice behind her and glanced back for a fraction of a second. Jak was being led out of the car along with a handful of children, heads bowed and chains wrapped around their wrists, marching forward like a chain gang. The man with the longblaster led the group in the direction of the central dais, while a second man brandishing a crossbow took up the rear, urging the party onward.

As they walked, J.B. and Mildred saw a similar group of chained children being forced from the car next to Jak's. Mildred nudged J.B. softly in the side and caught his eye, raising one eyebrow. J.B. shrugged in response and continued marching toward the front of the train.

The sec men led the two groups of children through the crowd toward the center of the vast room. As they watched them depart, Mildred and J.B. hastily reevaluated their objectives. It would be difficult to free Jak now without bringing down the wrath of the whole room.

"I'm going to create a disturbance," J.B. told Mildred, "but it'll take some doing." He gestured toward the middle of the train. "I need you to cover my back while I go get something."

Eyes alert, Mildred walked beside J.B. until they reached the eighteenth car from the engine. The Armorer had memorized the important units of the train, and he knew precisely what he was looking for. This was the car where he and Ryan had found stocks of construction equipment, including that enticing stash of explosives. There was no side door on this unit, so he stepped between the cars and pulled himself up on the lip beneath the foremost door while Mildred tried to look casual as she checked for anyone watching. There were sec men milling around, and suddenly one of the men on the dais shouted something and a group of sec men moved into position to surround a lone figure. Mildred wondered what was going on there, and realized, with a start, who the figure was.

"DO WE HAVE SUCCESS?" the hooded figure on the dais asked, his voice a painful rasp. He was addressing the lead whitecoat, the older man of the three-strong team. Adam stood beside the hooded man, and the *bruja* sat in her wheelchair with a sec man waiting behind her should she require to be moved.

The eldest whitecoat stepped forward and dipped his head toward the hooded man in supplication. "We've tested the network as much as we can without going fully live," he explained. "It's been on stand-by condition for one week, as you know, idling until we set the final phase in motion. I foresee absolute success, Baron Burgess."

The hooded figure, his face in shadow, nodded slowly, considering the whitecoat's words. "Absolute," he muttered, his voice strained.

"We have seen definite vagal nerve stimulation in the subthalamic nucleui of test subjects," the dark-haired female whitecoat explained, consulting her notes. "The tests have been brief, of necessity, but the results have proved entirely satisfactory."

The head beneath the heavy hood turned, and the baron addressed the *bruja*. "Well, mutie witch?" he asked, contempt in his tone. "What do you say?"

The trace of a smile crossed the woman's cracked lips and the creases deepened around her wise, ancient eyes. "He who controls the network will be puppet master. I can feel its power pulsing throughout the system now."

"Good," Burgess stated simply, turning back to look over the crowd.

But the *bruja* spoke again, after a moment. "I am not the only one who feels this," she said quietly.

Burgess, Adam and the three whitecoats all turned to look at her, stunned by her statement. Adam was the first to speak the question on their minds. "What? Who are you talking about?"

"There," the *bruja* whispered, and her clawlike right hand moved toward the crowd around them. Her index finger slowly stretched out and she pointed at a figure in the audience. "The woman."

Adam looked in the direction that the *bruja* pointed and scanned the crowd. After a moment he saw her—a tall woman that he hadn't seen before. She wore a dirty, brown blanket over her shoulders to disguise her form and a battered fedora on her head.

THE SCARRED MAN on the platform called out to the sec men who were near her and suddenly Krysty was surrounded by hostile forms. A man grabbed her from behind, yanking her arm painfully high up her back, and she snarled.

"Get off me," she growled, looking at the five armed men who stood in front of her.

"Adam says you're needed up there, sweetmeat," said a blond-haired man with a white scar running through his hairline, a patch over his right eye. "Don't make it awkward for yourself."

Krysty bent forward, flipping the man who had grabbed her arm so that he flew over her head and into the man with the eye patch. The pair stumbled and they both fell to the floor along with J.B.'s hat, which had disguised her vivid red hair.

To Krysty's right she saw Doc whip the hidden sword from its sheath inside his ebony cane, but more sec men had turned at the incident, and he was suddenly lost to her in the shifting crowd.

She needed to get out of there, to get away from

these people, but as she looked left and right she realized that there was nowhere to run. She ducked her head and steamed into the nearest sec man, knocking him flat on his back and charging forward.

DOC WATCHED Krysty fight her way through the sec men until they finally overwhelmed her. Even in her weakened state, sick and feverish, she fought like a hellcat. One punch dislocated a man's jaw, another pulled away from a man's face with a fistful of teeth. She kicked and she slapped, she clawed and she punched, but the sheer weight of numbers brought Krysty down and there was nothing Doc could do about it.

The older man stood there, his sword still in his hand, considering what a few well-placed shots from his LeMat might gain him.

As he watched the sec men drag Krysty to the dais, Doc formed a swift plan in his mind. He had spied a group of chained children being marched across the room a few moments before, and he had recognized the unique figure of his albino companion, Jak, among them. Doc stood no chance fighting alone against this crowd, but with Jak's assistance and whatever J.B. had hidden up his sleeve he might just be able to free Krysty.

He resheathed his sword and made his way through the crowd toward the chained children.

FROM HER SPOT beside the train, Mildred watched as the blur of red hair appeared in the middle of the skirmish.

Krysty had been discovered.

She looked back to the car door, inwardly cursing J.B. for how long he was taking. "Come on, J.B.," she muttered, "time's a-wasting."

She turned back to look at the proceedings in the crowd and saw Krysty being dragged up the steps onto the dais. The figure in the hood was leaning forward, examining Krysty the way a jeweler would evaluate a precious gem or a butcher a piece of meat. This situation was getting further and further out of their control, Mildred realized.

A noise from her right made Mildred turn, and she saw a large man swinging a heavy mace toward her.

Mildred ducked as the mace rushed toward her face, and the spiked ball slammed into the wall of the car, denting the metal side. The man growled at her, aiming a blaster in her direction with his free hand. "You're one of them, ain't ya?" the man blurted. "I slept with every whore on this train, and I ain't never seen you. You come here to rescue your lover boy?"

Ryan. The man was talking about Ryan, Mildred realized as she sprinted along the side of the train and weaved in between two cars. She heard the heavy footsteps behind her as the sec man followed. Just another minute and she and J.B. would have been away scot-free, unnoticed among the throng. It was bad timing that this guy realized that she didn't belong. It had all been going so well.

Mildred clambered over the coupling that linked the two cars, then leaped out the other side and ran along the starboard edge of the train toward the engine. She looked back, seeing the man pulling himself through the tight gap between the cars, blaster at the ready. As soon as he was clear, he fired a shot at her retreating form, and Mildred dived to the floor, the bullet whizzing overhead.

As she slid along the rough floor, her momentum driving her forward, she fired a single shot from her

Czech-made ZKR 551 revolver, clipping the sec man across the left arm. He brushed at the wound as a line of blood began to form, but the bullet had passed him, just scuffing his bicep. He looked up again, aiming his heavy blaster at the woman now lying prone on the floor. She rolled underneath the train as he blasted off another shot.

Target revolver in hand, Mildred crawled beneath the train, pulling herself along with her elbows and driving forward with her knees and feet as she tried to put distance between herself and the sec man. Hanging spikes of metal plucked at the pack on her back, slowing her, but she kept going, urging herself forward.

She turned and saw the man's feet as he ran alongside the train. A second man was running toward him from the front of the train, and she could hear shouting—a reinforcement being given instructions.

Mildred turned, rolling on her side, and aimed her revolver at the first man's feet. She pulled the trigger, the explosion loud in her ears in the enclosed space beneath the train. The bullet ripped through the man's left foot, and she heard him screech in pain as blood sprayed from a rip in his boot.

She turned, targeting the second man and reeled off a further two shots into the guy's feet. There was no time to be subtle. She needed to quieten the pair of them before more men were alerted, and she trusted that the noise of the blaster would be lost to the loud thrum of the crowd.

The closer man fell to the floor, blood gushing from his feet, and his face lined up with Mildred's for a moment. He howled in pain and raised his own weapon toward her. Calmly, keeping her breath steady, she snapped off another bullet into the man's face, demolishing his pained expression in a burst of crimson.

In car eighteen, J.B. stuffed as much plas ex into his pockets as he could and grabbed a handful of the sticks of dynamite. Looking at it closely, he realized that this was all predark military issue.

From discussions with Mildred and studying his ancient maps, J.B. had located an old Air Force base in the area now known as the Forks. All this stuff—the train, its contents, the crazy "station" that they now found themselves in—all of it had echoes of predark military equipment. From this evidence, he concluded that the baron and his crew had built their wealth and their plans on the Air Force remnants, which accounted for a lot of the impressive technology, such as the gosling gennys, that he had seen them using.

In J.B.'s experience there was a lot of trouble associated with old military equipment in the wrong hands.

Baron Burgess watched as the impressive, Titian-haired woman was forced up the steps to join him and his advisers. He closed his eyes, a long blink, and felt her there in his mind, burning like fire. Opening his eyes again, he fixed her with his stare. "What manner of woman are you?" he asked in his pained, rasping voice.

Krysty shook her head, her lips tight, trying to pull away from the baron's stare. But she found, somehow, that she couldn't do it, couldn't look away. The low hood left his face in shadow, but his eyes—their whites tainted to a sick yellow, their irises a vivid emerald—burned into her from its depths.

"Answer your baron," the man with the horrific scarring on his arms and face stated, looking angrily at Krysty.

"I…" Krysty began, her breath coming in gasps, "I'm just…just a norm."

"It is pointless to lie to me," the baron snarled. "I can feel a lie as you speak it, and I can unpick your thoughts at will."

Krysty tried to look away, turning her head from the hooded figure in front of her. She couldn't seem to look away. It was like she was trapped by the hypnotic stare of a cobra. "I don't…" she started, but it was becoming harder to string complete sentences together. Her head was pounding, her brain felt as though it was swelling, pushing against the sides of her cranium.

The robed baron clapped his hands together. "A demonstration," he said. "A demonstration for…Krysty Wroth."

Krysty gasped. He knew her name. This baron, a man she had never seen before, knew her name. And she had felt him—he took it, plucked it from her mind, wrenched it from her thoughts like a tiny thing, a splinter pulled from under a fingernail, a little pop of pain. What manner of man was this baron?

HIS WRISTS CHAINED, Jak shuffled behind Humblebee and Marc in the line of his cell mates as they were guided toward the raised platform in the center of the vast room. Maddie's voice whispered behind him. "What's happening, Jak?"

Jak turned back, glancing over his shoulder at the girl. "Not know," he stated.

One of the sec men that was marching beside them

shot forward and slapped Jak across the face with the back of his hand. "No talking, Whitey," he shouted.

Jak stumbled but retained his balance, recognizing the familiar metallic taste of blood in his mouth.

"You," a voice boomed from the dais in front of them. It was Adam, the scarred commanding officer from the train, the one who had chilled Francis-Frankie. "We got the resources this far, let's not ruin 'em now." He was talking to the sec man who had slapped Jak, chastising the man.

A hooded, robed figure leaned across, standing beside Adam on the raised platform. He muttered something, and Adam nodded before instructing the sec man to step forward.

As the man walked toward the platform, Jak scanned its occupants. A sec man stood behind a wheelchair-bound old woman at the right of the platform. Beside them, the three whitecoats that he had seen tending to the tower back in Fairburn were waiting patiently, riffling through notebooks and talking quietly among themselves. Adam and the hooded man were standing near to the front of the dais, watching as the sec man stood in front of them. At the far left, with an armed man on either side, stood Krysty Wroth, her figure hunched over as though she was having trouble standing straight, and her arms wrapped around her chest as though to keep warm.

The man's head twisted beneath the hood and he brayed at Krysty. "Your demonstration, Krysty Wroth."

Jak watched in growing concern as the sec man who had slapped him moments ago pulled his sidearm from its holster and calmly positioned it beneath his own chin.

Jak turned back to Maddie. "Look 'way," he told her and the other children.

It was over in an instant. The man pulled the trigger to his blaster, casually, as though sleepwalking, and his head wrenched back as the bullet drilled through his jaw, behind his nose and into his brain before bursting from the back of his head in an explosion of bone, blood and gray matter. The sec man's form keeled over as his legs buckled and he fell to the floor.

KRYSTY TOOK A STEP back from the hooded figure of Baron Burgess and bumped into one of the sec men behind her. She looked up at expressionless faces. These men had been full of life a moment before, yet now they were completely impassive at the horrific fate that had just befallen their colleague, their comrade-in-arms.

She wanted to scream because of the blacksmith's anvil pounding in her head, wanted to pull her hair out by the roots, wanted to collapse and curl up and die for the pain that lashed through her body. The whole atmosphere was charged, something she could almost taste now, something so very wrong about everything around her.

Baron Burgess turned to look at her with those piercing, emerald eyes once more and she felt herself shrink under his stare.

"You've gone pale," he rasped. "But I see that you are beginning to understand. You see, they are all my puppets. Everyone in this room, everyone in the state, and—soon—everyone in the whole of the Deathlands."

The driving pain in Krysty's head reached a crescendo, and all that she could see was the baron's eyes through a pinprick in the darkness of her failing vision. Then nothing.

Chapter Twenty-Two

Mildred scurried beneath the train, pulling herself away from the sec man as his blood-drenched boot trod toward her with an audible squelch. She was at the end of the car now, and she would have to break cover to crawl beneath the next one. She looked ahead, mentally preparing herself before diving out between the cars.

"Ah-ah." The sec man laughed, swinging his heavy blaster at her the very second she appeared. "Now, I got—"

His sentence was abruptly cut short as a burst of bullets split the air. From the ground, Mildred watched as red spots appeared on the sec man's shirt. He staggered forward before slumping against the car at her rear. J.B. stood behind him, holding his Uzi low to his body with a steadying hand beneath the barrel. "Come on, Mildred," he told her, "let's keep moving."

Mildred rolled out from under the train and put a restraining hand on J.B.'s shoulder as he started to jog in the direction of the rear of the train. "Wait, I think we have another complication."

J.B. looked back at her, urging her to go on.

"They've got Krysty," she told him.

The frustration was visible on the Armorer's face and he growled through his clenched teeth. "Just when you think it's as bad as it can be, the whole deal finds a way of going even farther south." He looked up and down the length of train. "Eight minutes. Find Ryan and get him off the train."

"Eight minutes. Check," Mildred said, looking at her wrist chron as she leaped into the nearest car and started making her way forward through the cages. J.B. stopped her long enough to hand her a pack of thermals and an instruction to "Distribute them every few cars."

KRYSTY FELT SOMETHING plucking at her head, something inside her skull. Slowly, warily, she opened her eyes to narrow slits and surveyed her surroundings in a long-established survival tactic.

"That's it, Krysty," a voice rasped, "wake up now."

She tasted a rich, thick flavor in her mouth and realized that she had vomited. She could feel it sticking to the side of her face and she spat out a thick string of gunk as she sat up.

The strange witch woman and the hooded baron were looking at her closely, along with a man that she recognized as the psychopathic leader of the train crew who had ordered the burning of the people that had attacked his train.

"What happened?" she groaned, her tongue feeling thick in her mouth.

Baron Burgess turned to Adam, his second in command, and laughed. "I've never known someone to be affected so completely," he said. "It's exquisite."

Adam looked piteously at Krysty's fallen form. "Why does it affect her, do you think?"

The *bruja* never took her eyes from the red-haired woman sitting on the floor in front of them. "Because she's like me," she said quietly. "An earth witch."

"Is that right?" the hooded baron asked in his painful, cracking voice. "Are you a witch, Krysty Wroth?"

Krysty shook her head heavily. She was still wiping the remnants of her stomach lining from her face.

"She doesn't know it," the *bruja* said with conviction, "perhaps, but she is one of mine. The power of nature flows through her, I felt it back on the train."

"What's going on?" Krysty asked. She had started to cry, some strange involuntary side effect of the power that was affecting her.

"Can you feel it?" Burgess asked. "In the air, all around you. That is my power."

Krysty looked fearfully at the eyes that burned within the shadowy hood. "I've felt it for so long," she admitted, "here in my head, kicking like a mule."

Burgess nodded, his hood swaying. "It hurts now," he rasped, "but it is a good hurt, I promise you. It is the power of good. Something so rare in this accursed land."

"Good?" Krysty breathed the word, a question.

"Once upon a time," Burgess began, "there was a fantastical nation called the United States of America. A nation so fantastic that they actually called it 'the land of the free.' But the land of the free had enemies, and so it protected itself until the nukes came and it could protect itself nevermore. One of the ways that this great nation protected itself was by exerting control, Krysty Wroth. Control of hearts and minds."

Krysty was trying to comprehend the fairy story that Burgess was presenting to her. He was belittling her, she knew, patronizing her with his prepared, satirical speech. But it was so hard for her to think straight, so hard to think at all. *Hearts and minds*. What did that mean?

"There were many programs," Burgess continued, "MK-ULTRA, MKDELTA, CHATTER, Osterley, ARTICHOKE, Paperclip. Hundreds of these systems were tested, each experimenting with ways to control the one great unfettered—the human mind. Do you see it yet, Krysty? I think that you do."

Krysty pushed the tears from her eyes, trying to hold all her thoughts in one place.

"The theories were all here, locked in the vast underground vaults of this base," Burgess told her. "I just needed a way to make them work."

"Why?" Krysty asked, her voice quiet and fearful.

"To save the world," Burgess told her, not a trace of irony in his rasping voice. "The land of the free—the freelands—became what you see around you, the Deathlands. In one hundred years mankind has reverted to a semisavage state, preying on one another, creating nothing but pain and violence. But I shall change all of that, once my Grand Project is engaged."

"I don't see how..." Krysty began, struggling to frame her thoughts through the fog in her brain.

"Discipline of the mind," Burgess shot back. "Everyone working for one true purpose, cleansed of their impure desires to steal and to hurt and to kill. Under my control those thoughts will be purged."

Mind control, Krysty realized. She saw it all in a brilliant flash of comprehension. This man, Baron Burgess, had a noble dream to unite all the deathlanders into a society, into a true civilization once more. Except... except something was not right, that was obvious. Somehow, his noble dream had corrupted. The death and violence that went with the train wherever it appeared was proof of that.

And then the thought was gone, coherence lost, the pain returned in her mind. In the distance she heard a child shouting, crying not to be hurt and she tried to turn, to open her eyes to see what was happening. Her head was so heavy now, the pain so intense.

MILDRED HAD CHECKED every one of the cage-bearing cars as instructed by J.B. There was no one aboard, no sec men, no children and certainly no sign of Ryan.

She had sprinted through all the empty cages, through a store car that showed clear signs of a firefight, two crew quarters, a laboratory car coupled to a car full of equipment. After that was a bland room with heavy drapes over the windows, another car filled with techie stuff including spotlights on a rig with a portable generator painted in a familiar military green, and finally out onto a flatbed with a heavy cannon on it.

She checked her wrist chron. She had less than four minutes left. Standing on the flatbed she looked ahead. There was the vast unit that presumably held the fuel for the loco wag, and then there was the engine. "Sorry, Ryan," she muttered to herself, shaking her head. He just wasn't onboard.

She stepped off the flatbed unit on the starboard side, away from the congregation in the vast chamber.

RELUCTANTLY, MADDIE stepped forward. Despite her reluctance, she held her head high, looking challengingly at the people on the dais above. A sec man behind her slammed the butt of his longblaster into her back to hurry her along as she marched toward the dais. She turned back for a moment, and her eyes locked with Jak's. "Goodbye," she whispered. Jak saw that this brave thirteen-year-old girl had accepted her fate with utter, faultless courage.

J.B. weaved through the crowd and joined Doc. "What's going on, Doc?" he asked.

"I have no idea," the old man replied, "but it seems that this may be our last chance to free both Krysty and young Jak."

"I've set charges throughout the loco wag," J.B. whispered. "We got about two minutes before they blow and then this whole place will turn into chaos."

Doc smiled grimly as he looked at the Armorer. "And what of Ryan?" he asked.

"Mildred's on it," J.B. said.

"She's going to have to be quick," Doc concluded.

They watched as the girl in the white nightdress was made to stand in front of the raised dais. "I don't like the look of this," Doc told J.B.

"You and me both, Doc," J.B. agreed. He looked across to the other chained children, instantly identifying Jak standing among them. "Reckon you can get the blaster to Jak?"

"I intend to do my level best," Doc replied, reaching a hand beneath the tails of his frock coat and feeling for the butt of Jak's Colt Python.

"It works best with the young," Baron Burgess told Krysty as he focused his stare on the Asian girl standing in front of him. A pained expression showed on the girl's face now, and she screwed up her eyes and brought her chained hands up to rub at the sides of her head. "Their brains are still forming," Burgess rasped. "They still have the capacity to accept me."

Krysty shook her head as she watched the girl,

feeling a tightness in her chest. The girl's mouth was wide open now and she was screaming, screaming for her father. "I don't think... No, she's not accepting you. That girl is not accepting you," Krysty muttered.

Krysty turned away as the girl dropped to the floor and began punching and kicking at it with all her strength.

JAK LOOKED FRANTICALLY around, trying to find a way to break the chains on his wrists, to get a blaster in his hands. Maddie was beating at the floor; her knuckles were bloody where the skin had ripped away with her beating. "Maddie," he said quietly. "Don't, Maddie."

Maddie looked at him and Jak saw the tears streaming down her face. She was still shouting for her father, but her voice was so overused it had gone hoarse. Jak watched as she wrenched at her hair, pulling it away from her scalp in great clumps.

All around, the sec men watched the display, casually indifferent as though they had seen this many times before. Probably they had, Jak realized.

"Please stop," Krysty called from the dais, but the hooded figure continued to stare at Maddie as she squirmed on the floor.

Then Maddie pulled herself upright, kneeling as she looked up at the baron. Suddenly, violently, she pushed forward, bending at the waist, and slammed her forehead into the solid concrete floor, headbutting the unforgiving surface again and again. Each time her head hit, her cries for her father became higher, as if she were hiccupping.

There was blood on Maddie's face now, seeping through from her hairline, trickling into her eyes, over her nose and down her cheeks. But she wouldn't stop. She just kept slamming her head into the floor, screaming for her father to come help her, over and over.

On the podium, Adam stepped forward and said something quietly to the hooded figure before walking across to the steps, accompanied by the sec men who had brought Krysty to the dais. They made their way down the brief staircase to the floor, and Adam gave an instruction to a nearby sec man who carried an ax next to the blaster on his belt. The man handed over the ax, and Adam tested its weight in his hands. Then he walked over to Maddie where she continued hitting the floor in a strange mockery of genuflecting.

Whatever happens, Jak told himself, this one dies.

Adam grabbed Maddie's long hair, patchy though it now was after her own assault. He held her upright as she tried to yank herself away and pulled back the ax. With a mighty sweep, he brought the ax down into the back of the girl's neck, cutting through it like a tree truck, beheading her in a single stroke, and abruptly halting her pleas for her father's help.

The girl's headless body knelt in place as Adam carried his bloody trophy back to the hooded figure on the dais.

IT WAS ONLY BY CHANCE that Mildred had decided to walk around the front of the train. She had seen the exterior once, by night, from the window of the rented room in Fairburn, and she had been half-convinced it was something come alive from a nightmare. The jutting spikes and flaming holes along the matte-black sides still gave her that impression, even up close, and she suppressed a shiver as she admired the metallic beast.

Then, quite unexpectedly, she saw Ryan, tied to the front of the train, hanging just above the floor by his wrists and ankles. His face was caked in dirt and his head hung low, no strength left to hold it up.

Mildred looked behind her, making sure no one else was sneaking up, before she stepped over to him and used her pocketknife to saw through the ropes. "Ryan?" she said with quiet urgency. "Ryan, can you hear me?"

The one-eyed man's only answer was a groan. His head lolled on his shoulders. He was clearly well out of it.

Mildred untied the final strap binding Ryan's wrist and eased him gently down. "Ryan, wake up." He was breathing and didn't seem to have any obvious wounds. He was just exhausted. She slung the backpack from her shoulders and rummaged through it until she found the half-full canteen of water. She unscrewed the cap and put the canteen to Ryan's lips, letting a slow stream trickle into his mouth. "Come on, Ryan, we have to get out of here right now." She checked her wrist chron again. They had one minute before J.B.'s surprise kicked into action.

Ryan's right eye flickered in and out of focus and he spluttered out the water, choking on it. Mildred pulled the canteen away, told him to take it easy.

"What happened?" Ryan asked. "Mildred, 'zat you?"

"Large as life," she told him, smiling broadly. "But not for much longer unless we get away from this train."

Ryan tried to stand, but he slumped back on the ground. "Can't feel my legs," he told her, his voice slurring, "or my arms. What the hell happened?"

"I'd guess you've been hanging from the front of the train for the past three days," she told him, looking around to see if any sec men might have noticed them. "I'll help you get out of here, come on."

On hands and knees, Mildred shuffled along next to Ryan, half dragging him as he crawled slowly away from the train. She guided them over to a glass-walled control room that she had spotted across from the train, set against the wall.

"One second," she promised Ryan, standing and stepping to the door of the control room. Inside, the room was full of tracking and monitoring equipment, and Mildred recognized some of it as being the workings of an old signal box. There was a single operator sitting at the control board, smoking a rolled-up cigarette, the cloying stench of maryjane in the foggy air. He turned when he saw her step into the room. "Hi," she said as she raised the blaster in her hand and fired off a shot straight through his forehead. "'Bye." The signal controller slumped to his console, a neat circular hole between his eyes, the cigarette still clinging to his bottom lip.

Mildred dragged Ryan into the room and they sat together beneath one of the control desks. She glanced at her wrist chron once again as she started strapping up Ryan's torn wrists with bandages from her med kit. He had suffered some nasty wounds while hanging from the ropes. They had cut into the flesh of his wrists and Mildred could see signs of infection there.

"What have I missed?" Ryan asked, his voice hoarse as he sipped a little more of the water from the canteen.

"All of the sec men have gathered in the big reception room outside, Jak and a load of kids are chained up ready for the slaughter, and some insane baron has decided to make Krysty his pet," Mildred summarized.

"Nothing important, then," Ryan said, and Mildred stopped strapping his wounds and looked at him. There was a sly smile on his lips, and she knew he was already assessing the best way to deal with their current problems.

Just then, a loud explosion rocked the room outside immediately followed by two further booms, and the glass in the control room's windows shattered and crashed inward, showering over the desktops and floor all around them.

"Oh, almost forgot," Mildred added. "J.B. has a plan."

Ryan nodded, rubbing his hands together as he tried to get the feeling back into them. "So I hear."

Chapter Twenty-Three

J.B. had rushed through the train, placing explosive charges in every fourth car until he reached the storage cars at the rear of the vehicle. He had not concerned himself with finesse, just tossed the bombs on shelves, under seats, sometimes simply placed them on the floor and then continued on. He had counted out the cars as he worked through them, units fifteen through to sixty, trusting Mildred to pepper the foremost cars with explosives, as well. When he reached car thirty, he had placed a huge wad of plas ex with a timer, setting it to seven minutes, giving him and Mildred more than enough time to complete their designated tasks. He had hoped she would find Ryan, but he had chosen not to delay the operation just because of that, well aware that Ryan might have been thrown overboard after discovery. Holding up the whole plan on the basis of a man who was possibly no longer aboard would be foolhardy behavior based purely on sentimentality, and sentimentality had no place in the Deathlands.

When he had joined Doc in the midst of the mob, the Armorer had resisted the urge to check his wrist chron. Some sixth sense worked for him in these situations. He would know when the charges were going to blow. He remained calm as he watched the horrifying mental assault on the young girl in front of the dais. While not the most demonstrably emotional of men, J.B. had not enjoyed witnessing the awful fate of the girl, feeling it a relief when she was finally decapitated and put out of her misery. But rash heroics would do more harm than good now, so he continued to let the timer tick down— when the train went up it would be big and it would hopefully provide the diversion they needed.

The younger male whitecoat had been handed the dead girl's head by the scarred CO and had taken a powered bonesaw to it. He swiftly cut into the forehead, splitting the skull and flipping the top of the head back. Inside, the brain sat snugly in the cranium, gray and glistening with moisture. Beside J.B., Doc had gasped, as though hit by a sudden realization.

Rubber gloves over his hands, the whitecoat had removed the brain and squeezed it in his hands, watching the trickle of liquid drip from it. The brain was placed in a container where, J.B. saw, it swam in similarly colored, mushy gray liquid.

Doc turned to J.B. and started to say something, but it was cut suddenly short as a series of almighty explosions came from the far right of the vast room. The timer had reached count zero. The first explosion flowered into existence, fire and fury wiping out the thirtieth car and the spreading flames engulfing the cars to either side. It took several seconds, the heat of the flames spreading from the middle car, before the next explosions kicked in, the thermals taking up the symphony of noise and heat.

"Get to Jak," J.B. shouted over the ensuing chaos, turning away from the bright flames. "We need him now."

Doc shoved his way through the crowd, most of

whom were transfixed by the burning wreckage that had been the center of the train just moments before.

Finding himself beside the children, Doc yanked the Colt Python from its hiding place at the small of his back. Jak stood in front of him, his back to Doc as he watched the reactions of the strange group of figures on the dais, his hands straining at the chains that bound him.

"Might I be of some assistance, Mr. Lauren?" Doc called, raising his voice above the turmoil and explosions that filled the air.

Jak turned, his eyes narrowed in anger. Then he saw Doc and relief flashed across his sharp features for a fraction of a second. "Thought not see you 'gain."

Doc shook his head, showing Jak the blaster. "I am like the proverbial bad penny, Jak, you should know that by now."

Jak's eyes flashed over Doc's shoulder as the older man spoke, and he powered forward, his hands held high with the small length of chain links pulled taut. Doc weaved aside as the albino swung both fists fractionally to the old man's left. Doc turned in time to see a bearded sec man stagger back with Jak struggling to right himself for a further attack. The man spit a phlegmy glob of blood to the ground before raising his right arm. Clutched in his hand, Doc saw, the bearded man held a well-maintained 9 mm Browning Llama blaster. In a second the sec man had the blaster pointed at Jak as the young man used his powerful leg muscles to push himself at his enemy.

As soon as the first explosion rocked the cavernous room, Krysty felt her thoughts snap into clear focus once more, the pain in her head abating; still there, but abating. Being near this Baron Burgess was like holding her head in a clamp. She had to get away.

She turned, scanning the crowd of, what had been a moment before, revelers. They had all turned to look at the flames that engulfed the center of the monstrous train at the far side of the room. As she watched, two further explosions ripped through the train in rapid succession, and she felt the heat of the flames throbbing on her chest and face.

She glanced back, looking at the people on the raised platform. They, too, were entranced, watching the growing inferno that had engulfed their train, all except the strange old woman with the blood-colored tears painted on her cheek. She just sat in her wheelchair, a serene expression on her lips, almost as though she was unaware of anything amiss, instructing the man behind her with a fluttering of hand gestures. Krysty could see the hooded figure of Baron Burgess shaking, gripped with shock, his shoulders shuddering almost as though he was crying.

This isn't about a train, she reminded herself. It's more than that, and to walk away now would be nothing but weakness, weakness Mother Sonja had warned her all her life to avoid. Krysty took a determined step forward.

"My train!" the baron screamed. "What has happened to my glorious train?"

Adam shook his head and turned to look at his master. His eyes widened when he saw the red-haired woman standing beside the baron, pulling back her fist. "Baron Burgess, look—" he began.

Burgess's hood shook as he turned his head. Krysty

watched his fiery green eyes turn on her and she launched an upper cut the length of her torso before connecting with his jaw in a solid blow.

"What?" Burgess howled as the punch slammed hard into his chin and his teeth clashed together with a clap. His head snapped backward on his neck and the voluminous folds of his hood dropped to his shoulders.

Krysty stood staring, her follow-up punch forgotten as she looked into the revealed face of Baron Burgess. He was entirely bald, and his exposed skin looked old and haggard. His bright eyes were a fierce green within the bloodshot yellows where the whites should have been. Wiring sprung from the top and back of his head, linked through open wounds straight onto the pulsing mass of brain that could be seen through a Swiss cheese sequence of drilled holes. The man had been repeatedly trepanned, and she could see that the attached wires disappeared into the back of the robe and, most likely, through it and into the floor below. The baron, she realized, had never moved more than a few feet in all the time she had seen him.

Burgess tilted his head, recognition in his eyes as he looked at Krysty's shocked expression. He smiled and she saw the rotten teeth that lined his mouth, the gums that they sat in an angry shade of violet. "You look horrified, Krysty Wroth," he told her solicitously, as though to a child when his cruel prank has finally been revealed. To her right another explosion rocked the room as more cars burst into flame.

"What…?" Krysty began, unsure how to even voice the question that was forming in her mind. "Are you some kind of 'bot?"

Baron Burgess laughed as he shook his head, his

voice sounding as pained as ever. "To achieve perfection one has to be willing to make sacrifices," he told her. "This was the only way to truly ensure that the system would respond to my commands. So I willingly became a part of it."

Krysty looked at the bald man, the wires jutting from his skull, and she felt a twinge of sadness. Perhaps, somewhere in the distant past, Baron Burgess had been an idealist. Perhaps he had had not a plan but a dream, a vision. But somewhere on his quest to fulfill his ideal to create a working, ordered civilization from the wreckage that was the Deathlands, he had given himself over to the system of its implementation and he had given up a little piece of humanity in the process. She saw it all then—the harvesting of children's malleable brains that acted as the transmitters in the towers. "What kind of monster does this to himself?" Krysty asked, thrusting her left fist toward the cloaked man.

But Krysty's punch failed to connect. The strength in her muscles ebbed away, like water through netting, and she just sank, straight down, as though collapsing in on herself. Her legs folded beneath her, then she slumped back and to the side, dropping to the floor of the dais. Burgess stood over her, his fierce stare burning through her, sapping her will.

"We don't need my glorious train anymore, girl," he bragged. Krysty felt icy claws plucking at her memories, a burning sensation behind her eyes as though her optic nerves were aflame. Baron Burgess was there, inside her head, pulling and wrenching at everything that made her Krysty Wroth, pulling at her very self.

DOC RAPPED the bearded sec man across the knuckles with his lion's-head walking cane and the man dropped his blaster with a yelp.

Jak sprang forward, garroting the man with the small length of chain that bound his wrists. The man fell backward, slumping to the hard ground with the albino youth's weight atop him. The sec man clenched his hands around Jak's forearms, trying to pull away the pressure on his throat. As he did so he saw the older, white-haired man lean forward and point a blaster at his throat.

"Watch your hands," Doc told Jak as he pulled the trigger on the Colt Python. There was a loud report and the bullet drove through the chain links between Jak's wrists, splitting the chain before drilling into the sec man's throat, killing him instantly.

The crowd of people around them were starting to react now, and Doc handed Jak his blaster and pulled his trusty LeMat from its holster. Jak swung the six-inch barrel of his weapon toward the dais and fired off a quick shot at the sec man who stood at the foot of the small staircase.

"Shooter still good," the albino teen stated, a wide grin splitting his face as he headed toward the stairs.

"J.B. oiled it for you," Doc called back as he knelt in a defensive position beside the group of frightened children.

Jak scrambled up the abbreviated flight of steps and onto the dais. He could see Krysty flailing as she dropped to the floor, and a bald-headed man poised over her, grinning maliciously. Beside the bald man was the scarred man who had killed his friends, Francis-Frankie and Maddie, his face away from Jak as he watched the burning wreckage of the train.

Jak saw a movement across the room, at the other end of the dais behind the retreating woman in the wheelchair, but he dismissed it, keeping his mind on his primary objective. He raised the Colt Python and reeled off two shots at the figures in front of him. The bald baron swayed as the first shot glanced past him, missing him by barely an inch. Adam wasn't as lucky—the bullet punctured his left leg and he danced on the spot as he struggled to maintain his balance.

Adam's huge frame turned to face his attacker and he saw the wiry young albino sprinting toward him, a sliver of smoke emanating from the raised blaster in his hand. Adam still held the ax, and he tossed it in a rotating arc toward Jak in a flinch reaction.

Jak weaved below the onrushing ax and fired another shot at Adam's legs, the large-bore bullet shattering his left hip in a burst of bone fragments and blood. Adam howled as the bullet destroyed his leg, and his hand reached down to the Magnum blaster he had holstered in his belt.

"Not escaping," Jak said solemnly as he ran at the scarred man, toppling him as their bodies slammed together.

Adam had his blaster free now, but Jak was on top of him, too close to shoot. He used the blaster like a club, slamming the butt into Jak's back and the lowest part of his neck. The albino teen continued his savage attack, arms swinging as he clawed at Adam's face, his legs pumping to drive the pair of them on across the dais. Adam could feel the hot flood of blood pouring down his left leg, and he couldn't seem to use the leg properly to anchor himself. Suddenly there was no floor to step on and Adam found himself walking backward into thin air before falling at an angle toward the ground a few feet below, Jak still driving at him in an unrestrained rush of rage. With a slam, Adam's body met the ground below, shoulders and the back of his head first, knocking the wind out of him. His blaster went flying, spinning across the floor before halting barely two feet away from the frantic pair of combatants.

Adam rolled to his left, tossing his attacker aside. As Jak wheeled away, Adam howled, unspeakable pain assaulting his shattered hip. He watched the strange, albino youth across the floor from him as he grabbed for the blaster he had dropped. Jak rolled across the floor before coming up in a crouch. He pointed his blaster at Adam's face, and his red eyes narrowed in determination.

"Bullet for tongue," Jak said through gritted teeth, pulling the trigger.

With a burst of crimson, the lower half of Adam's face disappeared in the same way Francis-Frankie had been wounded back at the tower. His hand twitched and he ceased reaching for the blaster he had dropped moments before.

J.B. SPRAYED the crowd with bullets from his Uzi, forcing them away from the captive children and the dais as more explosions gripped the broken train. Flames were racing up the wall now, and he could feel the heat of the fire here, halfway across the vast room. He kept his blaster aimed away from Doc, Jak and the child prisoners.

The explosions had shaken up the crowd, and sec men were only now reacting, almost a minute after the first explosion, to the enemies in their midst. As far as

J.B. was concerned, it was a turkey shoot. Everybody in his line of fire was an enemy and every last body, dead or alive, provided more cover for him. All he had to do was keep moving.

THREE DAYS Ryan had hung there, with no food to eat and only the little rainwater that hit his face to drink. And all it had done was make him meaner, more focused than ever.

Mildred watched in admiration as the one-eyed man pushed himself up from the floor and rolled his shoulders to ease the tension in his muscles. Blood seeped into the bandages that Mildred had wrapped around his worn wrists as he flexed and tensed his hands, painfully driving away any lasting numbness. Standing amid the shattered glass, Ryan stretched his right hand to his hip and pulled the 9 mm SIG-Sauer from the worn leather holster. "Come on, Mildred," he said through cracked lips, "time to end this thing." With that, he strode determinedly to the door as another explosion rocked the room outside. Hefting her backpack on her shoulders, Mildred followed, the ZKR-551 target revolver ready.

Outside the control room it was turmoil. People were running in all directions as fire engulfed the monstrous train. Flames leaped up the wall next to the burning train, and Mildred realized they were lucky to depart their cover when they had. In a few moments those flames would spread and cover the doorway. Ahead of her, Ryan walked heavily, his muscles still aching. He led her around the front of the train, not so much as wasting a single glance on the area where he had hung for the past three days, no curiosity while there was a job to do. Flames lapped at the wheels and rear of the engine and the matte paint blistered as heat engulfed it. Ryan just continued on, surveying the scene until he spotted Krysty's bright hair on the dais at the room's center.

Head down, he marched toward the dais, with Mildred jogging along beside him, making their way through the startled mob.

J.B. WAS NEXT TO Doc now, firing short bursts from the Uzi into the air, keeping the crowd at bay. A number of the crowd had organized themselves, rushing around with buckets of water to try to douse the flames that stretched the length of the room along the train tracks by the right-hand wall. They were no longer concerned with guarding the children.

"How are we, Doc?" J.B. asked as he stood by Doc's side.

Doc glanced at the Armorer, amused to see that during all the chaos the man had still managed to retrieve his hat from wherever it had fallen after Krysty's disguise had been blown, along with Ryan's longblaster. "I've done a quick recce, but I can't see any keys for the handcuffs," he said, indicating the children huddled behind him. "We're going to have to break the chains manually, I think."

J.B. shrugged. "As long as they're alive. Any sign of Mildred?"

"None," Doc told him, blasting off a swift shot with his LeMat as someone in the crowd leveled a shotgun in their direction. The man fell to the floor, a bloody wound dead center in his chest.

J.B.'s head flicked back and he scanned the dais. Jak had disappeared but Krysty was still up there, scrambling along the floor, trying to get away from the baron. For the first time he noticed the transparent panels along the side of the raised platform and saw the gray liquid that swirled within, lighted in a strangely pulsing manner. Having witnessed the awful death of the girl, he knew now what that liquid was: brain matter. Whatever this insane baron was doing, it involved the transference of thoughts, and the ideal medium for thought transference was brain—the horrifying logic was inescapable.

J.B. saw something else, too—two familiar figures jogging up the steps of the dais from the direction of the train. "Looks like she found Ryan," he told Doc as he turned his attention back to the frantic crowd that surrounded them.

LYING SUPINE on the floor of the dais, Krysty kicked with her heels and pushed herself backward, away from the leering baron. The baron's intense grip on her mind had wavered when Jak's bullet glanced by his shoulder, and Krysty felt the fog in her head lifting once more. She reached into the pocket of her jumpsuit and gripped the handle of the .38 Smith & Wesson she had hidden there.

Looming above her, the robed baron smiled a fierce, horrible grin. "Come to me, Krysty Wroth," he spoke softly, "don't try to resist."

"Resist this, Burgess!" she shouted, revealing the .38 in her hand and blasting a shot at his face. The bullet missed him by a fraction of an inch, leaving a bloody gash on his cheek. The baron flinched, slapping his hand against the wound.

From the far end of the dais, Krysty heard a strained

voice call her name. Her eyes darted across for a moment and she saw Ryan and Mildred rushing up the steps and onto the stage. Mildred fired shots at the whitecoats, hobbling them to ensure they didn't escape. In the turmoil, the old woman and her wheelchair had disappeared, Krysty realized. When had that happened?

Ryan had his blaster raised, and he bellowed something at the baron as he ran across the stage. "You shouldn't piss off Krysty," he yelled, and the baron turned, piercing him with his stare. Krysty knew the power of that gaze now. It had caused the sec man to kill himself, made the pretty, young Asian girl harm herself in the most savage, brutal manner, and it had locked Krysty's mind to the point of complete seizure.

She raised the barrel of her blaster and targeted the back of the baron's head. At the same time, Ryan pulled the trigger on his SIG-Sauer.

The noise of the twin shots was lost in the general hubbub of the panicked room. From opposite directions, two bullets raced through the air toward the same target: the trepanned skull of Baron Burgess. Perhaps they hit at the same instant, no one would ever be sure, but the bald man's skull cracked as the bullets drove through it, and a mass of gray jelly and wiring splattered into the air as the now-headless body fell to the floor.

Ryan continued to advance, a determined expression on his face as he struggled to make his tired leg muscles work. He dashed past Burgess's sagging corpse and went to his knees as he reached Krysty, lying in front of him on the floor, the .38 still poised in her hand. Ryan pulled her close, wrapping his arms around her, the scarred fingers of his hands entwining her hair. "It's okay," he whispered. "It's all over now."

But it wasn't, and Krysty was the first to feel it.

Chapter Twenty-Four

Krysty's head was throbbing. Her headache had been getting disarmingly more urgent in the last three seconds, ever since Baron Burgess had taken two bullets to the head. Right now it felt as if a blacksmith was molding molten-hot horseshoes into shape with his hammer, the anvil located across the space between her eyes. She blinked back the pain, but it redoubled its efforts and she could hear the sound of her blood rushing through her ears.

"He's not dead, Ryan," she said to the one-eyed man who clung to her. Her voice sounded so loud in her ears, she wondered if she was shouting.

Holding on to her, Ryan felt something dancing on his head, as if the hair was being plucked out by its roots. Krysty had whispered something but it was mumbled, lost to the noise coming from all around the station. "What did you say?" he asked her, pulling her close as they sat together on the floor. His words seemed strange, jagged things, like knives in his own ears.

A few paces behind him he heard the crash of a body falling to the ground, and he heard Mildred curse. What was going on here?

Krysty began to speak again, and Ryan held her face between his hands, watching her lips move so that he could make her out over the sounds of chaos all around them. "He's not dead," she told him. "The baron is not dead."

Ryan turned, aware of the heavy weight of his own skull atop his neck. It was like deep-sea diving, moving through the pressured water, trying to get the momentum going. The robed figure of the baron lay there, a puddle of blood and brain matter spilled from the top of his head. Ryan watched, inwardly preparing himself, but the man did not move. What was Krysty talking about? The man was clearly dead.

Beside the corpse, Mildred had fallen to the floor, her eyes clenched tight in agony. Ryan saw her slowly raise a heavy head, open her eyes and look at him. The whites of her eyes had turned pink as capillaries burst within them. She grimaced and pulled herself upright, confusion on her face. "What's happening?" she asked him after a moment, biting off the words as though speaking had become difficult.

Ryan felt punch-drunk as the pressure in his skull mounted. Beside him, Krysty was speaking once more, and Ryan tried to make sense of her words. "He's in my head."

Ryan looked at her, shocked by the statement she had just made, trying to make sense of the phrase. But by then it was too late, and the baron was speaking to them all, everyone in the cavernous room, inside their very minds.

He began with laughter. A strange, happy sound, somehow wrong and out of context here as the people in the room sank to their knees or simply dropped to the floor. The baron laughed inside all their heads, enjoying his newfound freedom. "Of course," he stated, "so simple." The voice was loud, astonishingly loud, it seemed to obliterate all other noise in the room but it wasn't there at all. It wasn't carried by sound waves, it was carried by thoughts, a virus running through the minds of every person in the room.

It went farther than the room. It went beyond the spectators here, wending through the skeletal transmitters that sat in the earth beside the railroad tracks, rocketing across the whole state and staggering farmers working in the predawn fields, the villes, the broken wreckage of the shattered cities. Everyone, awake or asleep, felt that voice in their head. Some heard it softly, a whisper in the back of their thoughts like the voice of their conscience. Others, especially the young and those nearest the scaffold towers powered by brain matter, heard it loud and strong, like the instructive voice of a teacher at the front of the classroom.

In Fairburn, the late drinkers in Jemmy's bar stopped their conversations in unison and the room fell silent. The players held their fans of cards in front of them but their eyes glazed over. The domino players dropped their tiles to the tables and clutched at their aching skulls.

Similar scenes were occurring throughout Fairburn, where the emanations of the nearby tower were strong, at the dogfight arena and the stables and the little, single-story wooden shacks that the villagers lived in.

Similar scenes erupted all across the old state of North Dakota, wherever the ring of transmitters touched, broadcasting its shrieking message to the minds of the inhabitants.

Baron Burgess's disembodied voice spoke to everyone, though he really only spoke to himself. "I never even thought," he said, "freed of the body I have utter control of the mind."

All around the station, people were dropping to the floor as though swatted by a hurricane, blood streaming from their nostrils, ears and mouths. The voice was strong here, loud and all-consuming, a wrathful god pronouncing sentence on his subjects.

Mildred could feel the blood welling in her mouth as her gums split. A trickle of blood was pouring from her left ear and both nostrils, and she tongued the blood away as it swam into her mouth. Raising her hand carefully, driving herself on despite the confusion in her mind, she aimed her ZKR-551 revolver at the baron's limp form and fired, again and again until the clip was empty and the hammer caught on nothing but an empty chamber. The robed body jumped in place, shuddering with each impact, but the driving pain in her mind continued, pulling at her very identity as it violently overwhelmed her.

Still clutching Krysty where they sat on the other side of the baron's corpse, Ryan watched Mildred blast holes in the fallen body. The whole thing seemed to take a second or an hour, Ryan couldn't seem to make sense which. His perceptions were breaking down under the mounting pressure in his brain, and he struggled to hold on to his awareness.

When he saw the corpse move as Mildred's bullets drilled into it, Ryan noticed the wiring that ran from the body into the floor—the same type of wiring that could be seen spouting from the skull. Beneath the baron, on the floor of the platform, there were holes and circuits, the whole dais formed some kind of machine. The mad bastard had wired himself into the machine itself, his whole life stuck to this spot, attached by an umbilical cord of wiring.

"This is the ultimate," Baron Burgess howled in the minds of everyone within transmission range. "The Grand Project works better than I could possibly have dreamed."

Behind the dais, Jak was sleeping beside the faceless corpse of Adam. The pressure within Jak's mind was colossal, and he had willed himself to sleep as a defense mechanism. In his dreams, the insane baron was laughing, his words flowing like living things from his mouth of rotten teeth.

Doc was slumped on the floor by the fallen children. He couldn't move his head, the pressure there felt so tight, but he lay with his sky blue eyes wide open, looking at the faces of the children as blood poured in rivers from their ears, nostrils and mouths, from the split where their eyes met the skin. The children were dying; their brains could not endure the unholy pressure that was building within them. Doc knew that within minutes the children would die, their personalities wiped out, their bodies empty shells. If only he could do something. If only he could move.

Beside him, J.B. had dropped under the mental onslaught along with everyone else in the room. He remained focused, pushing the victorious words of the baron from his head, concentrating on keeping his own thoughts intact. His right hand still clutched the Uzi and he forced the muscles in his arm to move, to point the weapon at the dais. He had noticed the swirling brain goop within the floor of the platform and, freely admitting that he had no comprehension of how such a device worked, realized that the baron had amplified his own psionic abilities through some kind of alignment of brain matter in series.

J.B. squeezed the trigger and the Uzi spit a long stream of bullets at the base of the platform, shattering the transparent glass and spilling organic liquid, gray matter, all over the floor.

But still the voice continued, still the pressure pounded at everyone's mind.

"The system responds to my commands better than I ever hoped," Baron Burgess bellowed. "I just needed the absolute freedom to embrace it. I am control!"

J.B. saw Mildred lying atop the dais, the blood pooling beside her face, and he wished there was some way to help her. "Mildred," he called, forcing his own thoughts past the euphoric feeling that the baron was transmitting.

Mildred looked at him from the edge of the dais, her head moving slowly, her eyes cast a wicked, bloodshot red.

"How do you clean out a brain?" J.B. shouted, and he willed her to understand.

Mildred looked at him, struggling to comprehend as the weight pressed on her mind. She saw J.B. gesture toward the floor below her with the barrel of the Uzi, and she started to realize what he meant. She rolled, pushing herself away from the floor and shrugged out of the armholes on her backpack. In her mind, placed centrally in her thoughts, the baron was laughing once more, a delighted child with a new toy.

Mildred dug into the backpack. From the scrounged medical supplies in her backpack she pulled out a hypodermic syringe, her hands shaking as she held it up to her eyes, trying to see if it contained anything.

Liquid. It held liquid, crystal-clear with a trace of foam at the top of the container. She felt relief flow through her like a wave, and her pained, bleeding mouth smiled.

"Put him to sleep," she answered, her slurring voice low and strained. Still clutching the hypodermic, Mildred slumped to the floor, her thoughts trickling away like raindrops.

Ryan had heard her, had watched her rooting through the bag. He saw the syringe in her hand and he ignored everything else. His vision was almost gone, a narrow circle surrounded by thick, inky blackness was all that remained. The view flickered in and out, light and shadow, and he urged himself forward, letting go of his lover as he drove himself on.

Without Ryan to hold her up, Krysty slumped to the floor, blacked out from the pressure within her head. Flames billowed up the walls, lighting the room, making her red hair shimmer in a halo of light.

Ryan crawled across the dais on hands and knees, his eye focused on the syringe in Mildred's hand. He had dropped his blaster somewhere, but he didn't remember where, his thoughts were so muddled, so fuzzy. Suddenly, like moving at high speed, he was there, his hand falling over Mildred's, clasping the little plastic cylinder of the syringe. "How much?" he asked her, but she didn't answer. Mildred had blacked out.

The baron's voice was screaming maniacally now, the puppet master examining his creations. He laughed and howled, his thoughts weapons against his detractors.

Atop the dais, Ryan stood, his knees buckling a little at the stress, his frame unsteady, swaying as though a tree in the breeze. His right hand held the hypodermic syringe filled with sedative, the thin, metal needle twinkling in the flames of the destroyed train.

He looked down at the baron's corpse, looking for the strange wiring he had noticed that connected the baron's body to the machinery below. There were gaps there, small tunnels through the floor that held the wiring in place. Ryan staggered two steps forward until he was upon the baron's robed figure. Then he lunged, collapsing to the floor, his right arm extended above him.

There.

He ripped at the wiring, yanking a strand of it free, opening the hole into the base of the platform. The aperture was so slim, a tiny breach in the vast unit. Ryan imagined he might see the liquefied brain matter rushing beneath but it was just a hole, thin and characterless. He brought his fist down and drove the thin needle of the hypodermic syringe into the little gap in the surface of the floor. Then he pushed the stopper, his hands shaking with the stress of following his commands, until he had released all of the liquid into the thought amplification unit.

Once he was done, Ryan slumped to the floor as all the thoughts in his mind burned away.

BLACKNESS.

Nothingness.

The end of the all.

RYAN ABRUPTLY REGAINED consciousness as a hand pressed against his chest and rocked him awake. He opened his eye and looked up into Krysty's smiling face.

"Wake up, lover," she said. "We have to get out of here."

Something preyed on Ryan's thoughts, a strange sense of loss, a dream only half-remembered.

"What happened?" Ryan murmured, his jaw aching, his mouth heavy and dry.

"He's gone," Krysty told him. "But the whole base is going up in smoke. We need to get moving."

Ryan sat up, his muscles protesting, and saw the thick black smoke that was filling the hall beneath the high ceiling. All around the dais were the fallen bodies of the baron's men, many of them struggling to rouse themselves as though from a hard night's drinking. There was blood splattered across the room, and many of the people wore streaks of crimson across their faces.

Ryan scanned the area and saw J.B. crouched beside a group of a dozen children, shaking them awake. To his side, Doc was nodding his muzzy head as he tried to shake off the effects of the mental invasion. In the distance, the train was nothing more than a burning streak of tortured wood and metal, and the wall beside it and floor beneath were burning furiously. Whatever ammunition had been stored on the train had cooked off during the initial fires, adding to the chaos.

Mildred stood beside the steps of the dais, her familiar backpack strapped across her shoulders, and she looked all around until she saw something behind the platform. She dashed off, hurling a single word back to Ryan and Krysty. "Jak."

In the nightmarish past three days, Ryan had almost forgotten about their teenage companion, and he chastised himself for the oversight. If Jak needed anything, he assured himself, Mildred would be able to provide it. With Krysty's help, Ryan pulled himself up to a standing position, his frame crooked as he tried to urge it to movement.

"Come on, lover," Krysty said gently. "It's time I saved you."

The companions regrouped and, with the frightened child prisoners, made their way through the crowd and out of the burning station.

Outside, the sun was just tripping over the horizon in the east, a new dawn breaking.

Ryan leaned heavily against Krysty, but she took the burden with ease and good grace. Her strength had finally returned. "What happened there, in the end?" Ryan asked, his memory of the final moments a clouded, impenetrable morass.

"The baron's psyche was transferred into his machinery on death, I think," Krysty told him, "and the whole process boosted his psionic abilities to a terrifying level. Don't ask me how—the guy was wired into his brain transmitter, and I'm damned if I can figure the whole logic of the thing."

"The heck of it is," Doc chipped in, "the confounded system actually worked, at the end."

"For a while," J.B. added as he herded the children out into the crisp, dawn air. They still wore chains at their wrists, but that was a problem to deal with once they were clear of the baron's base.

Bringing up the rear, Mildred and a very tired-looking Jak made sure there were no stragglers among the child escapees. Jak had his Colt Python poised, keeping an eye out for anyone who was stupe enough to follow the companions. No one did. They were too busy saving their own skins from the burning building to worry about six outlanders and a handful of children.

"You think that was Burgess's plan?" Ryan asked.

Krysty shook her head. "He gave up so much to achieve his dream, it was kind of touching when he told me, but he would never have given up his body like that."

"So where is he now?" Ryan wanted to know.

Krysty took a deep breath, luxuriating in the fresh air as the sun rose in the distance. "He's gone," she said with finality. "The sedative was transmitted through the system, just like his alpha waves. When you put him to the final sleep, well, I can't feel *their* agony anymore. They're *all* sleeping now."

There were more than a dozen children with the companions, and many of them were sniffling quietly, tears running down their cheeks and mixing with the dried blood on their faces where they had suffered from the baron's devastating mental attack. Humblebee, the eight-year-old girl with the lopsided bunches in her hair, tugged at Jak's sleeve and asked him a question. Her face looked sad and frightened, but she wasn't crying, at least. "Will we see Maddie again?" the girl wondered.

Jak shook his head. "Asleep with others," he told her, trying to sound reassuring. "Won't come back."

Humblebee thought about that, her mouth turned down sadly, and then she nodded. "I miss her," she told him, a confident smile on her lips as she turned back to her ex-cell mates.

"Me, too," Jak solemnly agreed, scanning the horizon. Loping along, the albino youth parted from the group and pointed to a small shack on the outskirts of the old military compound. "Stables," he told them.

He was right. As Ryan and the others looked, they

saw several riders mount up and head toward the mountain paths to the north.

J.B. spoke up as the companions and the children made their way across the scarred landscape toward the low buildings. "Reckon they take orphans at Fairburn?" He indicated the children.

Doc smiled, thrusting his walking stick forward to keep his balance over the uneven terrain. "It seemed like a nice enough ville, so I should think that they will," he suggested. "Perhaps even help some of these lost souls find their rightful families."

"But not Maddie," Jak growled, thinking of the poor girl who had shown such courage throughout the ordeal.

Ryan turned back to address his companions. "Then let's head back to the redoubt in Minot, swing by Fairburn and make us a few apologies while we're there, see if they have people who will take these kids in."

Together, the companions each secured a steed and, with the children sharing two or three to a horse, made their way across the plain and away from the wrecked military base at Grand Forks. North Dakota, they agreed, was a hell of a place to visit.

The Executioner®

Don Pendleton's

FIRE ZONE

A U.S. gold heist turns an African nation into a war zone.

After the leader of an African rebel group hijacks a shipment of enough gold to fund a revolution, Mack Bolan must retrieve it before the killing starts. Unable to trust even the CIA, the Executioner must put his combat and survival skills to the test to infiltrate the rebel base and destroy the key players.

Available October wherever books are sold.

TAKE 'EM FREE
2 action-packed novels plus a mystery bonus
NO RISK
NO OBLIGATION TO BUY